What did her mother really know about the man?

Lan maintained that she'd married Skully, but couldn't produce documentation. She didn't know his last name, his branch of service or his serial number. And what if Tam's mother did manage to find him after all these years? In all likelihood he'd made a new life for himself that included a wife and kids. What if he'd always had one? Only a double life made a man that hard to find.

So what was Tam really afraid of? That her mother would never find her father or that she would?

With the slightest tremble, Tam forgot all about poachers and drug runners and soldiers underfoot. She ripped open the envelope on what promised to be her mother's latest progress report.

"Trouble in paradise?"

Tam spun around. Trouble? Oh, yeah. And she was looking right at him.

He stood just inside the open hangar bay. Like the rest, he wore a combat helmet and the uniform of a seasoned soldier. He was caked in mud. She'd heard it said the uniform made the man. In this case, however, the man made the uniform. And he made it look good. Not that she was attracted to the type....

Dear Reader,

In the summer of 1976 my grandfather took me to see the movie *Midway*. Three years later, in October of 1979, I had the privilege of meeting retired Navy pilot George Gay and hearing his firsthand account—in the movie, he's the guy who watched the battle of Midway unfold from the water.

Both left indelible impressions on me. I had entered the Navy between seeing the movie and meeting George, and I couldn't wait to get there! In the summer of 1980 I shipped out to Midway Islands, and to this day it remains my favorite duty station.

In 1988 Midway Islands became a national wildlife refuge while still under the jurisdiction of the Navy. In 1993 the Navy closed its base of operation altogether. And by 1996 the transition to the Department of Interior was complete.

At a formal ceremony in April 1997 the Secretary of the Navy described the changing mission of Midway Islands as a transition from "guns to gooneys." This is my purely fictional account of that transition. If in reading this story you can't tell fact from fiction, then I've done my job!

Enjoy!

Rogenna Brewer

P.S. If I were writing about my actual experiences on Midway Islands, oh, the stories I could tell!

Books by Rogenna Brewer

HARLEQUIN SUPERROMANCE
833—SEAL IT WITH A KISS
980—SIGN, SEAL, DELIVER

Midway
Between You
and Me
Rogenna
Brewer

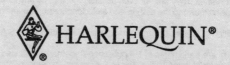

HARLEQUIN®

TORONTO • NEW YORK • LONDON
AMSTERDAM • PARIS • SYDNEY • HAMBURG
STOCKHOLM • ATHENS • TOKYO • MILAN • MADRID
PRAGUE • WARSAW • BUDAPEST • AUCKLAND

ISBN 0-373-71070-4

MIDWAY BETWEEN YOU AND ME

This edition published by arrangement with Harlequin Books S.A.

® and TM are trademarks of the publisher. Trademarks indicated with
® are registered in the United States Patent and Trademark Office, the
Canadian Trade Marks Office and in other countries.

Visit us at www.eHarlequin.com

Printed in U.S.A.

For my editor, Laura Shin, who once told me not all heroines have red hair. She proves it every day.

For my grandfather,
a Swiss immigrant and true American hero.
Gustav Adolf Amend
Born: 1904
(That's not a mistake—he's 98)

For my Midway friends,
especially the guys of NMCB133 det '80–'81.
How could I forget?

PROLOGUE

Spring 1972
Quang Tri Province, Vietnam

WAS IT POSSIBLE FOR A MAN to fall in love in the hours between sunset and sunrise? When he gazed into her beautiful almond-shaped eyes, he thought it was. Adoring. Brave. How many times had he been back since she'd saved his ass? Countless, in his dreams. Not enough, in reality.

He could never get enough of her.

The first time he'd left there'd been acceptance in those expressive eyes. The first time he'd returned and every time since, joy.

This time there were tears.

He'd be leaving Quang Tri Province, not just for a few days, but for a few months. For as long as his mission kept him away. "Don't cry, honey. I was born under a lucky star."

His Vietnamese was only marginally better than her English, and he sure as hell didn't have the vocabulary to say what needed to be said.

Instead he stroked the silk of her dark hair, trying to comfort her the way he would a child. And she was little more than that. Back home in the States she'd be jailbait. While he was twenty-five, fighting a war with no victor, only victims. But somehow when they were together nothing else mattered except what they felt.

What they did. And what they did was make love. He plucked a straw from her hair. He loved to feel its softness against his callused hands. They could hide from the world behind that curtain of hair—he inside her and she moving her slender hips to nature's enticing rhythm.

But her slow, sensual torture wasn't enough. Not today.

He sat up, taking her with him. Midnight-black hair fell past her shoulders to the curve of her spine. She wrapped her legs around him without hesitation, then touched his face. And finally her lips to his.

He growled low in his throat, deepening the kiss.

It was less an exploration than an invasion. He wanted to conquer her lips, to demand from her the level of passion she incited in him.

Reaching under her loose-fitting shift, he grasped her slender hips to drive her harder. And harder. As if anything would be enough to drive away his raging need to possess her.

He was a man built for endurance and she was a woman made to be treasured, not treated like some five-dollar whore in Saigon. Yet, she smelled of sweet grass and sex, an intoxicating combination of innocence and experience.

He'd always been so careful. But this time he held nothing back.

Sweat soaked both their bodies. He trailed heated

kisses, abraded her soft skin with his stubbled cheek. His mouth found one small breast, suckling her through the transparent fabric of her shift. The only cries coming from her now were those of sheer rapture. Maybe this was what he'd wanted, to drown out the tears.

Maybe this was what they both needed.

To communicate without words.

He wasn't her first. Not that it mattered. Not that he deserved her. But he knew by the way she clung to him he'd been the first to give her pleasure.

It was enough to give him the release he sought. His guttural cries became primitive, and when he was spent he couldn't even separate their bodies, wouldn't even look at her, afraid of what he might see.

So he closed his eyes. Rested his head between her breasts. And fought back his own tears, listening to her pounding heartbeat.

"Skully-san?"

He didn't respond. She cradled his head in her hands. Maybe she'd been holding him that way all along. He felt her fingers in his hair as she smoothed it away from his brow. Then she freed it from the ponytail he wore.

His kind weren't crew-cut soldiers.

The Viet Cong called them "men with green faces." Their own side called them "baby killers." As undeserving a moniker as any. The Navy's Special Ops forces had been misunderstood and underutilized since President Kennedy had created them eleven years ago. What they were—what he was—was a Navy SEAL.

A commando of sea, air and land, able to adapt himself and his fighting to any environment. Even the humid jungles of Vietnam. And because of that...

Feared. Despised.

A man with a VC bounty on his head.

And right now a man ashamed. He put her in danger every time he came here.

"Skully-san, look at Lan. I have displeased you?"

He raised his head to look into her innocent eyes. That she trusted any man after what she'd endured in her young life humbled him. "You could never displease me, Lan."

She smiled a watery smile and traced the skull-and-crossbones tattoo on his right biceps. "You take Lan with you this time?"

"It's too dangerous." At dawn his team headed west to the Mekong Delta in an effort to cut off supplies funneling into North Vietnam through Laos. Every day he'd travel a little farther north, upriver. A little farther away, up-country.

He didn't know when he'd be back.

Or if he ever would.

With gentle hands, he lifted her from his lap and pushed to his feet. He tossed her a jumper that looked and felt more like a burlap sack. He didn't have to search for his pants, they were around his ankles and back up around his hips in no time. His boots were still on his feet. They hadn't completely undressed. They never did.

He didn't know when Charlie would come calling, eager to collect his reward.

He zipped his pants and belted the holster for the

sheathed knife he wore. He didn't need more than that to survive in the jungle. But he carried enough to arm a small country.

Because his uniform was whatever he wanted it to be, he'd ripped the sleeves from the standard-issue green fatigue. He wanted his tattoo visible, wanted his reputation to preceede him.

She watched him, growing agitated as she always did when it came time for him to go. He tilted her chin so she had to look up at him.

"You're better off without me. You know that, don't you?" Who was he trying to kid? Like hell she was. He could marry her. Send her to the States. She'd be safe. Maybe a little scared at first.

But safe.

"If you say so, Skully-san." There was no mistaking the pout to her lips. Lips he wanted to kiss again.

"I say so," he almost barked at her, his gruff voice hiding more than it gave away. He always got a little testy when it came time to leave her.

If he married her, what would he do with her during all those months it took to cut through the bureaucratic red tape? It wasn't easy to send a war bride home. He didn't even have time to get her to Saigon. Some servicemen kept women, wives, set them up in apartments. But a village girl like Lan would be shunned by her family for such a thing.

And if anything happened to him, he'd be condemning her to a life on the streets. Too many young girls found that out the hard way.

Besides, with a bounty on his head she'd be a liability. They were better off keeping things the way they were. And she'd be better off with her family.

He wanted to laugh at that.

Her family had sons fighting on both sides of the war, drafted or recruited. He didn't know the right or wrong of it himself, so he could hardly blame them for choosing one side over the other.

Except her parents had betrothed their only daughter to a high-ranking North Vietnamese Army officer more than twice her age. An arranged marriage to an older man. Same thing as slavery. And he did find fault with that.

Her engagement to the NVA officer was to last until she turned sixteen, almost a year.

To hell with them all. She belonged to him.

There had to be a way *they* could be together.

She'd be exchanging one old man for another. Compared to her youth he'd lived a thousand lifetimes. Yet there was more than innocence in her eyes. There was wisdom, too.

And heartache. Too much heartache.

"I will come back for you. When it's safe. You know that, don't you?" He almost choked on the promise.

"San Francisco, U.S.A."

The corners of his mouth turned up at her careful pronunciation, and he pulled her close. "That's right. I'm gonna take you home and fatten you up." On his mother's cooking. With his babies. Lots of babies...

Shit, his old man would have a coronary. Amerasian babies? A Vietnamese bride? Maybe not

Northern California, near his folks. But they'd find a place to call their own. When the war was over.

Only one catch.

They both had to survive. And she had to remain his. He wasn't feeling that lucky. Before the month was out there'd probably be some G.I. to take his place. Some guy who'd do right and marry her. Or some guy who'd do her wrong. Maybe a lot of guys.

Because like him, she was a survivor. And survivors did whatever they had to do to stay alive.

His gut ached just thinking about it.

She was crying again.

She tried to bury her head in the crook of his shoulder, but he held her at arm's length, memorized every inch of her face. That beautiful face.

"Ah, hell." He whipped out the small notepad he carried in his shirt pocket and scribbled across the page. "This piece of paper makes you my legal dependent. My common-law wife. Do you understand?" He shook the paper in her face and waited for her nod. He'd written words to that effect along with his name, rank and serial number. "You're not to show this to anyone. Not your parents. Not your brothers. But if there's trouble, *big* trouble—" he emphasized "—you get to the U.S. base in Da Nang any way you can. You show this paper to the guard at the gate. He'll take care of you." He explained it all again in Vietnamese.

She sniffled and swiped at the tears, all the while nodding. He only hoped she really understood.

He could tell by the gaping holes in the sod roof that dawn threatened. Their time together had come to an end. He shoved a wad of bills into her hand. "Four hundred dollars, U.S." A month's salary for him. More than enough to keep her and her family for a year. "You don't spend this unless—"

"Big trouble."

"That's right. Big trouble. You'll need it for travel. And bribes. Understand?"

She nodded. *God, help her.*

Then he took one last thing from his pocket and handed it to her. A picture. The only thing he'd actually intended to leave behind. "Me and the guys," he explained unnecessarily. "Keep it hidden, too. But if you ever miss me…well, you just look at that ugly mug and know I'm thinking of you."

She pressed the items to her breast.

"You deserve better than me, Lan. But I promise I will come back for you." He looked for doubt in her eyes, saw only love shining there. "This is a hell of a way to get married."

There were no good choices. He could only hope he'd made the right one.

"You very good man, Skully-san. I make you good wife. Lan speak better English when you come back."

"Your English is perfect. You're perfect." He buried his nose in her hair. For the first time in a very long time he actually had something, someone, to live for. To fight for. To die for. He would take her earthy scent to his grave if it came to that. "Don't change a thing, honey. I love you just the way you are."

CHAPTER ONE

Spring 2002
Eastern Island, Midway Islands

PROFESSOR TAM NGUYEN lowered her video camera and hit Instant Replay. There it was again. Twice the size of her own bare foot. A single impression in the wet sand wiped away in the blink of an eye by the tide.

The fine hairs on the back of her neck stood on end.

Turning off the camera, Tam searched the surrounding darkness. The ocean. The island. She listened for unfamiliar sounds above the wind and surf, heard only the clapping beaks of young gooney birds trying to attract mates, and the occasional bark of a Hawaiian monk seal staking out his territory. The cacophony of Midway Islands.

Nothing out of the ordinary. Nothing human.

Except the catch of her own breath.

But Bigfoot was out there. Somewhere. And he hadn't bothered to introduce himself.

Tam hurried back up the beach to where she'd spent the better part of the past two hours filming a nesting green sea turtle she'd followed to the water's edge. Sometime during the night the air turned chilly. She'd just been too preoccupied to notice. She felt it now and shivered.

Putting on her windbreaker over her beachwear, she untucked her hair from the collar. The Fish and Wildlife designation on the jacket gave her some semblance of control.

She took a second to stake a No Trespassing sign near the mound of sand. If Bigfoot had come to collect turtle eggs, a posted warning wouldn't do much good. But her presence might make him think twice.

Poachers didn't like confrontation.

Neither did she. At least not unarmed.

Tam touched her holstered sidearm. She felt more comfortable using the video camera than the 9 mm Glock, but both served a purpose. As did the rifle she'd left under lock and key back in the boat.

Gathering her things, she shoved writing materials and penlight into the open gunny sack, then rummaged for her walkie-talkie.

Her quick search yielded several items that fell into the practical, but not-usable-in-this-situation category, like Tampax and Tic-Tacs. An unopened letter from her mother gave her reason to pause, but she didn't have time to stop and think about that now.

Radio in hand, she called for her lab assistant.

"Come in, Will. Over." Tam waited a beat for his response. No answer. Not surprising at four o'clock in the morning. And her admin assistant was even less likely to be awake at this hour. "Katie, are you there? Over." Tam's whispered pleas carried on the breeze, making her sound a little desperate even to her own ears.

But it never occurred to her to be afraid.

She felt safe on Midway. Safer even than in San Francisco. She didn't lock her doors. Or windows. The wildlife refuge staffers and scientists were a close-knit group, always watching out for one another. It just so happened tonight she didn't have backup.

Collapsing the tripod, she stuffed it and the video camera into the open sack, zipping it closed with an economy of movement. She kept the radio close at hand.

The prudent course of action would be to return to her boat and head back to Sand Island. Imprudent would be to retrieve her rifle and go after the poacher herself.

Having grown up on the streets of Ho Chi Minh City, the city her mother still called Saigon, Tam was nothing if not resourceful. And more than capable of handling any situation that came with her job. She'd known real fear in her life and this didn't even come close.

Opening a letter from her mother—now, that was scary.

Flinging the weighted pack over her shoulder, she made her way toward her boat. Toward her rifle. Ambient light from the full moon guided her cautious but hasty steps.

Eastern Island had not been inhabited by humans since the Naval Air Station moved to Sand Island in the fifties, before being downgraded to a Naval Air

Facility in the seventies. A few years ago the Navy had closed its base of operation altogether—though they still used the base for refueling—and left the management of Midway Islands to the Fish and Wildlife service. That's when she'd signed on as warden of the atoll.

The Navy may have abandoned them, but she could always count on the Coast Guard. It had small bases all over the Hawaiian Ridge. With any luck there'd be a patrol in the area. About to switch to an emergency frequency, Tam stopped just in time to catch the tail end of a garbled message.

"Warden?"

"Come again, Will. Over," Tam answered.

"Yeah, Warden, I'm at the airplane hangar. You may want to get back here. Something's up."

0420 Wednesday
NAVAL AIR FACILITY
Sand Island, Midway Islands

IN A MATTER OF MINUTES Tam had tied off her boat at the marina and joined Will on the tarmac in front of the airplane terminal. Amber light from the open hangar bays spilled onto an unmarked military C-130 Hercules. The cargo plane had landed for refueling. Not all that unusual, except this one stood heavily guarded by soldiers in full-battle dress uniform, armed with assault rifles.

"What do you think is in that cargo hold?" Will asked.

"I think they don't want us, or anyone else, to find

out.'' Tam eyed the milling flight crew and the re-fueling truck, then spotted more soldiers. Unlike the others they didn't seem to be standing sentry; their weapons hung from shoulder straps while they talked and laughed.

Still, the whole thing gave her the creeps. Until age seven she'd lived behind barbed wire guarded by sol-diers. Even after that, soldiers had been regular visi-tors to the two-room Ho Chi Minh City apartment where she'd spent the rest of a childhood that ended too soon.

Tam had learned a long time ago not to ask ques-tions when she really didn't want to know the an-swers.

And this was one of those times.

''I've got this covered, Will. You can get some sleep.'' She couldn't tell by his ''bed head'' if he'd been there already or not. He walked around with his blond-tipped brown hair mussed all the time. If it wasn't for his usual rumpled shorts and T-shirt she might think her grad student actually put some effort into his appearance.

''Are you kidding? This is the most excitement we've had on the island in months.''

''No sudden moves, okay? These guys don't look like they miss.''

Will laughed off her warning. ''You're the one who's armed. And might I add, dangerous.''

And since Tam served for what passed as law en-forcement on the island, she'd hang around for a while. ''I'll be inside if you need me.'' She started to walk away, but stopped and turned around. "Will, how long has that plane been on the ground?"

"'Bout an hour."

An hour. She really must have been lost in her own little world. Sound carried for miles at sea, but she hadn't heard the approaching engines of this aircraft or any other craft.

An hour would give someone enough time to get from one island to the other. And leave a footprint.

Deep in thought, Tam headed toward the terminal, carrying her satchel and rifle. The cinder-block building still served as an air hub for all branches of the American military, but like everything else on the island was run by civilian contractors. The first level of spacious hangars housed flight operations, airport terminal, billeting office, maintenance and storage depots. The second contained more offices. And an air traffic control tower capped off the center.

Along the way she exchanged greetings with fellow curiosity-seekers. An incoming flight represented their only real contact with the outside world. But her thoughts revolved around Midway Islands at the moment.

Once inside the nearest depot, she set aside her rifle, dropped her sack on a waist-high stack of empty pallets and dug out the video camera.

Twenty minutes.

That's how long it had been since she'd recorded the footprint. "Hmm…" She glanced over her shoulder at the cargo plane. She wasn't one to believe in coincidence.

Maybe she wasn't dealing with a poacher, after all.

She wished she'd thought to check the boats back at the marina for warm motors. Perhaps their military visitors had borrowed one. But for what reason?

Were there drug runners or smugglers operating out of the atoll? On occasion the Coast Guard and Customs agents tracked one down to the area. She'd make a point of finding out through her contacts.

Returning the camera to its proper case before putting it back in the sack, her hand came in contact with her mother's letter once again. An omen she could ignore once, but not twice. She picked up the sealed envelope and read her own name in her mother's careful print.

Tam's guarded expression softened to a smile. Her mother learned to read and write, as well as speak English, several years after Tam had already mastered the language.

The return address was San Francisco.

Home sweet home. Once Tam had been recognized by both the Vietnamese and United States governments as a U.S. citizen, she and her mother had been allowed to leave Vietnam for the States as part of the Orderly Departure Program fourteen years ago.

Some fifty thousand children born of Vietnamese mothers and U.S. servicemen fathers had been left behind after the war. Tam was just one of them.

Fathered by a man she'd never known.

With only a picture to remind her he'd ever existed.

But even after three decades her mother still hadn't given up hope. In the past year the woman had redoubled her efforts to find him. Tam couldn't foresee a positive outcome from that. If the man was alive he had abandoned them. And if he was dead…well, he had still abandoned them.

Tam could only hope her mother didn't get hurt any more than she already had been. So far the woman had spent thousands of dollars, all leading to the same dead end.

What did her mother really know about the man?

She claimed she'd married him, but couldn't produce documentation. She knew him only by a single name, probably a nickname. She didn't know his branch of service or the most crucial information for tracking him down, his serial number.

And what if her mother did manage to find him after all these years? In all likelihood he'd made a new life for himself that included a wife, kids…a family.

What if he'd always had one?

Only a double life made a man that hard to find.

So what was Tam really afraid of, that her mother would never find her father, or that she would?

With the slightest tremble she forgot all about poachers and drug runners and soldiers underfoot. She ripped open the envelope on what she knew would be the latest progress report.

Unfolding the single page, she began to read….

"Trouble in paradise?"

Tam spun around.

Trouble? Oh, yeah. And she was looking right at him.

He stood just inside the open hangar bay, at the Coke machine. Like the rest, he wore a combat helmet and the uniform of a seasoned soldier.

The jungle print was caked in mud.

He was caked in mud.

And judging from the stubble along his jaw, not only had the man not used a bar of soap in weeks, he didn't even own a razor. She'd heard it said the uniform made the man. In this case, however, the man made the uniform.

He made it look good. Damn good.

Personally, she'd never been attracted to the type.

He nodded toward the letter and rephrased his question. "Boyfriend trouble? You look upset."

"It's nothing." She folded the single sheet along the creases and stuffed it back in the envelope, then shoved that into her jacket pocket.

"Why didn't you just say it's none of my business?"

"Because that would be stating the obvious." Her hand shifted from her pocket to the butt of her Glock. He made her nervous with all that weaponry, a semi-automatic rifle slung over his shoulder, a handgun hanging from a utility belt slung low over his hips, a knife strapped to his thigh, and whatever else he carried concealed.

Her preoccupation with his equipment didn't go unnoticed, however. He smiled, showing off even white teeth. Apparently he'd only run out of shaving cream and not toothpaste.

"Between the two of us we could start a war," he observed. "Your finger isn't itching to pull that trigger, is it?"

"You haven't said or done anything to give me a reason to shoot you, *yet*. But I might decide to hose you down." She'd caught a whiff of burnt hemp. "Been smoking something, soldier?"

His laughter was hearty and genuine. "Uncle Sammy doesn't put up with that."

"Probably just jungle rot, then," she said with a trace of skepticism.

"Or something." He sniffed at his shirt. "Pretty rank, huh? Trust me, I didn't inhale."

"I guess that makes you a Democrat."

"Pretty. And witty." He turned to the Coke machine, emptying his pockets of change.

"Excuse me?"

"Whoever *he* is, he's a fool."

He? He who? She followed the direction of his thoughts to the letter in her pocket. Did he think she'd received a "Dear John" letter? Or rather, a "Dear Jane?" His eyes were shadowed by his helmet. Unreadable.

She wanted to know the color of those eyes. Maybe blue or green to go with that scraggly blond beard. "What makes you say that?" she asked, choosing not to enlighten him.

"Either he is. Or I am. I've been standing here for the past few minutes trying to get your attention." He punched a couple of buttons and two cans rolled out, one right after the other. "Can I buy you a drink?"

Trouble had the kind of voice that made even the simplest question sound like an invitation to the bedroom.

"No, thank you."

Taking her rejection in stride, he set one can on top of the vending machine, then casually leaned against it while he popped the top on the other and took a swallow. "Not much of a soda drinker this time of day, but I could use the caffeine."

She folded her arms in deference to his attempt at casual conversation. Or because the way he looked at her with those shaded eyes made her feel exposed. She'd added sandals to her attire, but still wore only her one-piece swimsuit and a loosely tied sarong under the Fish and Wildlife jacket. Not exactly the uniform for facing down your foe.

And she definitely considered all soldiers to be her enemy. "Look, I don't know what you think you want—"

"What does any man want first thing in the morning?" He gave her a dimpled grin, so completely male. So compelling.

She arched a brow in response. "I wouldn't know."

"Breakfast."

"Breakfast?" So the way to this man's heart was routed through his stomach. She pursed her lips to keep Trouble from getting the impression she found him amusing.

"Know where I can get a short stack of pancakes dripping with maple syrup? Bacon and eggs? Hash browns? About a gallon of coffee, strong and black?" He finished the last of his soda and tossed the empty can into a nearby recycling bin.

"Try twelve hundred miles southeast of here."

"I'll settle for an Egg McMuffin."

"You're two decades too late. The only McDonald's on the island closed in the eighties."

"Guess I'll have to make do with whatever I can scrounge out of these vending machines." Hitching up his untucked shirt, he dug into his back pocket and pulled out a billfold.

She couldn't help but notice the rest of his equipment, a firm, well-muscled backside.

"You cook?" he asked.

Her mouth opened, but no retort came out. Did he just ask her to make breakfast for him?

"This is supposed to be where you take pity on me and invite me to your place for a home-cooked meal," he confirmed, opening his billfold. "Last chance."

"For me? Or for you?"

"Chocolate bars and potato chips it is." He punched in the number combinations for his selections. Removing his helmet, he ran a hand through slicked-back, dirty-blond hair and squinted against the assault of the fluorescent light.

From what she could tell, his eyes were green.

He filled the helmet with breakfast booty, including the soda she'd refused. "Just don't tell my mother," he said in a conspiratorial aside.

He'd bought enough junk to feed an army. "Are you sure you haven't been smoking something?"

"I'm sure." He caught a bag of chips, then another as they threatened to topple. In the middle of his juggling act, he dropped his billfold. It fell open to a picture of a dark-haired boy and girl. Tam bent to pick it up.

"They must look like their mother." Feeling disappointed in him, and herself, she dropped the leather billfold into his upturned helmet, crushing the chips.

He winced.

She should have checked out his ring finger before she checked out his butt. She drew the line at military men. A married G.I. was far across the line and in quicksand. As a final dismissive gesture, she flung her sack over her shoulder and reached for her rifle.

"Kids?" He recovered from his stunned silence. "No, thanks. Not married, either. Never been in one place long enough. This is my niece and nephew. Aaron's ten, Mariah's three." He held it out to her for a second look.

She turned around to do just that and got a good look at his left hand. No wedding band and no tan line.

"Actually, they look like their father." He flipped to a picture of a handsome couple in uniform. "Aaron's adopted, but you'd never know it. Miller married my sister, Tabitha." The pair were opposite another couple in uniform. "Brother Zach and his wife Michelle." Then he flipped to the next photo and it all came together.

"I see you come from a military family." His coloring came from his mother, while just about everything else came from his father.

"My brother's no longer in the service. And my dad retired about the time I started school. But, yeah, I'm a military brat." She studied the image of the older man. His most noticeable feature was a scar from temple to chin.

He continued flipping through more candid shots

before coming to the end. He would have closed down the show then, but she stopped him, even took the billfold for a better look at the last picture. "Homecoming King? That is you with long hair and an earring?"

"Yeah, that's me. Rebel without a cause. Or a clue."

"But a girlfriend." She studied the brunette in the photo, all perky cheerleader smile and perky cheerleader breasts. The kind of girl who would have called Tam a geek, making her transitional years when she first entered the States as a teenager difficult. "Still your queen?" she asked, gauging his response.

"Married my best friend when I was in my senior year at the Academy. Guess she got tired of waiting." He shrugged.

But Tam thought perhaps the hurt ran deeper than that. He had quite a history in that worn wallet. Relations. Relationships. It must be nice to have a record of your past right at your fingertips. Did it make it any easier to forge your future?

She stood close enough now to get a glimpse into his eyes. They were deep, like the sea. Like him. Uncomfortable with the intimacy of getting to know this stranger through photographs, she handed back his billfold. So the guy had a family and tread marks on his heart.

So what?

So what was that look of expectancy in his eyes?

"I'm sure you're a nice enough guy and all, but…" He wore a uniform and never stayed in one place for very long. Getting to know him would be a mistake. *A big mistake.* "I'm used to your kind just passing through."

Tam picked up her rifle and stepped outside. Pre-dawn threatened to cut through the darkness, bathing the early morning in gray.

"Wait! Wait a minute. At least tell me your name?" he called after her.

"What does it matter? I'm sure your plane's been refueled by now." She kept walking, but he caught up to her in a few easy strides.

"Midway Islands, Where East Meets West. I read that off a mural in the terminal. Sounds kind of nice. And we haven't really introduced ourselves yet." She came to an abrupt stop. He put a hand on the small of her back, probably in an effort to steady her. *Probably.*

She felt the warmth long after he ceased to touch her.

"You're assuming an awful lot. I'm as apple pie as you are. San Francisco, U.S.A. Ever heard of it? I have no ties to the east." Not anymore.

"My unit has a motto—The Sun Never Sets on One Thirty-Three. We've traveled so far west from our homeport of Gulfport, Mississippi, that we're east again." He seemed to take care in choosing his next words. "I'm just returning from six months in Bangkok, Thailand."

She felt a surge of something... Wistfulness? But for what she didn't know. "I was born in Hanoi, raised in Ho Chi Minh City until I was fifteen," she admitted, but couldn't explain why she chose to confide in him.

She'd said too much.

But not enough to erase the compassion in his eyes. If he thought it unusual for an Amerasian to be born in North Vietnam, he didn't comment. Along with compassion she could see a spark of curiosity. Or perhaps interest that had been there all along.

"Maybe someday you'll go back for a visit. It's a small world and getting smaller all the time."

She could never go back.

"Not that small." Even if he wasn't referring to their obvious differences, he had to see that like Midway, she belonged neither east nor west.

"Not when you're a long way from home," he agreed, holding out his hand. "Lieutenant Bowie Prince, CEC, USN."

She read his name off his uniform at the same time he said it and realized all he'd had to do was read her jacket to find out hers. He probably already had.

She'd heard the loneliness in his words. They were both a long way from home. She should run away from him as fast and as far as her feet could carry her. She didn't want to find a kindred spirit in this man. Hesitating, she took a deep breath and put her hand in his. "Professor Tam Nguyen, warden of Midway Islands."

"Professor." He held her hand a moment too long.

She pulled out of his grasp and wiped her slightly damp palm along her thigh. "So, Lieutenant, what are you doing on my island?"

"Your island? I thought Midway Islands belonged to the Department of the Navy."

"The Navy likes to think so."

"My mistake." He didn't even try to disguise the amusement in his voice.

It took a second to sink in. Then she realized just what he found so funny. *Academy. CEC, USN.*

"You're not Army, are you?"

"'Fraid not. United States Navy at your service, ma'am." He offered a mock salute.

"Technically," she said, backtracking, "the Naval Air Facility and islands still *belong* to the Navy."

"I know."

"I guess it just goes to show you can't judge a man by his uniform." Her natural skepticism returned. Because to her they were all alike.

"Sure you can." He lifted his right collar. "Double bars make me a lieutenant, same as a captain in the Army. Both are O-3—officer, third pay grade. Like you're—what?—a GS-7?"

He had the Government Service part right. "GS-13."

"I guess we know which one of us makes the big bucks."

They were actually about equal on the pay scale. And about the same age, she surmised. She'd been making a lot of assumptions, now curiosity got the better of her. "What about the initials, CEC?"

"Civil Engineer Corps. Same as the speciality insignia on my left collar." He pointed to the cluster of gold leaves and silver acorns.

"A civil combat engineer? As if that's not an oxymoron."

"I'm trying to be serious." But his smile said he wasn't trying very hard. He wasn't the serious, studious type. He wasn't her type.

"So tell me what the insignia above your name means?" She studied the bee anchored in another leaf cluster between crossed rifle and sword.

"Seabee Combat Warfare Specialist. And the red kangaroo patch on my shoulder is for my unit, Naval Mobile Construction Battalion One Thirty-Three—the

Running Roos. Long story short, NMCB133 was first commissioned to deploy to Australia. But World War Two came along and they shipped out to the South Pacific instead.''

''And the one with the lightning bolt on your other shoulder?''

''Underwater Demolition Trained.''

That sounded dangerous. ''Is there a story behind it, too?''

''Never on a first date.''

She ignored the implication. This wasn't a date, only a chance meeting. ''I suppose some women find a dangerous man fascinating.''

''But not you.'' He made it a statement, not a question. But there was a question hiding behind those words.

She looked back up into those sea-green eyes. She could see herself drowning in them. ''Not me,'' she agreed.

She found fascinating men dangerous.

''I didn't think so,'' he conceded. ''So now you know everything there is to know about me. Let's talk about something more interesting.''

''Like?''

''You.''

She'd drown, all right, or at least find herself in over her head without a life preserver. Tucking a strand of hair behind her ear, Tam sought to change the subject. ''You never did answer my question.''

''What question was that?''

''What are you doing on my island?''

''I thought we decided this was my island?''

''You're just passing through, remember?'' She made a point of reminding them both. And just in case she needed a further reminder, instead of his eyes, she contemplated the combat boots that would be marching right out of her life.

His boots were caked in dried mud. But his trousers were wet to the knees and covered in sand and muck. Why was that?

Could it be she'd found Bigfoot?

Her gaze darted back up to meet his. "Been anywhere near Eastern Island tonight?"

"That's an odd question."

"Have you?" she persisted.

"I could tell you," he teased. "But then—"

"Let me guess. You'd have to kill me? I've heard that one before." Why wouldn't he answer her simple question?

"I'd have to seal your lips…somehow. But *how* is classified."

Ninety percent of all communication was supposed to be nonverbal. His message came through loud and clear on both levels, *I want you.*

But he represented everything she didn't want.

He leaned in. And she realized in about one second she'd either come to her senses or wish she'd popped one of her Tic-Tacs. Tam cleared her throat. "I'm not going to let you kiss me."

"No?" A trace of hope lingered behind that word.

"No." She shook her head.

"Because we just met?" He pulled back and searched her face. "Or because you don't want to kiss me?"

Did they just meet? He felt familiar.

Did she want to kiss him?

"What does it matter?"

"It matters to me. I swear—" he raised his hand

in oath like the Boy Scout he wasn't "—whatever the answer I'll still respect you in the morning."

"It's already morning."

"It's always morning somewhere in the world. What are you afraid of?"

"Bee stings."

For the first time an awkward silence fell between them. He'd taken her rejection personally this time.

She'd meant it that way.

"I guess you couldn't be any more honest than that."

A shrill whistle came from the direction of the cargo plane. They both turned toward the soldier waving his arms. "L.T.!" the man shouted. "Time to move out!"

"Guess you have to go."

"They won't leave without me." He adjusted the helmet full of loot at his hip.

But the refueling truck headed back to the hangar. And there didn't seem to be anything left to say, except goodbye. Though neither of them said it, their time together had come to an end.

"*L.T.!*"

"Coming!" he shouted, then frowned an apology to her, swallowing whatever it was he'd been about to say.

"You really should go...." She searched for something to break his hold on her. Or her hold on him. She focused on his boots again, then up his thigh. And stopped. "Did you get that in Thailand?"

"This?" He unsheathed the weapon strapped to his leg.

"Handle's ivory, isn't it? I'm going to have to confiscate your knife, Lieutenant."

"What?"

"Please hand over your weapon." She held out her hand.

"Are you trying to disarm me, Warden? Because I could think of better ways to do it." He made light of her request. That irritated her, not that she wasn't used to it, but it didn't deter her. "Your weapon."

"I happen to be the senior ranking officer on an American military installation—"

"Under the management of the U.S. Fish and Wildlife Service. I'm a civilian doing my job. And as a U.S. citizen on U.S. soil you have no authority over me, Lieutenant. A fact that's written into the United States Constitution."

"So we're at a standoff."

"No, I still intend to have your knife. You'll never get something like that through Customs. Importing ivory is illegal."

He sheathed the knife. She thought he'd walk away then, but he surprised her. Untying the thong with a jerk, he handed it to her. "Let's just say I know which battles are worth fighting. I'll be back for that." He nodded toward the knife in her hand. "And maybe we'll get around to having breakfast together, after all."

His words promised she'd have more than a fight on her hands. But it was the unspoken promise in his eyes that threatened her.

She liked him better with his helmet on.

Tam put her hands on her hips and tilted her chin to meet his steady gaze. "There's one thing you should know about me, Lieutenant. I don't cook."

"But I make a mean western omelet. And I didn't

buy that piece in Bangkok. It's a family heirloom. So take very good care of it for me.''

He walked away then, leaving Tam to squint into the rising sun. Each step took him farther away. She felt the tiniest tug at her heart, almost as if he were taking it with him.

Impossible. She didn't believe in love at first sight. She didn't believe in love at all.

Tam turned the ivory handle over in her hands. No question the knife had to be valuable—the craftsmanship alone made it a museum piece—but an heirloom?

She touched the tip of the well-honed blade. The prick barely registered. Even if she did believe in love, she wouldn't fall for a soldier.

"A sailor," she corrected herself, sucking her nicked finger. But it didn't stop the sting. "A Seabee.''

It didn't really matter, though. Because soldier or sailor, the last thing she'd ever do would be to repeat her mother's mistake.

CHAPTER TWO

0830 Wednesday
NAVAL STATION PEARL HARBOR
Pearl Harbor, Hawaii

ONE HUNDRED AND SIXTY commands operated out of Naval Station Pearl Harbor. Lieutenant Bowie Prince could only assume the cavernous underground bunker with high-tech security was one of them. They'd been taken there after landing, left alone in the interrogation room and not one member of his eight-man squad knew what to expect next.

Bowie removed his helmet and ran a hand through his hair. "There's enough grease on my scalp to replace a can of WD-40." The laughter released the tension momentarily. "I guess we wait." He set his helmet on a nearby conference table. Their gear and weapons had been left in a holding area. "Help yourselves to coffee."

A stainless-steel pot percolated in the corner. And several of his men did just that. Afterward they scattered to sit around the room.

While he remained standing.

Afraid he might fall asleep on his feet, Bowie paced from one end to the other. There were speakers in every corner, TV monitors built into the far wall, and a mirrored observation window framed the wall closest to him.

He debated addressing the mirror.

"Here." Dylan McCain handed him a longed-for cup of coffee and joined him in staring at the window.

"Thanks." Right about now he needed to mainline the stuff straight to his bloodstream. "I hate to even grumble when I know my every word can be overheard, but I wish they'd just get on with it."

"You and me both," the lieutenant junior grade agreed. He'd removed his helmet as well. His hair was just as dirty and he smelled just as bad. They all did. No less than to be expected after weeks spent in the jungles of Laos.

Thailand had been their official post in Asia, but after they'd run into a little snafu, the mission had turned classified—which was why they were here now waiting to be debriefed.

"Sorry I snapped at you on the plane," Bowie offered the awkward apology.

"Forget it."

McCain had been the first to comment on the fact that Bowie's knife was missing in action. Along with any chance of having breakfast with someone more appetizing than his squad.

"Still thinking about the one that got away?"

"You mean the one that got away with my knife? 'Man is the hunter, woman is his game,'" Bowie quoted. "Only, Tennyson had it wrong, sometimes woman is the game warden." And he wasn't likely to forget that anytime soon.

His next mission would be to get his knife back.

"I believe this belongs to you, college boy." Master Chief Russell "Rusty" Cohen handed over Bowie's wallet.

Bowie checked the contents and groaned, only one twenty dollar bill remained. His wallet had made the rounds along with his helmet full of junk food.

"I'll take that." Rusty snatched up the last of his hard-earned cash.

That would teach him to bet the entire squad he could scrounge up breakfast, a real breakfast. He'd never failed before. His stomach growled, as if in reminder. All he'd had today was a Coke and a Fig Newton.

And a few minutes of female company.

Company that had made it very clear she wasn't interested. In him.

"College boy, listen to your papa-san." Rusty slung his arm around Bowie's shoulder. "Forget about her. Tonight we're taking you to a little place I know."

"I don't know, Master Chief. I'm ready to crash—"

The door opened just then. Their battalion commander, Captain Harris, straight from Gulfport, Mississippi, walked in and the tension returned. Harris led from behind the desk, but always showed up to take credit for a job well done.

Rusty removed his arm from around Bowie and cleared his throat. "Attention on deck!"

The men stood as one.

The captain acknowledged them with a slight nod.

A dozen or so uniformed officers and civilians filed in behind him. Bowie assumed the men and women were with Intelligence and would take and analyze their statements.

Bringing up the rear was The Chief of SEALs. Admiral Mitchell Dann, his father's best friend since the Kennedy era, strode toward Bowie, walking stick in hand.

"Admiral," Bowie extended his welcome.

"Hell of a job, son!" The admiral clasped his hand, then pulled him into a bear hug in spite of their being in uniform and in company.

Bowie met Harris's disapproving gaze over his godfather's shoulder and pulled back. "Reclamation projects and roadways are a Seabee speciality."

"The monsoon season hit Thailand hard this year. I'm sure the relief efforts of your detachment were appreciated. But you know damn well I'm referring to the drug warlord your boys captured," the admiral said, dismissing his attempt at modesty.

Bowie puzzled over the comment. "The last we heard the Thai government let General Xang go."

"Xang is a very powerful man. The Thai government doesn't want border disputes with Laos and Burma to escalate any more than they already had. But that's not the whole story…. At ease," he ordered once he realized the rest of the men remained standing at attention. "There's someone I'd like you to meet."

When the room settled down, the admiral introduced one of the civilians. "This is Robert Stevens. Rob is a former Navy SEAL who served with dis-

tinction in Vietnam. Team Seven. Alpha squad,''
Dann noted for Bowie's benefit.

His father's unit.

The distinction the admiral referred to was the ru-
mor Stevens had had more than one hundred enemy
kills during a covert operation at Parrot's Beak, Laos.
He'd gone through the war with a VC bounty of fifteen hundred U.S. dollars on his head. A hell of a lot
of money in that place and time.

His dad had never mentioned more than that, except to say Stevens hadn't made it home. Bowie'd
assumed the man had died over there because SEALs
were known for never leaving a man behind. If he
had, then Bowie stood talking to a ghost.

And though Stevens may have grayed at the tem-
ples, he looked healthy enough. Like Bowie's father
and godfather, the ex-SEAL kept in shape.

"Sir." Bowie shook Stevens's hand.

"Lieutenant, I know I have at least twenty years
on you, but I'm uncomfortable with officers addressing me as sir when my highest rank in the Navy was
chief. Call me Rob.''

"It would be an honor.''

"And I'll try to remember to call you Bowie.
How's your mother? And that old son of a gun you
call a father?''

"Great.'' Bowie rubbed his thigh. Stevens had
given his father the ivory-handled knife, the knife his
father had entrusted to his youngest son. The knife
the game warden on Midway had taken from him.

"Rob is with the Central Intelligence Agency,''
Admiral Dann continued. "Former head of the Far

East division of Shadow Ops. And current head of that same division's Air America.''

"For the record," Stevens said, "neither of those organizations exist." He moved to the far end of the room and stood in front of the TV monitors. "Gentlemen, I'll be debriefing you this morning."

So Stevens *was* a ghost. A CIA spook. And unless he operated from behind a desk, probably deep cover.

"Congratulations," Stevens began. "You've managed to do in three weeks what I haven't been able to accomplish in thirty years. You captured General Bian Xang." Stevens held up his hands as if he expected them to deny it. Xang's face appeared on the monitors behind him. "I know you've heard Xang's been released. And it's true."

Disappointed murmurs followed the comment.

"Capturing General Xang was never our primary objective," Harris said. "His snipers were keeping us from completing our job on the reclamation project. We did what Seabees are trained to do, defended our job site."

Bowie bit his tongue. His C.O. had never even made it as far as Bangkok during their six-month deployment. And they'd been several hundred miles away in the northern highlands.

"But the fact remains," Stevens insisted, "your men crossed the border from Thailand into Laos to do that."

Bowie felt a little smug satisfaction. If Harris wanted to steal his thunder he could take credit for his mistakes, too. But Stevens looked Bowie right in the eye and it wasn't disapproval he saw there.

"A fact your government will deny." Stevens's slight smile told them all they needed to know. "This is not a lecture, gentlemen. Feel free to add your input. You've given us a look inside Xang's operation, which is no small feat. In the war on drugs you made a significant contribution. You made a bonfire out of two thousand kilos of cannabis...."

The picture of Xang on the monitors behind Stevens morphed into photos of burning fields.

Leave it to a woman. The professor had picked up on the scent right away. Until Stevens mentioned it, he didn't know exactly how many kilos they'd burned under the direction of the Thai government. But it was hard to forget that even standing downwind the Seabees had gotten a little buzz on.

Himself included.

Hopefully there weren't any drug tests coming up. He wasn't sure all his men would pass. Which just gave him more to worry about. Harris was likely to pull something like that after a deployment.

"You destroyed a methamphetamine lab," Stevens continued. "And aided in the release of Hmong highlanders being forced to serve as slave labor."

"Sir...*Rob*..." Bowie corrected himself, then waited for the older man's nod to continue. "I'd like you to know our big break came when Master Chief Cohen remembered working on a site in the highlands of Laos. The lab operated out of an interrogation center NMCB133 built for the CIA during Vietnam. We would never have found it without him."

Intelligence officers and agents, busy scribbling all this stuff down, started firing questions at the master chief in rapid succession. They wanted to know the who, what, when, where, how and why of everything.

Stevens held up his hands. "We'll get to the questions in a minute." He turned to the master chief. "Rusty, I didn't realize it was you. You mean they haven't forced you to retire yet?"

"Soon. Very soon." Rusty chuckled. "And before you go giving me all the credit, I'd like to point out that Lieutenant Prince spotted their man. Tracked him to the general vicinity of the lab before my memory kicked in. He even located the lab with that uncanny way of his."

Bowie studied the toe of his boot. It didn't surprise him that the two men knew each other. The master chief had seen action in Vietnam and every conflict since, long enough to know everyone.

Bowie had relied heavily on the man's experience. When Rusty told him to pocket his rank and scratch the distinction off his helmet or risk being used for target practice, Bowie had done just that. A move that had probably saved his life.

But nothing could have prepared him for the human suffering they'd seen. He and his men had entered the lab with protective gear, but the enslaved Hmong had had nothing. Every pound of meth produced five pounds of poisonous gas. Fires were a constant hazard and burn victims plentiful while emergency medical attention was nonexistent. The squad had arrived and done what they could to save the injured, exploited and sometimes addicted.

Stevens continued down the list of their accomplishments. "You captured fourteen metric tonnes, that's *fourteen thousand kilos,* of illicit opiates that won't be smuggled into the country this year.''

McCain leaned toward Bowie's ear. ''No, we only transported the stuff here ourselves,'' Dylan muttered under his breath.

''What's the street value on all that opium?'' one of Bowie's men asked.

''I think you're better off not comparing it to your paycheck, Jones.'' Bowie spoke over his shoulder to the man who'd asked the question.

Laughter and agreement filled the room. Their payment was in a job well done, not in dollars and cents.

''Laos is the third-largest illicit opium producer in the world. You wiped out ten percent of that supply in one blow. More important, you disabled the operation of the number-one drug warlord in the region.

''And while Xang may have slipped through the system this time, we're in a very good position to flush him out again. Next time he won't get away.''

The room broke into a round of applause.

''Gentlemen, I know you're anxious to get out of here and back to your homeport of…where is it, Gulfport, Mississippi? But I need your cooperation a while longer. We have some questions for you.''

0100 Thursday
THE PAPER TIGER
Honolulu, Hawaii

''SEABEES, CAN DO!'' Bowie raised his voice above the music, toasting their official slogan with his bottle of beer. He got distracted by the label. "What's this stuff called again?"

"Ba Muoi Lam. A Vietnamese brand," Rusty answered with great patience. Which told Bowie the master chief couldn't have been very sober or his natural impatience would have come through. "It translates to the number thirty-five or *butterfly*—as in *Madama Butterfly. Playboy,* if you're referring to a man."

"All that from one word." Bowie returned his attention to the label. "So a gal's considered a butterfly if she's a—"

"Exactly."

"Baa-mooee-laham." McCain tried to pronounce it phonetically. "I'm seeing all thirty-five of those butterflies right now." He seemed mesmerized by the mirrors behind the bar. The play of light and illusion became one, reflecting the topless dancer on stage.

The squad had mustered at the Paper Tiger shortly after the all-day debriefing, taking only long enough for a shower and a shave. The rest of the men were sitting right up on the dance floor, dropping dollars like they had money to burn.

Which they did. At least twenty dollars each of his cash money. Not to mention six months of accumulating paychecks they'd had nowhere to spend until now.

"Cadeo," Bowie called to the master chief's brother-in-law behind the bar. "Another round of Ba Moui…Lam!"

In quick succession the owner of the Paper Tiger knocked off the caps against the scarred surface and lined up another round of beer. They were running up the tab on Bowie's credit card. He couldn't remember, but he thought maybe there was some regulation against officers buying enlisted men drinks, though maybe it was the other way around.

Or maybe they couldn't drink together at all.

As far as he was concerned all rules were thrown out once you spent time in the trenches together.

But the three men in charge were sitting apart with their backs to the stage so they could talk over the latest development concerning their company.

Of course, they could peek if they really wanted to. But by this time Bowie had forgotten exactly what he really wanted.

Except for his knife. He'd managed a few calls that afternoon to his connections in Customs. He'd have the Pirate—as his father had always called it—back in short order and without ever having to step foot on Midway Islands again.

That made his promise to return an empty one.

Of course, he'd known at the time it was unlikely he'd ever see the professor again. She probably hadn't taken his threat too seriously to begin with. They were the proverbial two ships passing in the night.

Bowie took a swig from the bottle.

He would have liked to see her again. But he'd have to be content with the memory.

Long dark hair. Exotic dark eyes. Honeyed skin.

Seabees and honey. The two just naturally went together. But she was afraid of getting stung.

He couldn't blame her.

He'd been on the receiving end of a Dear John a

time or two. He'd also said more than his fair share of goodbyes. It was the price he paid for being part of a mobile military unit. He'd been places other men only dreamed of, he'd done things that really mattered in his life, but he didn't have anyone special to share it with. By choice.

Which was probably why he sat here with the guys.

If he squinted at the blurred image in the mirror, the exotic dancer could almost pass for the game warden. Bowie's eyes drifted closed, but he jerked them open again when McCain said something to ruin the moment.

"I can't believe Dick canceled all leave. Here we are standing by, instead of standing down." The unofficial nickname was an accurate description of Captain Richard Harris. "What about homeport? Not that I mind being stuck in paradise so much, just that I have business to take care of, know what I mean?"

"I'm meeting with Harris Friday. Guess we'll find out then."

"Friday," McCain scoffed. "Couldn't he have given you an extended weekend liberty at least? After all, you earned it. I'm telling you, the man has it in for you, Prince."

"My wife's none too pleased with me right now," Rusty added. "If I knew we'd be here awhile I'd fly her out to stay with her brother and his family."

"Don't make any plans just yet," Bowie warned, wishing he had something more concrete to offer.

The master chief's life wasn't the only one left in limbo. One thirty-three's Alpha company was a mix of marrieds and singles, men and women. Most of the

Alpha Dogs had been in Thailand when his squad had gone hunting snipers in Laos. The rest had been scattered around the South Pacific in smaller detachments.

The others had arrived in Hawaii a week ahead of his squad. After a six-month deployment, they should all be headed home. Instead they were awaiting new orders. After his meeting with Harris Bowie would know more. Then he'd have to break the news to his men and listen to their justified grumbles.

That's why tonight he was getting drunk.

"And what about the world free-diving championships?" McCain demanded. "If we can't get leave—"

"That's the least of our worries." But it looked like they might not be able to compete again this year. With one lung full of air, he could reach depths that challenged fully equipped scuba divers. The sport itself was as old as man's fascination with the sea. But his quest to be the world's deepest man would have to wait. Bowie understood duty came first. Nobody had drafted him into the service. He'd chosen his profession and he didn't have the right to complain. But that didn't mean he always agreed with his superiors. Or his peers. "I don't want to talk about it tonight. Let's wait and see what's up."

Bowie lifted his beer, putting an end to the subject.

"So what do you want to talk about?" McCain's raised eyebrows suggested a specific topic.

Rusty was a little more direct. "Why did you give a little bitty thing like that your knife? Afraid she'd hop on for a piggyback ride if you walked away with it?"

"That's the other subject I don't want to talk about." He'd been a little afraid her trigger finger would start itching. And if she'd pulled a gun on him, where would that have left her? Facing down an adrenaline-charged squad holding M16s? But he could control his men. The truth was he didn't know why he'd given it up. It was probably his most valuable possession, but he'd felt compelled to leave her with something. And she wouldn't accept a kiss. "Because I'm an idiot," Bowie confessed.

"Good enough for me." McCain saluted with his bottle as if he needed an excuse to chug his beer.

"I think you could come up with a little bit better one. Just a *ti ti*, little bit," Rusty said, continuing their education in Vietnamese.

"Tee tee." McCain tested the word.

"*Ti ti*, that oughtta impress her." Bowie's sarcasm wasn't directed at Rusty, but at their female subject. Most women at least liked the uniform, the grungier the better, if not the package inside. Not her. She hadn't seemed all that impressed by either.

He reached for a handful of beer nuts and popped a couple into his mouth. Breakfast had faded to a memory, lunch had been forgettable, and they were drinking their dinner.

"If you want to impress the lady, here's one for you, L.T. *Lai day*, pronounced lye dye," he enunciated.

"What's it mean?" Bowie asked, thinking maybe he would like to learn some Vietnamese. It never hurt to improve one's communication skills. If only he could speak the language of the opposite sex. Or at least understand it.

"Come to me. Add a *lam on*—lahon oon—and you've got *please*. I have a feeling you're going to need it." Rusty chuckled. "And if you're really brave take it further with *toi yen em.*"

"Toi yen em?" Bowie repeated.

"I'll let you figure that one out yourself."

"What about me?" McCain grumbled. "I might be in Vietnam some day. Heard they turned China Beach into a honeymoon resort."

"You're getting married?" Bowie asked.

"I'm getting married?" McCain repeated. "To who?"

"That's what I asked you."

"You're the one getting married. I'm not even in love. Though I could be in lust. With her." He pointed to the mirror, but the dancer had taken a break and the only thing reflected in their line of vision was a pole. "A little skinny for my taste, though."

"Women!" Bowie shook his head. "They give us the time of day and we drop to our knees in gratitude. Only they call it a marriage proposal. I can guarantee you I'm not getting married anytime soon."

"I'll take that bet," McCain said, extending his hand. "You'll be the first to fall."

"Who, me?" But Bowie shook on it.

"Okay, Abbott and Costello. Enough of that routine. Time to load you two into a cab," Rusty announced. "Some of the guys have already headed back to base."

"Do we have rooms at the BOQ?" Bowie asked.

The master chief assured them they had rooms at the Bachelor Officers' Quarters and helped them to their feet.

"Wait! My line," McCain demanded, like a temperamental actor.

"Here's one just for you," Rusty said, urging them toward the door. "*Xin loi*. Sorry 'bout that."

A blast of fragrant night air hit them as they stepped outside. Bowie felt woozy, but McCain looked worse.

"I think I'm going to be sick," McCain warned, barely missing their shoes. "Sin loyee."

"Uh." Bowie stepped out of the way.

"What the hell is wrong with you college boys? Don't they teach Ringknockers how to hold their beer?" Rusty had sure sobered up in a hurry, his patience completely gone as he hailed a cab. "I swear, you didn't have more than a six-pack between the two of you."

0550 Thursday
NAVAL AIR FACILITY
Sand Island, Midway Islands

TAM PUSHED ASIDE the mosquito netting from around the bed. Wearing a simple powder-blue tank top and patterned drawstring pants, she shuffled toward the kitchen. Confusing images of jungles and jungle-print uniforms, of knives and scars, clouded her first waking moments. She shouldn't have been surprised that she'd dreamed of *him*.

But she was.

"Get a grip, girl." She brushed a hand through her hair, freeing it from the loose braid she wore to bed. All this thinking before breakfast gave her a headache. That's one thing she and the lieutenant had in common—the need for caffeine first thing in the morning. Only she liked hers in the form of hot tea.

She chose a ginkgo blend to wake up her brain cells. Putting the tea bag in a chipped ceramic mug, she bemoaned the fact that they'd run out of bottled water a week ago. So she ran the tap water until the rust washed down the drain, filled the mug and placed the whole thing in the microwave, then waited for the timer to ding.

She really hadn't been kidding when she'd told the man she couldn't cook. Even if she could, there wasn't a single egg or a slice of bacon in the house. She opened her cupboards to see if anything interesting had materialized overnight, but closed them in disappointment.

Neither of the military flights this week had brought food. On Monday an unscheduled Coast Guard flight had dropped off mail, and the reason for Wednesday's flight remained a mystery along with the footprint—although she had her suspicions about that.

As for food, she had to make do with canned goods until the incoming log flight later today. And since she'd be leaving for Hawaii on the outgoing flight, she'd have a nice break from roughing it for a change.

A cool northern Pacific breeze blew in from the open French doors off her living room, billowing the hanging sheers on the other windows around the room. She slept with all the windows open and only ever shut them against the rain. Otherwise the house remained open and unlocked at all times. She didn't even own a key. She simply squatted in the deserted naval housing area. Soon it would become Fish and Wildlife Service property and wouldn't matter, anyway.

Mug in hand, Tam crossed the room and leaned against the door frame to savor her morning ritual. From there she could see ribbons of pink on the horizon. She didn't have a view of the ocean, but she liked listening to the island come alive as she sipped her tea.

Her mother had taught her to appreciate every single sunrise—and live in the moment because life could change in an instant. Only part of that lesson had taken hold. She loved to watch the sunrise.

She was too aware of consequences—past, present and future—to live in the moment.

In this peaceful setting, yesterday seemed so very far away. And her dreams were already beginning to fade as she looked forward to a new day.

But she believed in fate.

So there had to be a reason she'd met Lieutenant Bowie Prince. And a message in her dreams.

But why? And what?

Her jacket hung on the back of the desk chair in the corner. She remembered her mother's letter and went to get it. It wasn't so much what her mother had said, but what she'd left unsaid....

Dearest Daughter,

I'm so very sorry I missed your phone call the other night. Mr. O'Connor and I were out to dinner. He's such a dear man. Did I mention he and I met in Saigon all those years ago? He served at the American Embassy as a young marine corporal and I only saw him that one time, so I guess we never actually met. However, to see him again is like going home, not to the war I remember, but to the place in my heart that is Vietnam.

Which brings me to the point of this letter. When are you coming home for a visit? You're much harder to reach by phone than I am. You should memorize all my numbers or at the very least keep them handy. What happened to the cell phone I gave you for your birthday? Do you even carry it with you? I always have mine. And you really should, for your own protection. But I know you, you like your isolation and your island. It's not good for such a young woman to be so out of touch, not just from her mother, but from people her own age. From young men, especially.

Since I don't think I can wait until your next call or visit to break the news, I'll tell you now. Mr. O'Connor and I are making plans for a trip back to Vietnam in the fall. He's helping me look for your father. He's the one. I know it in my heart.

All my love,
Mother

The one, what? Tam puzzled over the question that had been bothering her since last night. Her mother hadn't even mentioned Tam's father except to say that Mr. O'Connor was helping her look for him. She'd mentioned O'Connor eight or nine times.

Could O'Connor be *the one* to finally help her mother forget? This could be a good thing, and Tam would keep telling herself that until she believed it. But he was a Marine.

A *former* Marine corporal.

That didn't make him career military. Probably an enlistee or draftee, and when he'd arrived home from the war he'd gone back to being a regular Joe with a regular job.

Tam had about a million questions. Like who was this O'Connor? What were his motives? Money or something more?

"Let it be something more." Her mother deserved that at least. Tam drank tea to wash down the lump forming in her throat. Folding the letter, she tried to think of it as a new beginning rather than an ending.

She'd call her mother later, but decided right then and there if O'Connor checked out, she'd do everything she could to encourage this budding friendship. She'd have to discourage the trip to Vietnam, though. That was insanity.

She slid the letter under the paperweight on the desk and picked up the knife from the cluttered desktop. Careful of the blade, she studied the polished handle that seemed to cast a spell over her like the country that still called her name.

O'Connor couldn't possibly know the danger that

awaited her mother there—unless Lan had told him everything, and Tam doubted that.

Even the lieutenant had assumed she was able to visit Vietnam. It was true. Americans were free to come and go, but she had other reasons for not being able to return to the country of her birth.

Had the lieutenant ever been there?

And who was he, really? A tall blond stranger who moved constantly, west ahead of the sunset and east ahead of the sunrise. Tam traced the words etched into the silver end cap of the handle. "The Pirate."

Like the owner?

She didn't approve of ivory, killing an animal for its tusks went beyond criminal to inhumane. Small consolation the man wasn't an ivory hunter. Or even an importer-exporter.

So why had he left such a valuable treasure with her? It wasn't like she'd wrestled it out of his hands. And as long as she had possession of his property, it meant they had unfinished business between them.

A connection.

Perhaps it was just an occupational hazard, but she couldn't help but make the comparison to courting penguins. When a male wanted a female he brought her a shiny stone and dropped it at her webbed feet.

If she accepted him as a mate she picked it up.

Tam dropped the knife into the open bottom drawer of her desk and slammed it shut. Penguins, like all her favorite birds, mated for life. She couldn't even see this guy settling down for a moment.

Even if he didn't go around killing for sport, he was still very much a hunter. Maybe the worst kind of hunter. And she had no intention of being his game.

Mug in hand, she stared down the closed desk drawer. She'd deal with the legalities and, if it was possible, figure out a way to return it. The sooner the better. He'd given her enough information about himself that she'd be able to track him down easily enough....

Double bars.

Breast insignia. Unit patches.

Identifies me...

But what if he hadn't been wearing any of those things?

Tam slammed down her mug and ran for the bedroom. The dresser. She yanked the top drawer off its runners, barely skipping back a step before it crashed at her feet.

Dropping to her knees, she tossed underwear to the floor until she found what she searched for.

The Polaroid taken thirty years ago.

Sitting back on her heels, she stared at the photograph. Her mother had given it to her when Tam had turned twenty-one, wanting Tam to have some sort of remembrance of the man.

She pushed to her feet and hurried to her desk. Picking up the magnifying paperweight, she took a closer look at the eight men crowded into the small frame.

They could have been Lieutenant Prince's men. They wore the same kind of uniform, except there wasn't anything to identify them, no bees or lightning bolts. She'd noticed the absence of dog tags and insignia before, but this was the first time she'd ever thought of it as a clue.

And the first time she'd ever considered the possibility that her father wasn't a soldier, but a sailor.

Their face paint concealed more than mere features, it hid a truth that had been right in front of her eyes. As she studied the photo of her father, she began to really see it. The red bandanna wrapped around his head. The sleeves ripped from a uniform shirt that hung open. This wasn't the uniform of a man who operated within the ranks of conventional warfare.

He carried many weapons, an automatic rifle over his shoulder, an ammo pack and knife belted to his waist. But the only identifying mark was that skull-and-crossbones tattoo with the evil red eyes on his right biceps.

She played with the magnifying glass to get a better look at the faces of the other men standing in the haphazard rows. To the far left a man stood out from the rest, dark hair, light eyes, and beneath the grease paint smeared on his face he had what appeared to be a very pronounced scar.

With shaking hands she set down the paperweight and the picture before she acknowledged what she saw. She was fairly certain the man standing shoulder to shoulder with her father was the father of the man she'd met yesterday morning.

"No, it can't be." She reached for the paperweight to disprove her theory and knocked over the mug. Tea poured onto the Polaroid. "No!" she cursed her own carelessness and the irony of fate. Lan Nguyen had managed to preserve that photo for decades. While Tam had managed to ruin it in an instant.

She bit down on her bottom lip, holding back her tears. Nothing could make up for thirty lost years, certainly not a photograph. So why did she feel like mourning the father she'd never found?

Or did she mourn something else?

She'd met the one man who held the key to her past. Did she dare let him unlock the door to her future?

That question unnerved her. He unnerved her.

And now she had to do the unthinkable—ask for his help. "Lieutenant Bowie Prince, don't make me regret we ever met."

Fall 1972
Quang Tri Province, Vietnam

MUCH TIME HAD COME AND gone since Skully had left Quang Tri Province.

Three months to the day he'd left, a fortune-teller had come to the village. Lan's mother had requested a reading, and the soothsayer had taken one look at Lan and predicted what she'd already known, her belly would swell before the month was out.

Lan stopped the oxen and pressed a hand to her aching back. The plow harness weighed heavily on her neck and shoulders as she tilled the soil for a small garden that would be planted in the only section of their land that was still workable.

Skully had been gone for seven months now. She didn't think a baby was what he meant by "big trouble.'' But if she'd still had the means to run away to Da Nang, she would have.

For now she had no choice but to play the dutiful daughter. She could see the smoke on the horizon, hear the explosions in the distance, and still she kept working.

Because she had no choice.

She only had today to live for. There was no tomorrow in Vietnam.

After the fortune-teller left, her mother had admonished her for not taking precautions. And as she had done once before, she'd brewed a special tea and tried to force Lan to drink it, but this time Lan had refused the abortifacient.

Then her father had got involved. He'd demanded the name of her lover. Still she'd resisted, not sure how her parents would react when they found out he was an American G.I. and not some village boy as they suspected.

So they'd searched the house, her person, everywhere until they found the evidence they'd been looking for.

The photograph. The money. The letter.

Lan had watched in tears as her father tore up her husband's words and threw them into the cooking fire. She'd tried to explain. But he wouldn't listen. And he couldn't read English.

Her father had called her a stupid girl for believing the soldier's lies. Lan couldn't read English, either, but she knew in her heart Skully hadn't lied to her.

Her father had been too superstitious to burn the photograph. And too smart to burn American dollars.

So he'd kept both. When things had settled down, her younger brother Bay had shown her where their father had buried the picture behind their hooch.

She'd dug it up and kept it in a hidey-hole in the root cellar. Every once in a while, when no one was around, she'd take out the photo and look at that ugly mug, which was oh, so very handsome.

She'd never seen eyes like his before she'd met him. They were as blue as the South China Sea.

And he said beyond that sea there was a place where they could be together. A place without war. A place where she wouldn't have to go to bed hungry at night because soldiers extorted crops for protection. Or stole them for food. Or destroyed them for no reason.

She missed the little cans of peaches Skully used to bring her almost as much as she missed him. But she could live without the peaches, she couldn't live without Skully.

Lan wiped away her tears. If she and her baby were to eat she needed to get the ox moving again.

She heard the heavy sound of a tank company approaching before she completed the row. Quickly she unharnessed the ox, then slapped it on its flank, knowing the beast would find its own way home.

Quang Tri Province had seen heavy fighting in recent months. Like brothers in a tug-of-war, one day it belonged to the North, the next day to the South. With the villagers caught in the middle.

Tanks meant Americans, since the VC and NVA didn't have any. She could go to her special place, the old barn, and wait for Skully. Just in case he'd returned for her as promised.

Her father owned many fields and many barns, all abandoned now. She'd stumbled on the old barn by chance, having forgotten it was there. Now it was a place she would never forget.

Aside from predicting babies, fortune-tellers also carried news from village to village. Which is how she knew both her older brothers were still alive and fighting.

She'd also heard either the Chinese or Russians had supplied tanks to the North. And that the NVA and VC were once again staging in Parrot's Beak, Laos, to attack Saigon from the southwest. If this was true, the North would soon have control of Vietnam.

With an instinct toward self-preservation, Lan hid in the tall grass as the tank passed by.

This wasn't an American company, but a ragtag band of Viet Cong. Her heart pounded until she thought it would explode. This was the same group of men that had raided her village before. The same group of men that had raped her.

CHAPTER THREE

BOWIE'S EARS WERE RINGING.

Head buried beneath the pillow, Bowie groped for the telephone on the nightstand. "This better be good," he grumbled into the receiver, expecting McCain's over-cheery greeting, but all he heard in return was the stutter tone that indicated he had messages.

The ringing persisted.

Tossing the pillow aside, he sat up and stared at the instrument in his hand as if he couldn't quite believe it wasn't making the racket. Then he realized the persistent noise came from the floor.

He hung up the room phone and reached for his cell phone without getting out of bed. "Yeah?" he answered in time to hear a click and a dial tone.

Who the hell was playing phone tag this early in the morning? According to the alarm clock it was only 0610. He wasn't expecting a wake-up call until 0800, an hour before his meeting with Harris.

But if it *was* already Friday, he'd slept for the past

twenty-seven hours. He remembered waking up briefly with a hangover, but only long enough to grope his way to the bathroom for a couple of Alka-Seltzer before crawling back into bed. "No more Ba Muoi Lam."

Wiping the sleep from his eyes, Bowie checked his calls. There were several from an area code he didn't recognize, a couple local, one from the base, and one from his mother.

He dropped his cell phone back to the pile of clothes on the floor. On the room phone he punched in his temporary retrieval number and checked his voice mail messages.

"You have twelve new messages," the prerecorded voice informed him. The first several were hang-ups...his mother wanted him to call home...more hang ups...

His pants started to ring again.

"Yo?" He answered his cell phone with an ear to the relaying messages. Harris had moved back their meeting to 1400...his godfather wanted him on the links at 0700....

"I need to see you," a female voice said without preamble. The word *need* registered first, then the fact her voice wasn't recorded. He juggled the receivers, hanging up on his messages.

"Yeah," he said, giving her his complete attention. He would have recognized her voice anywhere. He'd just never expected to hear it again. "I mean...I need to see you, too, Tam." Kicking his feet over the side of the mattress, he adjusted the sheet for modesty.

"Are you free for breakfast?" she asked.

Was he dreaming?

"Uh," he stuttered with an eye on the clock. "Where are you?"

"The Hawaiian Hilton. I realize this is short notice, but I flew in late last night, and I've been trying to reach you ever since..."

That would explain all those hangups.

He made a grab for the wrinkled heap of khaki on the floor and stepped into his pants before he remembered he was supposed to be mad at her.

"What's up?"

She hesitated. "I'd rather not say over the phone."

His heart started to beat a little faster.

Something serious. The kind of response guaranteed to scare him off in any relationship. But they weren't in a relationship. So he was more curious than anything else. A breakfast date signaled caution, unless of course it followed a night out. Now, there was a thought.

"How about dinner?"

"I'm afraid I can't. I'm only here for the weekend and my schedule's pretty tight. Breakfast tomorrow? Or brunch, perhaps?"

She seemed sincere enough, but as an excuse it sounded too vague. It wouldn't hurt for him to play a little hard to get. After all, she *needed* him. And he wanted...his knife back. "Did you bring my knife?"

"Yes, Lieutenant, I brought your knife," she responded in clipped tones.

He made a victory fist. But the battle wasn't over yet. "I can't make any promises about tomorrow, Tam. I may have shipped out by then." He counted down the seconds it took for her to rearrange her tight schedule. One, two—

"It would have to be a late dinner, eight or even nine?"

She *needed* him. And he wanted to be needed. "Perfect. The Hilton, right? What's your room number?" He reached for pen and paper from the nightstand.

"There's a lounge off the lobby. I'll meet you there."

Okay, he'd give her that one. "I'll be there, 2000 sharp."

"I might not get there until nine," she repeated.

"Not a problem. I'll wait."

"I guess I'll see you tonight, then."

She sounded nervous. He tried to picture her fidgeting with the phone cord, wearing the only outfit he'd ever seen her in. The image didn't fit. Take away the gun and the wildlife logo. Better.

He wasn't the kind of guy who had the time to take things slow. Or make things permanent. Maybe she needed to. "Tam, about breakfast. I have this thing with an admiral, but nothing I can't get out of—"

"No, don't do that. Tonight's better, anyway. We'll have more time," she reassured him.

Good sign, bad sign? He ran a hand across his flat stomach and felt the churning inside. Now which of them was nervous? It was nice to be needed, but he couldn't help but think it would be nicer to be wanted. Or loved.

"Okay," he said, reluctant to break the connection.

"I'll see you tonight, then."

But neither of them hung up right away—dead air followed. He decided to do something to make her hang up first, otherwise she'd think he was a heavy breather. "Don't forget my knife."

"How can I? You won't let me." Then she hung up.

Bowie smiled into the receiver as he disconnected.

He looked down at his uniform pants. Since he didn't have anything to wear except one wrinkled khaki uniform and a bunch of dirty battle-dress uniforms stuffed into his seabag, he had to do the one thing he hated above all else, go shopping. But first he'd better get out the iron or he wouldn't be going anywhere.

0630 Friday
THE HILTON HAWAIIAN VILLAGE
Honolulu, Hawaii

CINCHING THE OVERSIZE towel threatening to slip, Tam lingered near the phone, towel-drying her wet hair. She'd begun to feel as if she were stalking the man, she'd dialed his number so many times.

Well, this time she'd gotten through. And tonight they'd be dining together. Dinner, not breakfast.

That wasn't exactly her plan.

But she couldn't very well ask him to rearrange his schedule to suit her needs. She didn't want to make this situation any more awkward. Or complicated. She'd have to be very clear up front. She needed his help, but that was all she needed from him.

Stepping up to the mirrored closet, Tam thanked

her lucky stars the Navy hadn't shipped the lieutenant to places unknown. She'd tracked him down to Hawaii through his battalion in Gulfport, Mississippi. But the officer on duty had taken himself a little too seriously and refused to give her any more information.

That's when she'd thought of her Navy contact at Pearl Harbor. The captain heading up the transition of Midway Islands had accessed the lieutenant's numbers, including his personal cell phone number, and had given them to her without question.

Of course she'd had the knife as an excuse to make it sound official. *Had* the knife. U.S. Customs had the knife now.

Perhaps she'd be wiser not to bring that up until after she got what she wanted from the lieutenant.

Tam reached for her uniform, then hesitated. She had a long day of errands and meetings ahead of her. She probably wouldn't get a chance to change.

She made a rash decision and pulled out her light gray pinstriped suit and tossed it to the bed. Her mother had made her mark as a fashion designer by taking the traditional Vietnamese *ao dai* and adding western flare. The Mandarin collar, fitted bodice with long skirt slit to the waist, and loose pants were cut from a summer-weight wool rather than silk. A Lan Nguyen Original.

From half-starved worker in a textile factory to seamstress to top fashion designer, Lan Nguyen had come a long way. In all that time she'd never forgotten her roots.

And wasn't that what this evening was all about?

Tam grabbed a lavender silk bra and panties from her open suitcase and got dressed. She felt both professional and feminine and extremely proud. And just a *ti ti* nervous. She needed to hear her mother's voice.

Tam wouldn't give her mother false hope, just reassure herself that she was doing the right thing for both of them. She dialed out and the phone rang on the other end.

"Hello?"

A man answered, catching Tam completely off guard. "Who is this?" she asked, looking at the phone as if she could see through to the other side. She heard the good-natured chuckle and put the receiver back to her ear.

"I'm guessing you're Lan's daughter."

"That's right."

"Tam, this is Shane O'Connor. I know we haven't met, but I already feel as if I know you. Your mother just ran to the bakery on the corner for some bagels. She should be right back if you want to hang on to the line."

Tam picked up her watch from the bedside table and checked the time; six-thirty Hawaii time was eight-thirty California time. Still early. What was her mother doing having breakfast with a man? A man who felt comfortable enough in her mother's home to answer the phone!

"Do you always answer other people's telephones, Mr. O'Connor?" Tam realized too late she sounded rude.

He didn't seem fazed by her question at all. "We're expecting some long-distance calls this morning. You came up as 'out of area' on the caller ID, but even if I had known it was you I still would have picked up."

"It's hard not to like someone who's going out of his way to be nice to you," she admitted, then got straight to the point. "Do you care about my mother, Mr. O'Connor?"

"Very much," he answered without hesitation.

Tam felt a tightening in her chest. "That's all I needed to know. You can tell my mother I'll call her back later." Tam hung up the phone.

0700 Friday
THE NAVY-MARINE GOLF COURSE
Pearl Harbor, Hawaii

"LIEUTENANT PRINCE." Harris made a point of checking his watch. "Better late than never."

Bowie glanced at his own. According to Greenwich mean he was right on time. "Sorry 'bout that," he apologized to the threesome and their caddies as he joined them on the first tee. "I had to stop at the pro shop."

He'd purchased his Tiger Woods-joins-the-Navy outfit right off the mannequin after the salesclerk had assured him everything matched. His heart had been set on new cleats and clubs, as well, until he discovered he'd left his MasterCard at the Paper Tiger.

He had other credit cards, but the missing one gave him enough of a shock to rein in his spending. He'd bought a new pair of cleats, but rented a set of clubs.

Bowie shook hands all around, first with his godfather, Stevens and Harris, and then their caddies as he was introduced to each of them. He should have thought to ask McCain to caddy. The junior officer would have done it in a heartbeat and would have been better company. He hadn't realized his godfather's invitation had included his C.O.

"Let's get this show on the road," Admiral Dann said, stepping up to the tee. "No one likes to play through a five-star admiral. Bowie, you're bringing up the rear."

"Are you sure you're feeling up to this, Lieutenant?" Harris asked, taking the driver offered by his caddy. "I've managed to take four strokes off my handicap in the month I've been here."

"I'm feeling great." Bowie dumped his rented bag in the nearest golf cart and pulled on his gloves. The fact that his C.O. had been in Hawaii a whole month surprised him more than the older man's improved handicap.

"Really?" Harris questioned. "Because Stevens said he thought you might be feeling under the weather this morning.

Bowie looked over his shoulder at Stevens. Stevens, Admiral Dann, even Harris were all grinning at some inside joke. He knew what they were doing. Golf was a mental game as well as a sport; they were trying to psych him out.

"Youth is wasted on the young," Harris muttered, taking a couple of practice swings. The admiral and Stevens had already taken their turns.

Bowie's godfather squeezed his shoulder. "And

don't even pretend to know what that means. You won't until you're at least forty."

"Looking at life from the downhill slope instead of the uphill climb does have its advantages," Harris added. "Fore!"

"I know when I'm being suckered." Bowie had chosen a driver he felt would take the ball downrange and took a practice swing. "I just didn't know you had the spook spying on me."

Bowie ranked par for this course, so he played without a handicap. But he had a feeling these old geezers were about to give him a run for his money.

"It wouldn't take a shadow operator to see you staggering out of that club Thursday morning," Stevens said.

"But I was still on my feet," Bowie defended as he addressed the ball. Taking a deep breath, he waited until his total concentration was on the game. The club sliced the air and the ball rode the leeward wind, then fell far short of the other three golf balls on the green.

"Standard bet, loser buys lunch," his godfather taunted with a smile as they headed toward the golf carts.

Bowie sucked in his breath and let it out again. "To think I had a better offer this morning."

"What's her name?" Stevens asked.

"I doubt he can keep them straight with a girl in every port," Harris answered.

Her name stuck somewhere in Bowie's throat and he intended for it to stay there. "Afraid I don't live up to that reputation."

They divided into two carts. Paired with Harris and his caddy, Bowie offered to drive.

"That reminds me," Harris said, climbing in on the passenger side. "Did the warden of Midway ever get ahold of you? Said something about your knife and needing to return it. Funny thing is Customs called this morning, said the same thing." Harris gave him that all-knowing look of his.

"Oh, yeah?" Bowie was still trying to absorb the fact that Tam had spoken with Harris when he was hit by the realization that she no longer had his knife.

"So you did speak with her?"

"This morning," Bowie confirmed, replaying the conversation in his head.

"Did she happen to mention the transition meeting?"

"No." It appeared she'd forgotten to mention a few things.

"I may as well brief you now, before we meet with the warden this afternoon. We've been given the overlay project. A high-profile campaign like this puts One thirty-three in line for the Peltier Award from the Society of American Military Engineers."

"We're shipping out to Midway?" Bowie punctuated the question by putting on the brakes. "Sir, we need to discuss morale—"

"Save your breath, Lieutenant. I'm aware your men are giving up a well-deserved homeport. But I want my best man on the job. And that's you." Harris hopped out of the cart. "Don't forget to have your men report to sick call Monday morning for drug testing.'' With that parting shot, he strode toward the second tee.

Could today get any worse?

By the eighteenth hole Bowie realized he never should have asked himself that question.

"Don't forget your tee," Stevens reminded him for the second time.

Bowie turned back around and removed the tee from the ground. "Thanks."

Stevens studied him openly. "Red's my lucky color. Care to make a trade?" He held out a box of white tees for Bowie to take his pick.

Bowie studied the object in question. Stevens either knew or suspected that Bowie couldn't distinguish the colored tee in his hand from the grass at his feet when it was in the ground. Except by outline. And he'd become very adept at that.

Was this a test?

"Why not, it hasn't been that lucky for me." Bowie offered up the red tee and took a white one in exchange. "Did I pass or fail?"

He walked away from the CIA agent without waiting for a response. Shoving the club into the bag, he hopped into the cart with his C.O., thinking Harris seemed the lesser of two evils right now.

He didn't like it when people played games with him. Something he'd put up with all his life.

FOLLOWING THEIR GAME and lunch for seven—on him—at the 19th Puka Club House, Bowie found himself alone in a corner of the locker room with Rob Stevens.

"You need to loosen your grip." Stevens offered the unsolicited advice as they returned from the showers. Towels couldn't hide the ex-SEAL's many visible tattoos and scars.

"I'll keep that in mind." There was nothing wrong with his grip. He had plenty of reasons to be tense. Turning his back on the man, Bowie opened his locker and stowed his shaving kit. It struck him then that he'd sounded like a sore loser, which really wasn't the case.

Gripping the damp towel around his neck, he turned and leaned against a closed locker. Another towel hugged his lean hips. "As my master chief would say, *xin loi*. I got up on the wrong side of the bed this morning."

Stevens followed with a string of Vietnamese that left no doubt the man was as fluent as the master chief's brother-in-law. He sat down on the center bench looking as if he expected to carry on a conversation.

"I have no idea what you just said," Bowie admitted.

"I asked you to come work for me at the agency."

"The CIA?"

Stevens nodded. "I made the same offer to your sister when she finished SEAL training. The Teams wanted nothing to do with women, but I knew Tabby to be an invaluable asset. Eventually, they saw the light. My loss."

"I didn't know that."

"Zach and his wife both fly for me on occasion."

"Really?"

They were tight. Yet his brother had never once mentioned it. Not that he doubted Stevens for a minute. It sounded like something Zach would be crazy enough to do, but Michelle? Bowie just shook his head at the thought of two former Top Gun Navy pilots flying for Air America.

No wonder they didn't have any kids yet.

"I'm not really like my brother or my sister. I'd just as soon not pick a fight if I don't have to. I'm not the kind of guy who throws a punch, I'm the kind of guy who blocks it."

"I understand, more than you might think. And I need players on defense as well as offense."

"I appreciate the offer. But I'm going to stick with blowing up bridges and building roads for the Navy." Whipping the towel from around his neck, he dropped it to a growing pile on the floor.

"For what it's worth, I think you've made the right decision." Stevens pushed to his feet and turned his attention to his own locker.

Thinking the conversation over, Bowie did the same.

"Just curious," Stevens continued over his shoulder. "How'd you get through underwater demolition training being color-blind?"

"So that was a test?" Bowie asked, turning back around.

"A guess," Stevens answered, continuing to dress. "I'm trained to observe. That and something Rusty said about your vision tipped me off. We relied on color-blind spotters in Nam. The military has used them since World War Two. It seems you guys can't be fooled by camouflage because you're used to looking beyond the obvious."

"Adapted, memorized. Faked it," answering the man's earlier question, Bowie shrugged. "Been doing it all my life. The sky is blue. The grass is green. I see color by distinction. Not that faking it hasn't gotten me into trouble." He had an all-too-recent review board to remind him exactly how much trouble he'd gotten himself into.

"So when defusing ordnance how do you know the difference between the red wire and the green one?"

"Red-green color deficiency is the most common type of color blindness. But eyes are complicated. There are different degrees of impairment. In my case I receive all three colors, red, green and blue, but with reduced green sensitivity. The cones and rods work together, so it's more about distinguishing colors from one another. For me a red tee in bright sunlight is a red tee, but a red tee in green grass cast in shadow is a different story."

"Except there's not much on the line in a game of golf."

"You're right, and to answer your question, once the Navy found out I was faking it, they busted me and limited my speciality." But they couldn't take away his training. "Besides, I'm an optimist, which is why I have these." He removed a pair of glasses from his locker and put them on. The specially tinted lenses corrected his vision to some degree. "It's really not so bad seeing the world through rose-colored glasses." That wasn't exactly what is was like for him, but most people could relate.

Stevens nodded. "I certainly wish I could. Vietnam colored my world and changed it forever." Turning back to his locker, he reached inside for his shirt.

Once again, Bowie was struck by the pattern of crisscross welts on the older man's back. "If you don't mind my asking, did you get those in Vietnam?"

"I hardly remember they're there anymore. Bamboo beating. Courtesy of my stay at the infamous Hanoi Hilton. Ever hear of it?"

"Prisoner-of-war camp in North Vietnam." Bowie had a hard time believing the man didn't remember something like that every day of his life.

Stevens nodded. "If it wasn't for your old man I'd be dead."

"I'm sure he was just returning the favor. He said you saved his life over there."

Rob had a far-off look in his eyes, but a slight smile touched his mouth. "As a squad we relied on one another."

Bowie nodded in understanding. "Why'd you stay after the war?"

"There was still work to be done. Once a SEAL, always a SEAL." He closed his locker. "When did you get the tattoo? Not that I was checking out your ass," the man quipped, "just that it's hard not to notice around here."

"Couple years ago we started a fraternity, Sons of the Sixty." His father, godfather and Stevens were three of the original sixty SEALS. But the Navy didn't like its officers tattooed, so unlike Stevens, Bowie had the skull in a fairly inconspicuous place. "How come you haven't asked me why I didn't become a SEAL? I mean, everyone who knows my father asks. But then I guess you know because I just told you why I can never be a Navy SEAL. Or a Navy pilot—"

"Or a UDT Seabee?" Stevens finished for him. "Seems to me you can be anything you want to be. You're more like him than you know. I don't think the word *can't* is in the man's vocabulary. There's *won't* because he's such a stubborn cuss. But *won't* is a choice. I think you made yours. And I think your father knows that. I know he's proud of you. He once said, 'Bowie marches to a different drummer. He's traditional. He loves history. He knows Seabees were frogmen before Navy SEALs were ever commissioned.' And that's why he thinks, and why I think, you choose to be one."

Bowie thought about that for a moment. "Recruiting films depict SEALs as the guys who cleared the beaches in World War Two. The first frogmen were just Seabees who could hold their breath. The first SEALs were just Seabees trained in demolition. Hell, the SEALs still go through our schools."

"But you know the truth. And that's what matters." Stevens offered a wry smile. "How much do you know about Vietnam?"

"What I've read. My dad doesn't talk about it much."

"No, I imagine he wouldn't." He paused, as if gauging his next words. "We fought a Shadow War in Laos. It mirrored the Vietnam War, but started before and ended…well, let's just say it wasn't unusual for profiteers to flourish. Our side, their side, many ran drugs. The Vietnamese had the supply, the Americans had the demand and the connections to open trade routes.

"As an NVA officer, Xang kept a low-profile drug trade, but by the end of the war he'd hooked up with American deserters who were left behind. Within a few years he established himself as a powerful drug warlord."

Stevens seemed lost in another world for a moment. Bowie forgot about getting dressed and stood transfixed by the conversation.

"The CIA was in charge of military Special Operations back then," Stevens continued. "With the war winding down and the conventional military headed home, they were recruiting right from the ranks of Navy SEALs. I had nothing to go home to. As far as I was concerned Vietnam was my home."

Bowie realized he wasn't getting the whole story. "This thing between you and Xang, it's not just about drugs, is it?"

"No," Stevens admitted. "It's personal."

Fall 1972
Somewhere in Laos

"SEE WHAT YOU CAN GET out of him. He just looks at me and pisses his pants."

The scarred face of his commanding officer was

enough to scare anyone. It was probably a good thing the VC didn't know Tad Prince the way Skully did.

SEALs served a real purpose here. Only sixty strong and they were able to keep forty thousand VC busy and unable to fight in the war.

"Sure." Skully pushed away from the wooden support. The Seabees had just built the interrogation center for them deep in the jungle.

The wood smelled new, reminding him of a time he'd gone camping with his family in the redwood forests of California. They'd split logs for fire and toasted marshmallows.

His dad told the best ghost stories. Sometimes war stories set in the South Pacific Islands of World War Two. All his buddies were heroes. All "Japs" hated. He even hated the "Commie Chinks and Ruskies" fighting on the same side. His racist SOB of a father had opinions about Blacks and Jews, as well, but Skully still loved him enough to forgive his ignorance.

Even though the old man was wrong.

Hell, his father had strong opinions about everything. This war. The fact that Skully's own cousin had gone off to law school instead of Vietnam.

He sure as hell would have opinions about Lan. He considered the Vietnamese people "gooks," the racist term that had been carried over from the Korean War.

His father didn't see this war, this country, this people the way he did. With compassion. And he knew that's why Tad Prince had picked him to interrogate their young prisoner.

Mitch Dann was better-looking. Hacker, softer spoken. Doc, younger. H.T., big and intimating. Rodriges, short fused. Ketchum, just plain crazy. That left him.

Skully opened the door and had to hold his breath.

He leaned against the door frame and studied his quarry. God, how old was this kid? Fourteen, fifteen? The VC weren't picky. They recruited them younger and younger these days. And to boys who'd known nothing but war Skully supposed it just became a natural way of life.

With slow, deliberate movements, he tapped a tightly packed box of Winstons until one cigarette nosed its way out. By the time he lit it the kid was shaking, tears falling from his red-rimmed eyes.

Skully took a long drag from the cigarette, blew smoke toward the ceiling and stepped into the room. He crossed to the kid and struck the filter between the boy's trembling lips. If he was man enough to fight, he was man enough to smoke. One or the other would probably kill him.

Damn.

Next Skully untied the kid's hands. By the time the kid finished his first cigarette. Skully knew his name, Bay. His age, fourteen. That the VC had "recruited" or killed all the eligible men in his village when they'd raided it a week ago.

The only men left were the very young and the very old.

"They came in tanks."

"You're lying." The VC didn't have any. Hell, the whole NVA didn't have any.

"Yes, tanks," the kid insisted.

Something about the earnestness with which the boy spoke and the pleading in his eyes made Skully believe him. This was information they could use. He sat down across from the boy. "Which province?"

"Quang Tri."

Skully's blood ran cold, then hot again. "Your family name!" he demanded, all his patience gone as the instinct that had kept him alive screamed.

"Nguyen. Bay Nguyen."

Nguyen, common enough. Like Smith or Jones in the States. Ho Chi Minh himself was Nguyen That Thanh.

But Lan's last name was Nguyen. Hell, she was related to half the villages in and around Quang Tri. But he also knew she had two older brothers, and one younger.

"Your sister's name?" He couldn't keep the edge of impatience from his voice.

"No sister," Bay denied.

"You have a sister. I want her name!" Skully stood, knocking over his chair with a deliberate bang.

The boy jumped. "Lan." The word escaped on a whisper and he hung his head in shame.

Skully righted his chair and rammed his ivory-handled knife into the table. "Tell me everything," he demanded.

The boy shook his head even as he started to spill his guts. And Skully didn't like what he heard. If things were that bad, why hadn't she used the money he'd given her to get to Da Nang?

The fighting in Quang Tri had been sporadic throughout the war. Skully had reasoned Lan would be as safe south of the DMZ as anywhere in this hell-hole. She knew how to survive. But maybe he'd been wrong.

She was, after all, only a girl.

"Is she all right?"

Bay didn't know.

Skully couldn't be content with that.

CHAPTER FOUR

1300 Friday
THE PAPER TIGER
Honolulu, Hawaii

AFTER CHANGING BACK into his uniform, Bowie had headed to the Moanalua Shopping Center, where he stopped for a long-overdue hair cut.

He had mixed feelings about shipping out to Midway. On the one hand there were his men to consider. On the other there was Professor Tam Nguyen. He'd give her the benefit of the doubt about his knife. She'd probably wanted to tell him in person and that's what tonight was all about.

He'd flown enough MAC flights through Hickam Field, sworn out enough declarations for personal exemptions upon returning to the country and knew enough about U.S. Customs that getting it back shouldn't be a problem. All he had to do was flash his antique-weapons permit, fill out some paperwork and pick it up. Maybe pay a fine.

Not that he would complain about a little legwork. Because of George Washington's Tariff Act of 1789, customs revenues had built the United States Naval Academy where he'd graduated with a degree in engineering. And there was the fact that he should have saved himself the trouble by taking the time to show the permit to the warden of Midway Islands in the first place.

Leaving the barber shop with a "high and tight," he adjusted his garrison cap, then walked the few blocks to the Paper Tiger.

He'd left his pro shop purchases in his locker for his tee time tomorrow. But he still needed other necessities. The shopping center would have provided the perfect opportunity, except he didn't have the luxury of time.

He had the feeling the uniform would scare her off, though she'd see him in one soon enough. If she didn't like it, he'd be willing to take it off for the night.

Inside the dimly lit bar, Bowie removed his cap and tucked it into his belt. "Hey, Cadeo," he said as he approached the bartender. "I don't suppose—"

Before he could even get the words out the man hit the sale button on the old-fashioned cash register. "Figured you'd be back." The drawer popped open, and Cadeo dug out Bowie's credit card and a receipt for him to sign.

"Four hundred dollars?"

"You're the guy who ran up the tab, not me."

Bowie checked and double-checked, but everything seemed to be in order. Eight sailors in a strip club could sure run up a bill. And if the tips to some of the strippers seemed a little excessive, well, he supposed they deserved it.

Bowie signed the credit slip and pocketed the card.

"Can I set you up with a cold one?" Cadeo asked.

There was entertainment up on stage and a modest midafternoon, mostly military crowd to go along with the more sedate beat. He thought about one for the road, but had that meeting in an hour. "Make it a club soda."

"You sure?" One of the dancers slipped up beside him. He assumed she was off duty because she had her clothes on, a skimpy number with the shoulders and back cut out. "Just one beer, Lieutenant Prince?"

"Ginger, isn't it?" he asked the redhead. Of course he could tell she wasn't a real redhead. And obviously Ginger Snap wasn't her real name. In fact, there wasn't much about her that was real.

Except she was a *real* nice gal just trying to pay her way through college. Or so she'd said the last time they'd spoken.

"You remembered," she cooed.

"How could I forget?"

"You didn't seem all that interested the other night." She tried to run one manicured hand up his thigh, but he stopped her.

"You like to shop?" he asked.

"What girl doesn't?"

"Think you could do me a favor?"

"As long as it's before eight," she answered, cozying up to him. "That's my first show for the night."

"That'll work. I'll meet you back here at 1800 hours, six," he translated when he noticed the blank look on her face. But Ginger continued to stare past him with that same expression.

Bowie turned on his bar stool, expecting to find some rival stripper. Instead, Professor Tam Nguyen stood at the opposite end of the bar arguing in Vietnamese with Cadeo. She didn't look like the gun-toting game warden he remembered.

Wearing a pantsuit that appeared to be Miss Saigon on Wall Street, she looked both sexy and in charge. But what was she doing here?

She wore her hair up, and sophisticated tortoise-shell-rimmed glasses perched on the end of her nose. The glasses only added to her mystique, because he knew the beauty hidden behind them.

"Get out!" Cadeo shouted at her. "I told you never to come back here. You're nothing but trouble."

"I just want to use your pay phone, Cadeo." Ignoring the bartender, Tam headed in Bowie's direction.

Cadeo muttered after her. Bowie wondered about the bartender's objections. And why Tam felt it necessary to use *this* pay phone.

"I have to go," Ginger muttered before heading toward the back of the bar with Tam not too far behind her.

From the corner of his eye Bowie caught Cadeo's nod to the bouncer at the door. When Tam walked by Bowie without even looking in his direction, all he could do was stare in stunned silence. But when the bouncer followed, Bowie stood in his way.

The guy was built like a biker. A big, bald, badass with a Fu Manchu mustache and a Harley-Davidson

T-shirt that all but screamed *I'm going to kick butt and like it.*

Bowie smiled but put up a warning hand. "I'll get her out of here," he offered.

The bouncer crossed his arms but stayed put.

Bowie headed toward the back of the club. He followed a darkened hallway plastered with posters of the strippers and backlit by neon beer signs. Tam had caught up with Ginger at the end of the dim hall. He ducked into the rest room alcove out of sight.

The stripper and the professor conversed in low tones just outside a door marked Private. Ginger slipped Tam a piece of paper. And Tam slipped Ginger cash.

At least that's what it looked like to him.

The stripper stepped through a door to what he assumed were the dressing rooms. And Tam turned toward the pay phone. Bowie pressed his back against the wall so she wouldn't see him.

She dialed out, but he couldn't make out her whispered words beyond a date.

He continued down the hall, and when Tam hung up the phone a few seconds later, she turned and walked straight into him.

"Excuse me," she said, clinging to his biceps.

His natural reflex was to hold on. But what he really wanted to do was shake her until she told him what the hell she was up to. "We have to stop meeting like this."

"I know kung fu. And I won't hesitate to use it," she threatened in response to what must have seemed like a pickup line.

He would have laughed, but it was then he realized she didn't have a clue. He could have walked right by without her ever knowing it was him. He *should* walk right by. "I'm not the one holding on, *Professor.*"

Startled, she shifted her gaze upward, giving him the courtesy of eye contact. "Lieutenant Prince?"

He nodded.

She looked him up and down, then at her hands still clutching his arms. "You look…different," she finished, pulling away from him. "I mean, you're wearing a different uniform."

"Grunge is out this season. Thought I'd clean up my act and at least look like an officer."

"Oh…"

That trailing "oh" didn't quite make up for the disappointment he'd felt when she hadn't recognized him right away. Maybe she didn't *need* him as much as he thought she did. He'd recognized her even with her hair up and hiding behind glasses. Maybe he wanted her a little too much.

"I'm sorry, Lieutenant" she apologized. "You just caught me by surprise. I mean, I didn't expect to run into you here."

"That should be my line."

"I supposed you're right." She scanned the posters as if she just realized where they were standing. "Do you come here often?"

He couldn't help it, he chuckled.

Unable or unwilling to see the humor, she frowned up at him. She took herself too seriously and him too literally. She didn't get his jokes. Hell, she didn't even get her own jokes. He could think of a million and one reasons why he shouldn't be attracted to her. Except when he looked at her, then he couldn't think of one.

"Again, that should have been my line. So how 'bout we get out of here?"

"I think we should," she agreed.

"Maybe we could start our evening early with some shopping later this afternoon?" he asked, guiding her to the door with a gentle but firm hand.

"I have a meeting. In fact I should be there right now," she said, checking her watch as they stepped outside into the daylight. "Afterward, I'm meeting you for dinner."

She stopped and turned to him on the sidewalk, bestowing one of her rare smiles. His knees went weak as he fumbled with his garrison cap. Covering and uncovering while in uniform was as natural as walking. And right now he couldn't manage to find his feet or his head.

Either she hadn't made the connection between Harris and him, or she was playing it cool. As she had with his knife.

"I have to wait that long to get my knife back, huh?"

"What kind of shopping?" she asked, suddenly interested in changing the subject. "I have some errands myself and a wad of cash to spend that isn't mine. Will ran out of hair gel. Katie's craving chocolate. Just about everyone on the island wants something."

"Well..." he hedged. "If you must know, the real reason I joined the Navy is the uniform. I can't color-coordinate my clothes. I need someone to pick them out for me."

"In other words, you want me to dress you?"

"Or undress me, no pressure." Teasing a blush out of her made him feel all warm on the inside. "But we can talk about that later."

"Don't count on it." She checked her watch once again. "So six, sevenish…I really don't know how long I'll be. Where do you want to meet? Or should I call you when I'm through?"

"I don't think that will be necessary. I'll find you."

The door to the club opened and Ginger stepped outside. "I'll see you back here at six, Lieutenant. I can't wait to take you shopping," she said, grabbing his arm and giving it a squeeze. "You're going to look so *GQ* when I'm through with you."

Tam looked at the redhead. Then at him. "Shopping…huh, Lieutenant Prince?" she asked, over those oh-so-prim-and-proper rims. "Don't you mean shopping around?"

Bowie disengaged himself from the stripper. He could only wish the Volcano Gods would accept him as a sacrifice right then and there. "I, ah—"

"I didn't know he was your man, Professor," Ginger gushed. "The girlfriends never understand," she added in an aside to him.

"He isn't *my man*. But he is my date for this evening."

"I saw him first," Ginger said mistakenly.

"Xin loi, minoi!"

"Troi oi!" Ginger clicked her tongue and walked off in a huff.

"Chao."

"I recognized 'sorry' and 'good-bye,' but I'd really like to know what you said to make her so mad. I usually like to break my own dates without stomping on someone's feelings."

"Too bad, honey!"

"Sorry I asked."

"Xin loi, minoi. Too bad, honey. Sorry about that...I feel sorry for you... It's not always an apology."

"I take it she wasn't apologizing to you, either."

"Troi oi is just an emphatic expression. It can mean anything. I'm sure she meant it exactly the way she said it." She raised her eyebrows above her glasses for emphasis.

He was a man who could appreciate having two women fighting over him. But he felt the guilty pleasure of a little boy caught with his hand in the cookie jar. So instead of pulling his hand out, he reached right in. "I just stopped by to pick up a credit card I left here the other night. And I ran into Ginger..." He shrugged. "I really do need help with shopping. And I didn't know you had the time."

"You don't owe me an explanation, Lieutenant," she said, fussing with her delicate wristwatch. "I can see why you'd find her attractive."

"Because she's independent and makes six figures?" he asked, baiting the hook.

"Try mammary glands."

"You think I'm a breast man?" He grinned.

"No, I think all heterosexual men are hardwired to appreciate a young woman's breasts. But what you don't realize is that you're not really interested for your own sake. It's all about picking someone to carry and suckle your young. So you spend your entire lives running from the truth.''

"Which is?"

"Something you have to figure out for yourself. I'm going to be late," she said, digging into the side pocket of her soft-sided briefcase. She handed him a business card. "You'll catch up with me later?"

"Definitely."

1400 Friday
NAVAL STATION PEARL HARBOR
Pearl Harbor, Hawaii

"I THOUGHT WE'D BE MORE comfortable in here." Captain Harris ushered Tam through the door of a small cluttered office to an equally small but less-cluttered conference room. "Please, make yourself comfortable, Professor Nguyen. Temporary office space is never ideal, but we're trying to make do."

"Thank you, I'm fine," Tam reassured him, setting her briefcase down beside her chair.

"As you know, this is just a formality."

He'd already apologized several times for the inconvenience of having her flown out for the meeting. But the captain looked haggard, probably too busy to travel. And for her this was a chance for R and R. So she really didn't mind.

"Midway Islands became an 'overlay' refuge in 1988 while still under the jurisdiction of the Navy," he continued. "With the closure of the Naval Air Facility the mission changed from national defense to wildlife conservation. The brass is calling this operation Bullets to Birds.''

"I like it already—"

"So do I," said the man standing in the doorway. Tam sat in stunned silence.

The captain checked his watch. "Lieutenant Prince has this annoying habit of always being precisely on time."

"Definitely," she agreed, repeating the last word the lieutenant said to her before they'd parted company. No wonder he was so positive about catching up to her later.

"Sorry 'bout that," he apologized.

He hadn't taken his eyes off her since he appeared in the doorway. She couldn't be sure, but she thought he winked when the captain wasn't looking.

Why hadn't he just told her he'd be here?

"I understand you two have already met," Captain Harris said. "Lieutenant Prince is here to answer any questions you may have on the role of the Seabee detachment."

"It's always a pleasure to see you again, Professor."

If there was such a thing as a seductive handshake, he'd mastered it. His words emphasized her title, but his touch emphasized the pleasure.

It wasn't until Captain Harris cleared his throat that she tugged. And the lieutenant let go. He sat down opposite her. Long, lean. Athletic. He stretched out his legs under the table. The first time he tapped her toe she thought it happened by accident. The second time, she kicked him.

The captain handed out thick reams of paper on the proposed transition. Tam flipped through to find the Navy's responsibilities detailed down to the letter. Of course, she'd known this was the Navy's project, but she was just beginning to realize this was the Seabee's project. One Seabee in particular.

"Care to give us the history of Midway Islands, Lieutenant," Captain Harris invited.

The lieutenant looked as though he'd just been put on the spot, but he recovered smoothly. "Late 1800s Marines were sent to Midway to evict squatters—"

"From exploiting bird life," Tam added, thinking to rescue him. "Midway was the last link in a global telegraph system laid by the Commercial Pacific Cable Company—"

"Inaugurated by a message from President Teddy Roosevelt on July 4, 1903," he said, cutting her off.

She accepted the challenge with a tilt of her chin. "In the short-lived clipper era of the thirties Midway was a landing site for Pan Am Clippers en route across the Pacific."

"August 1, 1941—" he leaned forward in his seat "—the United States was preparing for war and Naval Air Station Midway Islands was commissioned. The islands are best known for what is considered to be the turning point in World War Two, the Battle of Midway."

Check.

"You needn't take pity on the lieutenant, Professor," Captain Harris interrupted their byplay. "It's rare that I don't see him with some sort of book in his hand. And I never ask him to do anything he's not capable of.'' The captain's gaze shifted to the lieutenant.

There may have been one conversation on the surface in this room, but there were two undercurrents. The one that flowed between her and the lieutenant. And the one she felt between him and Captain Harris.

"As detailed in the proposal in front of you," Captain Harris continued, "we anticipate it will take up to three years to restore Midway Islands back to its natural habitat. At which time it will be turned over to the Department of the Interior, under the management of the Fish and Wildlife Service. The project will begin with the arrival of NMCB133 next week. Any questions?"

Tam had plenty.

But she'd only ask those pertaining to the islands.

"This says your unit will rotate every six months," she said. "Can you explain that in nonmilitary terms?"

The lieutenant closed his proposal. "For an unaccompanied tour like this, a detachment serves six months before rotating back to homeport. Or at least that's the way it's supposed to work." His gaze shifted to the captain.

Again that undercurrent. *Didn't he want the job?*

"Unaccompanied?" she asked.

"Without dependents," he said, and anticipated her next question. "Without wives, husbands, families. In other words, you'll have six different detachments in those three years."

So he wasn't staying.

"What about project continuity?"

"It'll go a lot smoother than it sounds. Since the battalion is managing the entire project, any necessary equipment will arrive with the first detachment and leave with the last. The incoming company commander will be briefed by the outgoing company commander and so on, with Alpha Dogs leading the way."

He was definitely the Alpha Male.

"Dogs? You'll have to excuse me, gentlemen—" she included both of them even if she wasn't quite sure the lieutenant qualified "—I'm not up on all these military terms."

"*Dog* because this is not a glamorous job," he said. "It's mostly grunge work, demolition, earthwork, waste removal…a lot of sweat and *cold showers,*" he emphasized.

She'd be happy to dump a bucket of ice on him right now.

For being just a formality, the particulars took up the next two hours as they went through the project page by page. And all she could focus on was the fact the lieutenant would be spending the next six months on her island. Six months. Only six months.

She wasn't sure how she felt about that.

What did it matter, anyway? In the end he'd rotate out like the rest of them.

Captain Harris checked his watch again. "It's getting late and I think we've gone over everything. Lieutenant, I'm going to assume you and the professor have it covered from here. I expect you two to work together very closely on this project." The captain gathered his things. "I'll leave you to lock up."

With that Captain Harris left them alone.

"Well, this is awkward," Tam admitted, tucking the proposal into her briefcase and pushing to her feet. "I don't know if I was more surprised to bump into you at the Paper Tiger or meet up with you here."

The lieutenant stood, as well. "Not trying to back out of our date, are you?"

"I'm afraid so." She clung to her briefcase with both hands. "I may have given you the wrong impression when I called this morning. And again when I told Ginger you were my date this evening. I didn't think I'd see you after tonight."

Hitching up his pant leg, he sat on the corner of the table nearest her. "I'm not a one-night-stand kind of guy, but I suppose I could make an exception if that's what you're hinting at."

Was he having a little fun at her expense because she was being so vague? Luckily she wasn't the type to blush easily. She set her briefcase on the table between them and replied, "That's not what I had in mind. And I think under the circumstances any relationship beyond professional would be uncomfortable for both of us. We're going to be stranded on the same island for the next six months."

"I've been on islands before. I know how small they can get. So what did you have in mind when you called this morning? Other than hit and run?"

Tam fidgeted with the handle of her briefcase. Nothing had changed except their circumstances. She still needed his help to find her father. She just didn't know how to approach the subject now. Or how to expose herself emotionally to a man who would soon become a part of her everyday life.

"It was nothing," she said, discouraging him from digging deeper. "How long have you known about your orders to Midway?" Before he'd landed on her island? That would explain why he left his knife.

"This morning. Just before I bumped into you."

"Why didn't you say something?"

"When were you going to tell me about my knife?"

She'd just lost her leverage.

"That is why you asked me to dinner, right? To break the news? Customs confiscated it when you got here."

"I suppose I owe you an explanation—"

"What do you say we call it even?" he offered.

"You're not angry?"

"Why should I be?"

"I didn't mean to be deceptive—"

"I'd call it more of a delay of the inevitable. Either you'd get around to telling me in your own time, or sooner or later I'd find out about it in mine. Either way we both wound up here, so why not make the best of it? Come on," he said, pushing to his feet. "Let's grab a bite to eat."

AFTER THE LIEUTENANT locked up the office, they left the clapboard building and passed a dozen others just like it. He saluted periodically with his right hand. Tam noticed he kept her to his left side and intentionally followed a path along sidewalks that put him curbside, as if he were a barrier between her and oncoming traffic. This was the kind of man who protected instinctively.

But was this the kind of man she wanted to trust?

Outside the base they headed in the general direction of the nearby Moanalua Shopping Center. "Where would you like to eat?" he asked.

"Do you know what I would dearly love right now?"

"Oh, no," he responded, spotting the street vendor on the corner. "Not a hot dog." But he soon gave in to the inevitable. "Two, please," he said, reaching into his back pocket. "What do you want on yours?"

"Everything."

"One with the works. And one plain." He opened his wallet and hesitated. "Where's the nearest ATM?" he asked the hot-dog man.

Tam clicked her tongue. "Don't worry about it. After all, I did ask you to dinner first." She dug through her briefcase for her billfold.

"But then I asked you," he argued.

"Hot dogs were my idea."

"Would somebody please pay up?" the impatient hot-dog vendor asked.

"I have the money," Tam said, handing it over and effectively putting an end to their nonsensical argument.

"Thank you for the hot dog," Bowie said, handing over hers.

"You're welcome for the hot dog." She smiled up at him, pleased she'd gotten her way. They continued walking up the street with the setting sun over their shoulders. "How come you don't have a dime in your pocket? Been stuffing too many g-strings? Not judging, just asking," she qualified.

"I guess you could say that, but not really. I lost a bet." He polished off his hot dog with the third bite.

"What was the bet?"

"That I could scrounge up breakfast for the squad when we landed on Midway."

"I take it the chocolate bars and potato chips didn't go over too well. You may seriously want to consider counseling for your sexual and gambling addictions." She kept as straight a face as possible when she said it. "Not to mention your drug habit."

"Oh, yeah?" he countered. "You might want to ask yourself why your favorite food is a phallic symbol." Tossing the wrapper in a nearby receptacle, he brushed his hands in triumph.

She choked and wound up sticking her nose in the works. And then she couldn't stop laughing.

"Hold steady." He took her napkin from her and wiped relish off the tip of her nose, his touch matter-of-fact. And even though there were sexual undertones to their verbal sparring, she appreciated that he kept things light.

She waved the napkin away. "I can't eat this anymore," she declared, laughing, then threw it away.

"Good! Now we can go get a real meal. I'm starving."

"You did that on purpose," she accused, wiping the tears from her eyes with the back of her hand.

"Oh," she sighed, catching her breath. "Just for that I'm going to make you go shopping first."

He stopped on the sidewalk and turned to her. "Lead the way."

Several stores later he'd relieved her of her brief-case and numerous shopping bags. They no longer even attempted to keep their purchases straight.

"Let's go in here," she said, picking the cheesiest tourist trap she could find so she'd be able to finish off her list. This time he actually groaned and she realized he'd reached his limit. "Just this one more," she pleaded, dragging him through the door. "Besides, you still have to pick up something for your niece and nephew," she reminded him. "And you know your wardrobe won't be complete without a Hawaiian shirt."

Tam picked up chocolate-covered macadamia nuts for Katie. She found a cute muumuu for Bowie's niece. He picked up a Hang Ten T-shirt for his nephew while she searched racks of bright-colored clothes for the gaudiest shirt she could find for him. She came across something equally garish and held it up. "Try this on."

"A man skirt?" he said in alarm from the next rack over.

"It's called a sarong. Besides, it's gender neutral."

He didn't look as if he believed her.

"Don't you think he'd look sexy in this?" she asked the older couple in matching leisure wear by her side.

"He'll look ridiculous," the old man grumbled.

"I think he'll look hot," the wife said. "Try it on," she urged.

The old man cupped a hand to his mouth. "Run!" he encouraged playfully.

Tam walked up to the lieutenant and handed him the garment. "So are you going to run? Or are you going to be a man about it?"

"You can run from 'em, but you can't hide from 'em," the old man offered sympathetically. "May as well try it on."

Bowie grumbled good-naturedly all the way to the dressing room.

Tam picked up a plastic lei and brought it over to the louvered door. He'd tossed his uniform shirt over the top.

"No peeking," he said as she reached in and hung the lei on an exposed hook.

"I'm not tall enough. Anyway, I'm not interested." She draped his shirt over her arm so it wouldn't fall to the floor when he opened the door. "Step out here where I can see you—don't be shy. And don't forget the lei."

"I'm not coming out there in this."

"You don't want me to come in there, do you?" she offered. "Because I'd be happy to bring more stuff for you to try on," she threatened, knowing he'd had enough of that already when she'd helped him pick out civilian clothes to get him through a week of leisure hours.

He'd insisted on neutral colors with a preference for khaki and white. Some blue. And she'd insisted on at least one green shirt to go with his eyes. He'd given in only after she convinced him khaki went with anything and everything, even green. Men! They just couldn't see the obvious.

The hardest part were his socks. They'd gone to three stores for the one brand in the one color he would wear, white. White socks were everywhere, the man was simply too picky for his own good.

"I'm counting to three," she stated.

He pushed through the louvered door.

She'd been prepared to have a good laugh at his expense. After all, she'd earned it shopping with him, but... He stood there, barefoot and bare chested with the sarong slung low on his hips. He stood akimbo, the look on his face comical.

But the look on hers must have been awestruck.

"Had enough fun?" he asked.

The older lady started clapping and complained to her husband that he'd never looked like that in all the years they'd been married.

Few men did. He had the body of a swimmer, incredibly tight pecs and abs. And his biceps and broad shoulders and narrow hips weren't bad, either—in fact, they were perfect. When he moved, the slit in the sunset-colored skirt showed off hints of one muscular leg all the way up to his tan line.

"I'm buying it," Tam declared. "Consider it a welcome-to-the-island gift."

"Over my dead body." He stalked back to the dressing room.

"And a lei," she added as if he hadn't said anything.

The stripper had wanted the sailor to look *GQ?*

That would have been a mistake. You could make a man over on the outside, but you couldn't make him over on the inside. And inside this man was no sissy boy, not even in a "man skirt."

For a moment she forgot why she was holding his khaki uniform shirt and it caught her off guard. She brushed the rank and insignia on the collar as if it would burn at the touch.

In a city like this where military uniforms were almost commonplace, Bowie Prince attracted his fair share of female attention. She'd noticed heads turn. And had felt a little feminine pride—even if he wasn't really her man.

She hadn't recognized him in his uniform at first. For one thing, he'd cleaned himself up with a shave and a haircut. For another, she'd avoided all eye contact with the uniformed crowd at the Paper Tiger.

She draped his shirt back over the dressing room door and snagged the sarong.

"Where do you think you're going?" he asked over the top of the door. "You're next."

"Oh, no," she declined. "I already own several. You saw me in one the night your plane landed on Midway."

She decided to get while the getting was good and left the lieutenant in the dressing room while she went to pay for her purchases. She put two fresh gardenia leis around her neck and picked out a dozen postcards at random. He lined up behind her to pay for his gifts, grumbling about horses and water.

But the real awkward moment came when they left the store loaded down with all of the day's purchases.

The sun had already set and she suggested they catch a bus to her hotel on Waikiki Beach.

"There are something like twenty restaurants to choose from and we could drop off this stuff in my room."

"Perfect, but let's stop by an ATM so I can get cash and we'll take a taxi."

"That's just male pride talking," she said. "There's nothing wrong with public transportation."

"There is on a date."

"It's not like this is a *real* date," she said, trying to qualify it. "We're just—" But she couldn't think how to finish that sentence.

"Not on a date, eating, shopping and taking the bus together?"

"Exactly."

Leading the way toward the bus stop, he tried to take more bags, but she wouldn't let him. He carried enough already.

At the well-lit bus stop she unburdened herself. And thinking to appease him, she removed one of the leis she'd bought. She offered it to him, and he dipped his head so she could reach around his neck.

"Now we really look like a couple...of tourists," she added in haste, feeling bright spots burning her cheeks.

"Doesn't a kiss come with that lei?" he asked. And not in that teasing tone she'd become comfortable with.

"I don't know. Does it?" She pretended ignorance, looking up and down the street for signs of a bus. Any bus!

"It's tradition." He stood there loaded down with shopping bags and expectations. He wanted her to make that move. She wanted to run.

She could already feel the Big Island getting smaller. What would happen when he came to her little sandbar in the ocean?

"And you're a traditional kind of guy?"

"I am."

Fate had brought him to her for the here and now, not for keeps. She should consider it her good fortune and just ask for his help. First she needed to ask herself to trust him.

She decided to take a hesitant step. "I think we have more in common than I first realized."

"I hope so," he said, putting his bags on the bench with hers.

"We're both military brats," she confessed. "The difference is you know your father and I don't know mine. My mother was fifteen when he got her pregnant...and left us behind in Vietnam."

His once-smiling lips were now in a firm line.

"I need..." The huskiness of her voice betrayed her raw emotions, and she struggled for control. "I need your help," she expelled on an anxious breath.

"You know, there are whole organizations that re-unite veterans and their families?"

"That route hasn't worked so far."

He crossed his arms. "Why me?"

It wasn't the response she'd been expecting from her white knight. Shouldn't he be mounting his trusty steed? Swooping her up in his arms for a kiss? Riding off into the night to slay her dragons? This is why she'd never believed in fairy-tale endings.

"Forget I asked."

And she'd forget she just shared the most intimate details of her life with a total stranger.

She backed away from the wariness in his eyes.

But he stopped her by reaching for her arm. "Just humor me. Why do you think I can help?"

She looked at his hand, then his face. "I think our fathers served together in Vietnam."

Her words worked like a stun gun. He dropped his hand immediately.

"I have a picture—" she dug into her briefcase for the proof. "It's water-stained, or rather tea-stained, but there's your father, right? And here's mine. The one with the tattoo."

He took the photograph from her.

"His name's Skully, that's all I know."

Deep furrows of concentration formed above his brow. He neither confirmed nor denied his father's presence in the picture.

She found it hard to catch her breath when he didn't say anything. Too big a favor? "I don't expect you to help me beyond information, of course," she said, letting him off the hook, before he started to wriggle and she lost him. "I just thought that if you could tell me the name of the unit, it would be something to go on at least. Or maybe you could put me in touch with your father?"

He handed back the photo and met her uncertain gaze.

"Are you sure that man is your father?"

"Of course!" She felt outraged that he'd even asked. "Do you think my mother would lie to me about something like that?"

"I wasn't accusing your mother of anything," he said with quiet calm. Too quiet. "I'll see what I can do. You have to understand, these men are legends to me. They're Navy SEALs. I've always looked up to them—"

"And now you're afraid to knock one of these legends from his pedestal?" Her spine became rigid. "You're embarrassed for him, his family. He should be ashamed to have a daughter like me, right?"

"You're putting words in my mouth. As a man I'd want to know. And I'd want to do the right thing. I'm shocked, that's an honest reaction."

"You know him," she accused.

"I can honestly say I don't know the man at all." He worked gravel loose from a crack in the sidewalk with the toe of his polished shoe. "I don't know if you can understand this—it's going to sound like a bunch of bull when I say it out loud—but there's an unwritten code between military men. What happens on the road stays on the road. You have to be able to trust each other with your life and that includes keeping one another's dirty laundry a secret."

He finally looked at her.

And she glared in righteous indignation. Now she was some man's dirty laundry? "Like I said, forget I ever asked."

Tam scooped up her bags from the bench. As the bus rolled to a squeaky stop, she rushed the opening doors.

"I never said I wouldn't help." He followed her on board, loaded down with bags and patting his pockets for change.

"All you had to say was that you would. As for your macho military code, you're right. I think it's bullshit!" She paid her fare and had the satisfaction of witnessing the driver kick him off the bus.

CHAPTER FIVE

2000 Friday
THE HILTON HAWAIIAN VILLAGE
Honolulu, Hawaii

"DON'T HANG UP. I'm in the lobby, holding your macadamia nuts hostage until you give me your room number."

"If I was going to hang up on you, Lieutenant, I simply wouldn't have bothered to pick up the phone," Tam countered without the same humor as his request. She'd known it had to be him and thought about not answering, but realized she'd have to face him again sooner or later. And not just because she had half the man's wardrobe in her hotel room. "I'm in the Kalia Tower," she said, then rattled off her room number and hung up.

She prepared to wait by raiding the minibar.

It had never occurred to her that he wouldn't want to help her. But she'd seen the conflict in his eyes. Did he think she didn't know that lives would be affected, even changed, if she did find her father?

Including her own.

Because she'd been unable to reach her mother, she had her own uncertainty to deal with. She didn't need his as well. Or did he simply not want to get involved?

She rarely touched hard liquor, but she believed this occasion called for a good stiff drink. She twisted the cap off the small bottle of gin. "Bottoms up."

Not bothering with a glass, she simply poured back the contents. The bitterness matched her mood, stinging the backs of her throat and eyes.

It was less than five minutes before she heard that first tentative knock on her door. She'd managed three different shots in that time. But if courage could be found in a bottle, she hadn't managed to find the right mix.

She tossed the empties into the trash and swept up his shopping bags on the way to the door. She opened it feeling nothing at all. He stood there in his uniform and her lei, leaning into the door frame with those soft, sympathetic eyes and that hard, heartless body.

He offered her bags without a word.

And she dropped his at his feet.

"Are you okay?" he asked. "You look a little flushed."

"I'm fine, not that it's any concern of yours." She had her hand on the door, but couldn't bring herself to close it in his face.

"Despite what you must think," he said, "chivalry is not dead, just AWOL. But I'm here now and I want to help you. Forgive me?"

She broke eye contact first. Her chest felt tight, the back of her throat burned, and when she raised her eyes they were on fire.

"No," she said dispassionately. But the single tear-drop rolling down her cheek gave her away.

He brushed it away with his thumb. "Don't cry, honey. I'm the right man for this mission. But you have to trust me to do it my way."

She sniffled. "I'm not crying, I have allergies. As for trusting you, we'll see."

Bowie had convinced her to have dinner with him, but they had to wait for their table so they were seated in a nearby open-air lounge. He really didn't know if he was the right man for *this* mission. He sure as hell didn't think he'd escape unscathed.

He'd recognized his father. Her father. And every man in that photo. But he had to handle things his way.

With as little collateral damage as possible.

Her defenses were back up after he'd spent all day working to tear them down. So he resorted to small talk.

"So this is how the other half lives," he said, looking around. They were far enough away from the waterfall that he didn't have to talk above it.

"Per diem doesn't even begin to cover it, and I can't really afford it on my salary," she admitted. "But I like to splurge when I get a chance to come to the Big Island."

"How long have you been warden of Midway?" He took a sip of his beer.

"Three years. With another three to go on my new contract. And while I'm not the Crocodile Hunter, I do have a cyber classroom series that's taken off. Who knows where that will lead.''

She absently stroked his bottle when he set it down. She'd ordered a diet cola. So it surprised him to see her taking a nip of his beer. He wondered if she realized how much of a sexual charge that was for him.

''Watch yourself,'' he warned.

She glanced across the table at him, then at the bottle in her hand, as if she just realized what she'd done. ''I'm sorry,'' she said, pushing it back toward him.

''I just meant it has a bite. Swore I'd never touch the stuff again, yet here I am.'' He took a swig, imagining what she would taste like on his tongue instead of the beer. Flagging their server, he ordered them both one this time, along with an appetizer to stave off his hunger.

He nudged their shared bottle toward her.

''It's an acquired taste,'' she admitted before taking another sip.

''I figured you for the fruity-umbrella-drink type. But you're full of surprises. Take the Paper Tiger for instance—''

''I just stopped in to use the pay phone,'' she said, anticipating his question. ''I've been trying to reach my mother.''

He didn't believe it for a minute.

''Aside from the fact there are other pay phones in this city, you'd been in there before. Cadeo and Ginger both knew you. And from what I gathered, Cadeo at least doesn't want you hanging around.''

She shrugged. ''You caught me—''

He had to wait through the arrival and departure of their server before he could get to the bottom of that answer. "Care to explain?"

He dipped a tortilla chip into the pineapple salsa.

Taking a deep breath, she folded her arms across the table and leaned in before she started. "Cadeo doesn't like me coming around because I try to talk the girls into another line of work. And Ginger is...a sad story, really."

"Is that why you gave her money for whatever was on that piece of paper she gave you?"

Her hand stilled around the bottle. "Information. Nothing that concerns you."

He leaned back in his chair and studied the tilt of her chin and the challenge in her eyes. "Tam, if you want me to help you, then you have to come clean with me."

"My business with Ginger is just that, my business." She washed down her words with beer.

"Let me be the judge of that." Getting to know her would help him decide how best to break the news about her father when the time came. Besides, he had the ulterior motive of being interested.

"Ginger had information on a flower auction," she offered with more defiance than grace.

"Don't tell me you two belong to the same garden club?" He took another swig, trying to decipher her code.

"You have no idea what I'm talking about, do you." She looked smug. "That precious flower known as virginity?"

He sputtered, then pounded his chest.

She handed him a series of napkins until he regained control. "And here I thought you were a man of the world, Lieutenant."

"Maybe you'd better start from the beginning."

"When I handed over your knife, I spoke with an agent friend of mine in Customs. We got to talking and compared notes. It seems a large shipment of opium arrived Wednesday via military transport, then vanished. All traces of the flight, the manifest, the drugs, gone. Nothing but a memory. And all they're being told is it's in the right government hands. Except word on the street is supply is up."

The pounding in his chest almost drummed out her words. Drugs didn't just vanish. Into government hands? Stevens came to mind.

"What was in the cargo hold of your plane, Lieutenant?"

He put on his best poker face. "That's classified. And what, if anything, does all this have to do with the auction?"

They were both leaning forward, speaking in low tones. "Opium and *ba moui lam* go hand in hand." She tapped the label of her beer for emphasis.

"Butterflies?"

She took a deep breath and removed her glasses to rub the bridge of her nose. "It's another word for—"

"I know what it means."

She raised her eyebrows.

"I've never paid for sex," he said, offended that she'd even think it.

Her lips compressed to a thin line "I make it my

business to keep on top of things. And I've noticed a pattern over the years. An auction usually follows a large shipment. Ginger hears things. I pay her for the information. Then I place anonymous calls to the proper authorities. Sometimes we get lucky."

"Except you haven't explained what this has to do with you or even Ginger."

She put her glasses back on. If they were playing poker he'd call it a "tell." She was hiding something. So he listened very carefully.

"Like I said, it's a sad story. We met a little over three years ago. I did my graduate work here at the University of Hawaii." She picked at the label on her bottle. "Ginger worked the streets. I helped her get clean."

"She's a pro?" He sat back, stunned.

"Not anymore. Every once in a while I'll get her thinking about college and a career. Unfortunately her self-esteem is so low that even though she got herself off the streets, she doesn't believe she's got more to offer than her body. But she's managed to stay clean so I can't fault her on that." She stopped picking and cradled the bottle in her hands.

While his brain processed the information, he dipped another chip. She reached for one and pulled back when she brushed his hand. He devoured the chip like the starving man he'd become.

"It wasn't her fault."

"It never is."

"In this case she really was the victim. Ginger's from Vietnam. At fifteen her father sold her to a drug warlord to pay off his opium debt. She was shipped to the U.S., her virginity sold to the highest bidder. Then she was introduced to opium to keep her manageable so she would ply her new trade for a very exclusive clientele. She had the courage to run, but wound up on the streets making a living the only way she knew how.''

"Does this drug warlord have a name?" He was almost afraid to ask, afraid he already knew.

"Xang."

Information overload set his mind reeling.

"You transported opium from Thailand, didn't you?" she accused. "Did you even think to ask why?"

"I'm not going to justify that with a comment."

Tennyson had long been his favorite poet because the man knew a soldier's mind. *Theirs not to reason why. Theirs but to do and die...* A code he lived by.

But suddenly he *was* asking himself why.

Armed with Tam's revelation and his knowledge, Bowie had every reason to protect her from the truth. At least until all questions had been answered to his satisfaction.

"My 1-800-TATTLE-TALE calls may not seem like much to you, but at least I'm trying to do something—"

"Your table's ready," the hostess interrupted. "I can seat you now and get you another round of drinks if you like?"

"Do you mind if we skip dinner?" Tam asked him. "I seem to have lost my appetite."

"As a matter of fact I do."

THEY ATE IN RELATIVE silence. Tam picked at her surf and turf. She'd expected the lieutenant's polite consensus, not his high-handedness. Never mind he'd been starving and she merely sulking because she'd been unable to force an admission about the shipment from him. She still didn't know how it all connected to her islands and the footprint in the sand.

But she wouldn't find out by running away from him.

"More wine?" he asked. The balcony overlooked a stretch of Waikiki. Whitecaps rolled over the sand and receded again in a quiet crescendo that matched the cadence of his voice.

She placed a hand over her glass. "I don't know if you're counting, but I've imbibed more than my share tonight."

"Two beers and a glass of wine with dinner doesn't exactly make you a lush."

"And half of your first beer..." Perhaps she wouldn't mention those three shots up in her room. "I'm feeling just a bit light-headed," she admitted.

"Okay, I'm cutting you off," he teased, setting the bottle aside. "A walk along the beach might be just the ticket."

While he took care of the bill, the fog lifted enough for her to realize that would be a mistake. "I think I'll pass on the romantic moonlit walk." Dinner seemed to be enough of a risk. She played with the stem of her glass. "I realize you may have expectations—"

"Maybe I'm just enjoying the company and don't

want the night to end," he suggested, rising to his feet.

She looked up at him. "It has to end sometime, right?"

"Ever consider that those expectations you keep seeing in my eyes are a reflection of your own?"

She wished he wasn't so good at word play. She had very little experience flirting. And didn't know how to read his mind.

"I don't know what you mean."

"I mean, my help doesn't come with a price tag. I have my own reasons. So let's just say Uncle Sammy's picking up the tab on this one—he owes you that much at least." He held out his hand.

They hadn't talked about her father, which only seemed to reinforce to her that he knew something he wasn't telling her. But she'd decided she had no choice but to trust him, at least until he proved untrustworthy.

She put her hand in his and stumbled to her feet.

"Thought I just said I didn't expect you to fall all over me in gratitude."

"I'm pretty sure that was more wine than gratitude."

"Lean on me," he urged, wrapping her arm around his waist and his around her shoulder.

"I certainly hope I'm not embarrassing myself." It was all she could do to put one foot in front of the other.

"We're just another couple strolling through the village," he reassured her.

With that she relaxed against him, allowing him to

take the lead. She'd try not to think about how right it felt to lean on him. Or even that his shoulder made a comfortable place to lay her head.

Somehow, between her eyes drifting closed, then open again, they made it to a bank of elevators. He pushed the button and pulled her in with him when the door opened, then over to a corner where he propped them both up.

An older woman getting on behind them jabbed her husband in the ribs. "What did I tell you? They're a honeymoon couple."

"All the more reason for you not to bother them," he said.

Tam recognized them from their matching leisure wear as the couple from that afternoon.

"How come you never put your arms around me anymore?"

"My arms don't fit around you anymore." He pretended to try and the woman swatted him for his efforts.

"This clown is what I've had to put up with for fifty-seven years," she said, drawing them into the conversation. "How long have you two known each other?"

The lieutenant checked his watch. "Sixty-six hours, twenty minutes and twelve seconds."

Startled by that revelation, Tam looked up at him. He'd made that up, right? He looked down at her and winked.

The old lady stared at them both. "Oh, my!" Her mouth softened to a smile. "Am I blushing? I didn' think young people waited for their wedding night anymore. Of course I saved myself for marriage—"

"Gertie, nobody wants to hear that—"

Gertie ignored her husband. "We met when Bert was in the service, a Marine, stationed in the South Pacific. I was a Navy nurse, myself. Where did you two meet?"

"Midway," they said in unison.

"But—" Tam tried to explain. "We're not—"

"That's going to be one to tell the grandkids."

"No kids," Tam managed to say as the elevator doors opened on her floor.

"Of course not, dear, give it a few months. Bert, hold the elevator door while I snap a picture of these two lovebirds with the new digital camera."

Before Tam could utter a protest the deed was done.

"See how you can preview the picture?" Gertie showed off her new toy. "Give me your e-mail address and I'll send it to you as a download."

"I don't have e-mail," Tam said.

Bowie offered his address. "We'd love a copy, thank you."

Tam started down the hallway before Bowie even exited the elevator. "I hope she bothers you every day asking about our kids and grandkids. The woman thinks we've *known* each other in the biblical sense for sixty-six odd hours, which she thinks is the amount of time that's passed since our wedding. How did you come up with that number, anyway?"

"That's when we met."

She stopped in the middle of the hallway to stare

up at him. "Oh." That sixty-six hours seemed like a lifetime ago.

He turned her around to face the opposite direction. "Your room is that way."

"Anyone can make that mistake in a hotel."

"A lot of mistakes are made in hotel rooms. Do I need to carry you over the threshold?"

"No!"

"Then keep putting one foot in front of the other."

She did until he turned her once again, this time to face a door. "Is this it?"

"This is it."

After some difficulty, she managed to insert the key card and get the green light. She opened the door a crack. "Are you coming in?" she asked, turning around to face him.

"Are you asking?"

"Your things are still here. Besides, I owe you a kiss, not as payment, but because it's tradition," she said in a voice so husky it didn't even sound like hers.

"Well, if it's tradition."

She leaned back against the door and unceremoniously fell on her butt.

"On your feet." He bent over to pick her up.

She became rag-doll limp. "I think I'm drunk." She hiccupped, then giggled.

"I know you're drunk." He got her up only to have her go down again.

"I've never been drunk in my life." She sat there stunned by the possibility.

"There's a first time for everything." He switched on the light and the door swung shut behind him. He half dragged, half carried her to the bed. "This would go a lot easier if you helped some."

"You're a big strong man, you should be able to wrestle me to the bed."

"Not when you alternate between dead weight and hanging all over me." He dropped her to the mattress.

She sprang back up and wrapped her arms around his neck, trying to pull him down with her. His lei fell forward, and she had to spit a gardenia petal out of her mouth. "I always knew we'd wind up in bed together."

"Not tonight," he said, unlocking her arms.

"You sound so serious." She'd meant to sound light and flirty like earlier—but they were way beyond that now.

It had been a day of emotional ups and downs for her as well. Sixty-six hours of ups and downs. She needed a physical release. Before she bottled her emotions back up again. Funny how being tipsy gave her that clarity.

"Can you get undressed yourself? Or do you need me to help?"

"This afternoon you wanted me to undress you." She reached for his belt buckle.

He tethered her wrists. "Slow down, Tam. Let's start with your shoes and be glad you're not going to remember any of this in the morning." He knelt beside the bed, removing first one shoe, then the other.

She fell back against the mattress and worked the buttons at her collar while staring up at the ceiling. She wanted him to hold her. To take her to a place where her father hadn't abandoned her, where she didn't have to be afraid of men in uniform...

He rubbed her instep with expert hands.

Her eyes drifted closed and she moaned. "You learned reflexology in Asia."

"From a book."

"You do know it's possible for me to orgasm—" she sucked in her breath "—while you're doing that."

His hands stilled. "Maybe we won't go there, just yet."

"I'd like to go there with you." The bed started spinning. "Oh, no, this isn't good," she groaned. Opening her eyes, she forced herself upright. "The bed— The room— They won't stop moving."

"Look at me," he said. "Tam, honey, did you take something for your allergies?"

"What allergies?"

"Just making sure."

"Rub my feet?" She wiggled her toes in his direction.

He sat back in his crouched position. "Ask me again when you're sober. And I'll rub all night long, I promise."

"Please," she begged.

When he responded by shaking his head, she slid off the bed onto the floor beside him. Reaching across the space, she slipped her hand between two buttons on his uniform shirt until her fingers touched his T-shirt right at the breastbone. He stilled her hand by covering it with his.

"Your heart's beating so fast." She brought their other hands to her breast. "Feel mine?"

"I feel it," he admitted in a husky tone filled with hunger.

She could convince herself that was enough. And if she let him ease his body, he wouldn't leave. Not tonight, anyway.

"Our heartbeats are one. That's the nature of attraction."

"I never said I didn't want you. The timing's off is all." He pulled his hand back and began to push to his feet.

"I don't want to be alone."

"I know."

She held out her arms. *"Lai day, lam on."*

COME TO ME, PLEASE.

Only a fool would resist the invitation. Now he was a cramped fool, sitting on the floor, cradling a passed-out woman in his arms.

A beautifully exotic, highly erotic woman.

Bowie waited until Tam's breathing became even before he stood and laid her on the bed. He stared down at her, and decided to finish what they'd started, at least as far as undressing her and putting her to bed.

He worked the row of buttons from the bottom to the top until the jacket fell open. A gentleman would have averted his eyes, but he'd already done his duty for the night. He could at least appreciate the silky bra that pushed her small breasts together. He was a breast man, but size didn't matter. He liked her compact frame.

He liked more than that. Tonight she'd touched him on many levels, not the least of which was his heart.

"Don't even go there," he warned himself. He would have been better off taking what she offered and leaving it at that. Never mind the favor he still owed her. And the fact that she'd been too wasted to honestly offer him anything.

He searched for and found the back zipper of her tailored pants, then tugged the pants off to find thong panties in the same silky material as the bra. That and the thigh-high stockings made him click his tongue at all she had hidden away from the world.

Sitting on the edge of the bed, he lifted her up to peel off the jacket. She cuddled his chest in her sleep and he smiled, breathing in her soft scent. Brushing the left sleeve from her shoulder, he stopped and pushed aside the bra strap.

She had a small butterfly tattoo.

Snatches of their predinner conversation played in his head. *"Flower auction…precious flower…opium and* ba moui lam*…butterfly…it's a sad story, really."*

Then the other night at the Paper Tiger. Flashes of mirrors and light. Strippers on stage.

Ginger had that very same tattoo.

If Tam thought his heart had been beating fast earlier, she needed to feel it now. He held her close, pressed his lips to the butterfly on her shoulder and felt a gut-wrenching pain. "Ah, Tam. You didn't tell me everything."

TAM AWOKE TO A QUIET CLICK and opened her eyes just in time to see Bowie slip through the door. She lifted her pounding head from the pillow to check the clock. After six. He'd stayed the night?

Panic set in. She sat up in bed.

She noticed the package of Alka-Seltzer on the nightstand. The half-empty glass of water. The post-card beneath it. Underneath his number, he'd written: Take two and call me in the morning. The lei he'd worn hung from the lamp, along with hers. She turned the postcard over. Reading it, she groaned. *I got laid in Hawaii.*

The mirrored closet door stood ajar. Her favorite suit hung neatly in the closet. She checked under the covers. Bra. Panties. Stockings? Who wore stockings to bed?

Unless *he* thought that was a turn-on.

Snatches of erotic imagery from last night clouded her brain. He'd undressed her. Held her. Kissed her. Had he kissed her?

She'd clung to him. Touched him. Unbuckled his belt...

Why didn't she remember any more than that?

She threw back the covers and searched the room. His things were gone. And he must have showered because of the damp towel and wet tub. Not to mention the fresh scent of shampoo.

In desperation she dumped out all the waste baskets, hoping to find a condom, condom package, something! She didn't. But she had three empty bottles to remind her a lot of mistakes were made in hotels.

0700 Saturday
THE NAVY-MARINE GOLF COURSE
Pearl Harbor, Hawaii

"YOU SON OF A BITCH!" Bowie's fist connected with Rob Stevens's jaw.

Unprepared, Stevens ended up on the ground.

"Get up!"

All night long he'd watched over Tam from a chair in her hotel room. His head throbbed with the thought of first Stevens, then Xang. Finally one thing became clear. The two men were connected.

And both of them had hurt Tam.

Bowie would have rushed Stevens again, but his godfather stepped in between, calming everyone down after Harris threatened to call the SPs.

Stevens got to his feet and wiped blood from his mouth.

"What the hell happened to that cargo?" Bowie demanded.

"It's all right," Stevens said. "Let him go."

Breathing heavily, Bowie shook himself free of the admiral's restraining hand.

Stevens kept his distance. "You can either tell me what this is about or beat me to a pulp. Because I'm not going to fight you."

"Look me in the eye and tell me that shipment of opium didn't make it to the street. Tell me you don't know anything about girls from the east being sold to the highest bidder.'' Bowie dropped his voice an octave. ''Tell me you had nothing to do with the Thai government letting Xang go—''

He'd hit his mark on all three counts.

''I could look you in the eye and lie, but I'm not going to.'' Stevens turned to the admiral and Harris. ''Go ahead and play through.''

Bowie stood in stunned silence, the fight still in him, but curtailed by the man's admission. Stevens nodded toward a golf cart where he put away his club.

''Do you want to walk it off or ride?''

''Walk,'' Bowie said.

''For a guy who doesn't throw the first punch you have a mean left hook.'' He grabbed a towel and used it to wipe his mouth, then tossed it aside.

They followed the path toward the tree line, where they'd be less likely to be overheard. Stevens remained calm, and Bowie wary.

''You have a top-secret clearance so I don't need to tell you this is strictly confidential,'' Stevens began. ''Imagine my surprise when a renegade squad of Seabees took down a drug warlord just as my men were moving in on him.''

''You didn't mention that during the debriefing.''

''You didn't need to know. But a simple straightforward bust isn't always the best when trying to bring down a whole organization. Yes, we arranged to have Xang let go. But only so he can be completely ruined. Thanks in part to you and your men, Xang now believes he's above the law in not two, but four countries—he's also desperate to make up for his losses, which has made him careless. An opportunity will present itself sooner or later. One thing I've learned over the years, this job takes patience.''

"You think doing it your way is worth the thirty years he's been free?"

"It took him ten years after the war just to establish himself. It took us longer than that to even find him. He's not our only concern over there. We hack off at the bottom and work our way up, otherwise the serpent just grows a new head."

"Or maybe the serpent has two heads," Bowie suggested.

"If you want to believe that, then there's nothing I can do to change your mind. I'm in so deep my own mother doesn't know me."

"And the cargo?"

"It takes big bait to catch big fish. Xang has orders to fill and nothing in his warehouses. He's already started production again, but he might be in the mood to buy, so I have a man working that angle. He must be moving drugs from distribution centers we don't know about, too, because we're not responsible for the influx of drugs on the street. As for the girls, that's the other side of this ugly business. Poverty-stricken addicts can't pay cash so they pay with their offspring."

And what did Stevens know about his own offspring?

The man hadn't told Bowie much he hadn't already discovered—except to confirm that the CIA agent had his own way of doing things. Bowie had no reason to trust the man and every reason to distrust him.

"So the girls are just more pawns in your game?"

"I was young once, and an idealist. I'm trying to tell you there are always more drugs and more girls and there always will be. Maybe you don't realize this, but I don't work for a law enforcement agency. I'm just a pair of eyes in a foreign country. The INS received a tip-off yesterday about a girl. We may be able to save one. We're looking into a couple of leads. Do you know a Seaman Nathan Jones?''

"He's an Alpha Dog, a member of my squad. Why?''

"Know if he has an actual love interest in Thailand? Or if he's hard up for cash? He just swore out an affidavit for a fiancée visa yesterday. That's how they bring these girls into the country legally. Dupe some poor serviceman short on cash or smarts. Get him to swear he's actually met the girl, even though he never will. If it ever comes under scrutiny—and it usually doesn't—the paper trail leads back to the guy, who pays the fine and does the time.''

"We were over there six months.'' Bowie felt he had to defend Jones. "It's possible he fell in love with a young woman. It happens all the time.''

"I know.'' Stevens got a far-off look, but no smile came. "I'll keep you informed.''

"That 'something personal' between you and Xang, does it have anything to do with a girl you met in Vietnam?''

"Don't go there.''

"I thought SEALs never left a man behind? Any man who'd leave a woman behind, carrying his child, is a coward in my book. Maybe she was better off with Xang.''

"Where the hell did you hear something like

that?" Stevens became outraged. "I know it wasn't from your father or godfather!"

"You want to try taking that swing at me now?" Bowie asked, itching for that fight.

Fall 1972
Quang Tri Province, Vietnam

THERE WAS NO TOMORROW in Vietnam.

The Viet Cong had rounded up all the young men in her village, including her youngest brother, Bay, and marched them off. Then they rounded up all the young women and sorted them into groups. Those who had consorted with the American GIs and those who hadn't. Lan found herself in the first group. Even if she hadn't been with child, neighbors were only too willing to cooperate with the VC if it meant saving their own lives.

In her case, however, they had found the picture of Skully to use against her. They pinned it to her, marking her as lower than dust.

Five of them were lined up and forced to their knees. The man in charge spit on the ground. He ordered a soldier to pour honey over their feet. And another to release fire ants. As the man with the ants walked down the line the screaming began.

Lan had been barely holding on from the moment the VC had arrived. She couldn't control her shaking, but she'd bite off her own tongue before she'd scream.

But the VC weren't finished. Whimpering in pain and fear, the five women were each made to hold a grenade without a pin. Lan knew if she let go, she would die. She knew if the girl next to her let go, she would also die.

So she held that grenade in her shaking hand and forced her mind to go blank. She didn't want to die. She didn't want her baby to die.

The screams, the biting ants, became unbearable.

She prayed to Buddha. To all her ancestors.

To Skully.

Then the girl at the end of the line let go. That girl and the one beside her fell after a loud explosion, and Lan was spattered with flesh and blood. The second body had taken the brunt of the impact, her grenade still clutched in her dead hand.

The girl next to Lan wet herself.

Lan tried to mouth words of comfort, but none came.

The girl got up and ran away. With amazing nonchalance the VC trained their weapons on her and shot her dead once she reached the edge of a field. Her grenade went off, and Lan ducked her shoulders as dirt came raining down, getting in her eyes and mouth, making her gag.

But she was still alive. Two of them were still alive.

Time passed. She couldn't even feel the ant bites anymore. Her limbs, her entire body and mind had gone numb. She swayed on her knees and fought to stay awake.

She knew the VC would get tired of their game and then they would kill her, but she didn't let go of the grenade.

She wanted to throw it at them. But they remained spread out among the villagers. Her own mother was on her knees crying and begging for her release. Her father just stared past her as if he already mourned her death.

The shelling that had been going on around them continued lighting up the night sky with an eerie beauty. More tanks and trucks rolled in. The band of VC now had jobs to do. She dared to hope they would become busy enough to forget about her.

Headlights blinded her. A jeep pulled up to a stop. An angry voice called out.

Then gentle hands closed over hers. She looked up into the man's face. For a moment she thought it must be Skully, but that was only a hallucination.

"Xang" was all she could manage to say past her parched throat.

He took the grenade from her and lobbed it into the night. He ordered the other woman released while ushering Lan to the Jeep.

Her father slipped General Xang the American money he'd stashed away, all of it. Lan knew right then and there Xang would take her away. Away from her family. Away from her home.

It was to be the last time she ever saw either of her parents. The last time she ever saw her home.

And she knew for all Xang's gentle handling, the anger would come. She was his property now. He could do what he wanted to her and no one could stop him.

CHAPTER SIX

0900 Thursday
NAVAL AIR FACILITY
Sand Island, Midway Islands

FROM THE WORLD WAR TWO vintage watchtower, Tam peered through binoculars. She could have been bird watching. But on this occasion she found bees more interesting.

Seabees, to be exact.

"The fleet has landed," she muttered in pure frustration. An exaggeration on her part, no doubt. It was, after all, only one vessel. Carrying one detachment of Seabees. Not an entire fleet.

Not an invasion force.

She shouldn't feel as if the enemy had landed. Except she did. And *he* had.

She craned her neck for a clear view of the harbor and marina in anticipation of getting a look at the man she'd been avoiding for almost a week. After several unsuccessful attempts she lowered her spyglasses, letting them dangle from the cord around her neck.

"Well?" Katie Dewitt, her administrative assistant, called up from the base of the tower. Katie, being afraid of heights, had chosen to keep both feet planted firmly on the ground.

"They're here," Tam repeated for her assistant's benefit.

"How many?"

"Just one, that I can see, anyway," Tam answered.

"Only one?"

"Bob Hope."

"Is he really cute and wearing a uniform like the guy on the Cracker Jack box?"

"The USNS *Bob Hope,*" Tam clarified. "Please don't tell me you're too young to have heard of the ship's namesake? I'd heard of the man before I even came to the States."

"Well, duh! You grew up in Vietnam. Didn't he like invade your country or something?"

No wonder Will called her Katie DimWit. *Please, someone, tell me she failed history and restore my faith in the education system.* "That's right, we hold Bob Hope personally responsible for the entire American War."

"Huh?"

"The Vietnam conflict."

"Why didn't you just say so?"

It wasn't just Katie's lack of wit, everything about the younger woman made Tam feel really old. Compared to Katie, Tam had lived two lifetimes in her twenty-nine years.

She made her way down the ladder one rickety rung at a time. She'd taken her life in her hands by climbing the abandoned tower in the first place.

A missing rung halfway down meant a long stretch

to the next step. It hadn't seemed so bad on the way up, but this time she lost her balance. A splinter snagged the tender flesh of her palm as she hung on for dear life.

Hearing the crack of rotting wood a split second before the ladder gave out, Tam let out a helpless shriek as she fell the last few feet to the sand. It wouldn't have been so bad except she picked up more splinters on the way down and landed on her holstered sidearm.

"Troi oi!"

"What did I tell you?" Katie rushed to her side. "That tower isn't safe."

"You said it was *too high*." Tam rolled off her hip and pushed to her feet, brushing the sand from the seat of her uniform shorts with raw palms.

"Same thing."

She supposed it only fair that Katie got the last word since Tam had been thinking unkind thoughts. She'd learned a long time ago not to argue with her assistant's brand of logic. Somehow to Katie it all made sense.

Regardless of what the young woman actually said, climbing the tower had been a risk. One worth taking for a peek from a safe distance. Not that she'd be able to keep that distance much longer.

"I think there's a first aid kit down at the marina," Katie offered helpfully.

Traitor. "Go ahead. I'll catch up with you later."

"Here, wear this." A green construction helmet flew by.

Katie caught it and Tam wheeled around.

"Thank you, Lieutenant Prince." Katie correctly identified him. "Nice binoculars."

Tam immediately regretted confiding in the only other female on the island. But she stood staring at an even bigger regret. His eyes were shaded, not by the helmet he'd just given up, but by sunglasses.

As Katie had pointed out, they both wore binoculars around their necks. So who had been spying on whom?

"You know," Katie continued, "I've always liked shorts on UPS guys, but I think I like them much better on Seabees."

Tam noticed he had no problem wearing green socks with his green uniform.

"Thanks, I think," Prince said as Katie gamboled past. "Try not to distract the men too much. They're operating heavy machinery." Once Katie disappeared down the path, he turned back around and peeled off his sunglasses. "From now on the watchtower is off limits."

"What happened to you?" Tam asked, getting her first good look at the butterfly bandage above his right eye that matched the bandaged knuckles on his left hand.

"There you go again, stepping on my lines."

"I can't seem to help it." She shrugged. Was his heart beating as fast as hers?

He leveled an unsympathetic stare. "You never called."

It wasn't a question, but an accusation.

She searched her brain for some plausible excuse. In truth she'd just wanted to put off this encounter.

She dug at her splintered palm. "Were you in a fight?"

"Something like that."

Why did she have the feeling that "something" had to do with her?

He reached around the back of his utility belt for what turned out to be a first aid kit. She noticed he was wearing his knife, too. She couldn't help it, her hand automatically went to the butt of her Glock.

Ripping a length of surgical tape, he rolled it sticky side out. "Let me have a look at that."

He took her hand in his and pressed the tape to her palm in a painless operation. Almost painless. There was his touch to contend with.

She studied his bent head. "What does the other guy look like?"

He lifted his gaze to meet hers and held it for one breathless moment. "I had something to tell you, but when I got back to the hotel you'd checked out. Why?"

It did have something to do with her. She could tell by the way he'd avoided her question. She pulled her hand back. He'd removed most of the splinters, anyway.

"I called Hickam," he continued. "Your flight back to Midway wasn't until Tuesday, and by then I'd boarded the ship. I had every intention of keeping you in bed all weekend long." The teasing quality had completely disappeared from his voice.

"I'm sure you did." Which is why she'd checked into another hotel. No use making the same mistake twice. She licked her suddenly dry lips. "I need to know if we used protection."

He pulled back and studied her face. "Naturally I would take advantage of you in your intoxicated state."

"I know I threw myself at you," she snapped.

"And I found you irresistible. You don't think very highly of me, do you? The morals just disappear when I put on the uniform?"

"Did you use a condom or not?" she demanded.

"No," he said through tight lips, "because nothing happened."

Something had happened. In those few seconds before relief set in she'd mentally counted backward through her menstrual cycle and her mind's eye had started building a baby...his eyes, her nose, his smile...

Her heartbeat accelerated.

"Are you certain?"

"When you're certain, come find me." He turned and headed down the path, then turned back around. "We're throwing ourselves a little welcome party tomorrow. The whole island is invited."

"Thank you." She didn't know if he realized it or not, but she wasn't thanking him for the invitation.

1500 Thursday
THE MARINA; NAVAL AIR FACILITY
Sand Island, Midway Islands

"CRAP." BOTH LITERALLY and figuratively Bowie had gotten more than his fair share today. He eyeballed the fresh stain running down the front of his puke-green undershirt. The parrot perched on his shoulder cocked its feathery head to one side.

"Like you don't know," Bowie growled, untucking his T-shirt by the fistful.

Crackers squawked in protest. The bird was smart enough to realize it had worn out its welcome and fluttered to the ground before Bowie raised his arms to peel off the soiled shirt.

Puke green joined jungle print on a nearby weathered post. Bowie's battle dress uniform shirt had been an earlier casualty of war. "That's the last time you stay up all night playing poker and drinking with a bunch of merchant marines. Got that?"

"Sore loser!" Crackers strutted away from the bustling dock like cock of the walk, repeating the only words the mariners had been able to teach the bird under their care.

Bowie shook his head. He really wasn't mad at his parrot. In truth he'd missed the little nuisance. And it was hot enough that he didn't need a shirt.

His "fowl" mood had more to do with lack of sleep and his return to Midway.

Captain Harris had bailed at the last minute and stayed in Hawaii. The C.O.'s shiny silver eagles carried more clout than Bowie's own lowly double bars. And who could blame a man for preferring golf over grunge?

Bowie removed his construction helmet and swiped at the sweat beading his forehead before settling it back on his head. Until he earned back his lieutenant commander cluster and got elevated to X.O. of

NMCB133 he was stuck here unloading six months' worth of supplies and equipment.

Because of Tam there was nowhere else he'd rather be. But she'd ditched him in Hawaii and dumped on him here. All he'd wanted to do was make things right for her. To take her in his arms and keep her there. To wipe away the past by being her present. Even after she'd run he'd almost convinced himself he was the man she needed, until he'd learned for certain just a few short hours ago he wasn't the man she trusted.

"Here she comes," McCain warned in passing.

After this morning Bowie figured she'd be itching for a fight. He just hadn't counted on it being so soon. He tugged at his work gloves and motioned a forklift operator into the warehouse of company stores just as she approached.

She wrinkled her pert little nose, and he resisted the urge to lift his arms and sniff. If she didn't like the way a working man smelled that was her problem.

"We need to talk."

"Put on a hard hat," he instructed, pointing out the stack of extras. "Is this the official meet and greet?" he asked, putting his arms through the sleeves of a frat-boy, party-animal Hawaiian shirt he'd picked out himself. "Or is this personal?"

He'd spied her from the bridge of the ship. When she didn't show up to meet it, he'd gone to her so they could have a private moment to put all the awkwardness behind them. Or so he'd thought.

"Katie tells me you've brought a parrot to the island?"

"That's right."

"You can't do that, Lieutenant. This is a wildlife refuge—new species can't be introduced without affecting the habitat. Birds carry disease, which they might pass on to one another and humans."

"I think you'll find all the paperwork in order."

McCain produced a clipboard, and Bowie handed it to the professor.

She looked it over carefully, then gave it back. "This says the parrot is imported from Thailand."

"That's right. Crackers is a gift from the Thai government. I had special diplomatic dispensation to bring him into this country. Uncle Sammy didn't want to offend an ally. It's all there in black and white."

"The U.S. stopped all importation of parrots three years ago. I'm going to have to quarantine your bird."

"Crackers hasn't been off the *Bob Hope* since it left Thailand, not even when it docked in Hawaii weeks ago. He's not sick." Well, not the kind of sick that counted, anyway.

"I'm still going to have to quarantine your bird, Lieutenant. If he's healthy you can have him back in thirty days. If not he'll have to be destroyed. I'm responsible for over two million birds on this island and I can't risk introducing an epidemic. Please put him in his cage."

"What's the difference if he stays with you or me?" Bowie shooed the bird back in its cage. "I'm setting up office in the brig. We'll quarantine Crackers there."

Her hand went to the butt of her Glock.

"You know it really makes me nervous when you do that," he said. "Do you see anyone here armed?"

"Do what?"

He ingored the question. "Hand over the gun and I'll hand over the bird."

Leaving the cage where he'd stood, Bowie stepped closer to her. Most of his men were using the excuse of dusting themselves off to watch as they gathered around the water coolers.

"I'm taking the bird. It's the law."

"I'm the law around here."

"As I said before—"

"Before the island came back under the management of the Navy? This time I'm taking your weapon." He reached over and disarmed her, tucking the handgun in his belt. A place he knew she wouldn't reach for it. "Now we're even." He offered her a hand in truce.

She refused to shake. Folding her arms, she tilted her chin. "If I were you I'd check the safety."

He followed her gaze to the gun. He checked the safety, then tucked it behind his back. Taking a deep breath, he counted to ten. She'd had the safety off! "We're going to have to figure out how to get along."

Whether she agreed or not, he didn't have the chance to find out. A commotion on the docks demanded his immediate attention. With all the excitement going on no one had noticed one of the equipment operators crash into a post, tearing down a pier. A steamroller had gone into the drink.

He rushed to the disabled dock.

From what he could understand the driver was still underwater. He made the split-second decision to dive in. Several of his men followed.

Tam rushed to the edge of the pier with the others. Heads bobbed as men came up for air. The lieutenant didn't. Something was seriously wrong. She could see the outline of the steamroller in the clear and relatively shallow water.

Finally the lieutenant emerged. He had a crowbar in one hand and the unconscious body of a young woman in the other.

"Katie!" Tam screamed, rushing over. Tam grabbed the girl's wrist and checked her vital signs, ready to help administer CPR before he even laid her out on the pier.

He rolled Katie's limp body onto her side and got her to throw up water, but she remained unconscious. "Katie," he said, patting the girl's cheeks. "Can you hear me?"

No response.

He laid her back down. Tilted her chin. Pinched her nose. And administered a few quick breaths. Following those breaths, Katie coughed and sputtered and finally roused.

He helped her sit up. "You okay?"

She nodded, coughed some more, then finally answered, "Yes, sir."

Tam helped Katie to her feet. "Are you sure you're okay? Let's get you home and dry. I'll make some hot tea."

Several of the young men crowded around to tease Katie about women drivers. Tam glared at them.

But it was the lieutenant who put a stop to it. "Which idiot let her play with his *equipment?*" he demanded.

Three hands went up. "Crap! Owens, Brown, Gonzales and Jones. Follow me."

"What did I do?" Jones asked. "I didn't raise my hand."

"Master Chief—" Bowie continued to issue orders "—get a crane over here to get that 'dozer out of the drink. McCain, get a work detail busy on the pier. The rest of you keep off-loading on the other side."

He turned his attention to Tam and Katie. In a calm, but cool voice he said, "Ladies, I think that's enough excitement around here for one day."

"You're not holding us responsible for that?" Tam pointed toward the crane rolling into position.

When he would have walked right on by, she reached out and grabbed his arm.

He shrugged her off, then stopped. "No I don't," he said evenly. "It's always the man's fault and the man's responsibility." He picked up the birdcage and handed it to her. "Take the damn bird! In fact," he said, whipping the gun from behind his back and handing it back to her, "take the damn gun. You may as well shoot me now and get it over with. I'm sure you'll come up with a reason sooner or later. But you might want to clean it first. I'm afraid I got it wet." He scooped up his long discarded hard hat and stalked away.

Tam was left holding the bird.

1600 Thursday
THE BRIG; NAVAL AIR FACILITY
Sand Island, Midway Islands

BOWIE STOOD BEHIND a dust-covered desk in the
brig's office, staring down the four men standing at
attention. "I don't want to know—"

"It was my fault, sir," said a tiny voice from the
doorway.

"Flynn!" The confession came from one of the
only four women in his company and took him by
surprise.

Owens snickered. "The Navy has a don't-ask,
don't-tell policy, Flynn."

"Shut up." Brown elbowed him in the ribs.

She clicked her tongue. "Just 'cause I'm not
easy—"

"Okay, enough of that. What happened, Flynn?"

"I got tired of waiting my turn to off-load just because these losers were acting all stupid and showing
off. So I told the twit to get off the pier. And I got
into it with her. I said something like, I didn't learn
to drive from a guy's lap. And she said something
like, any idiot could learn to drive a stick, but it takes
a woman to know how to use it. So I said, if you
think it's so easy go ahead. Then I walked away,
thinking I'd cool off, and she'd be gone when I came
back. But—"

"I get the picture. And I'm going to let *everyone*
off the hook this time. Flynn, see the master chief for
a refresher course on safety."

"Yes, sir."

"You're dismissed. Guys, same refresher course. I don't think it would do any good to make Ms. Dewitt off limits. Just keep in mind what comes around goes around. Dismissed."

"I think Brown's got a hard-on for Flynn," Gonzales said as three of the four males followed their female cohort out the door.

"Knock it off," Brown said.

"Sir," Petty Officer First Class Jones said. "I wasn't messing around with Ms. Dewitt."

"I know, but you're their leading petty officer."

"Yes, sir." Accepting the responsibility, he turned to leave.

"Sit down," Bowie invited. "Actually, there's another matter I've been meaning to discuss with you. I understand congratulations are in order." Bowie pulled a dusty chair behind the desk and sat down, as well.

"Sir?"

"You're getting married."

Jones looked around the room, everywhere but at Bowie.

"You are getting married to a young woman you met in Thailand, aren't you?"

Jones finally met his gaze. He nodded. "I'd appreciate it if you didn't tell the guys just yet. They like to tease me because her parents were strict and wouldn't let us alone together, if you know what I mean."

Bowie nodded in understanding, relieved that Stevens had turned out to be wrong about Jones.

"I couldn't stop thinking about her, you know, when we went off to Laos. Then when we got back to the States…that first night some guy came up to us and said he was having trouble getting his cousin to the States, wanted to know if we could help him out. He needed someone to swear he'd met her in Thailand. He'd even pay."

"None of the guys—"

"No, sir. We just blew him off. But the next day I checked into fiancée visas and there really was such a thing. So I figured why not bring her to the States and get married."

That didn't sound like solid reasoning to Bowie, but men had done stupider things for lust and love. "Thanks, Jones. That's all for now. Let the guys know everybody came up clean on the drug test."

"Thanks, L.T." Jones left to spread the good word.

Bowie picked up the desk phone to call Stevens. "How's your jaw?" he asked by way of greeting.

"Last time I counted I still had all my teeth. How's your eye?"

"I can still use it, but I have a part in my eyebrow."

"You were too much of a pretty boy, anyway. So what's the scoop?"

"I just wanted to let you know Jones checks out okay. I also wanted to apologize for what I said the other day. Age aside, you really cared about her, didn't you?"

"She didn't seem so young at the time."

Fall 1972
Somewhere in Laos

"DON'T GIVE ME THAT LOOK, Skully." Tad Prince shook his head as if he already knew Skully was about to make an impossible request. "We're going home," he admonished softly. The word had just come down. They were to turn everything over to the South Vietnamese.

After eighteen months in this jungle hell those words should have been music to his ears. To Quartermaster Chief Petty Officer Robert Stevens, they were anything but. While the rest of his teammates whooped it up with 35 beer and blew entire bankrolls on boom-boom, he sat on a crate beside his tent. Home is where the heart is, after all.

His heart was about to be left behind in Vietnam. "I have to go."

"The Navy has other plans for you."

"Tad, I gave her my word." He didn't mind making it personal. As long as it got him what he wanted. "You were there when she saved our asses."

"The Paris Agreement says we're out of here."

"The hell with the Paris Agreement. And all those fat-assed politicians. This war isn't over...for us, maybe, but not for her. If I marry her, they gotta let me bring her back to the States, right?"

"Don't you mean adopt her? Skully, she's a baby."

"That's why she needs me."

Tad Prince took one long breath and released it. "I'll get my gear and go with you."

"I can't let you do that. You've got a wife and three kids waiting for you. This is personal. I'm going alone. But you can do me a favor. If I don't make it back, get Bay to the States for me—he's Lan's kid brother.''

Prince cursed under his breath. ''They're going to think I've been smoking some of that wacky weed. Go on, get the hell out of here. If you're not back in seventy-two hours—''

''I'll be back.'' He didn't need to let him finish. Navy SEALs never left a man behind. He'd have a squad of pissed-off teammates after his sorry ass. And he couldn't let that happen. Every last one of them had already earned their ride home.

''That seventy-two hours started thirty seconds ago.''

''Aye-aye, sir.'' Skully pushed to his feet, shouldering the AK-47 he'd picked up on their last mission. The Russian-made assault weapon was less likely to jam in the humidity than the M16 and ammunition was easy to come by, but it had a distinctive pop so there was always a chance someone from your own side would mistake you for the enemy.

''Skully, where you going? Come join the party,'' Chief Howard Thomas invited.

''There's something I've got to do.''

''WHERE IS SHE?'' Skully demanded.

The man stood in the doorway of the bamboo hut. He looked past Skully, refusing to acknowledge his existence. He could have been forty or four hundred.

''I asked you a question. Now, where the hell is she?'' Skully grabbed the other man's collar and forced him to meet his gaze. This was no way to treat his future father-in-law, but his patience had its limits.

It had taken him longer to reach Quang Tri than he'd anticipated. He'd only been able to catch a chopper for part of the ride. America had pulled out of the Vietnam Conflict. Only fifty advisers to the South Vietnamese Army would be left behind.

He'd wound up walking most of the way. Running, really. Entire armored tank divisions passed him on the road, heading in the opposite direction. He'd have to hurry to even catch the tail end of the retreat for the ride home.

He'd be damned if he let anyone stand in his way. He let go of the man's collar and pushed his way inside. "Lan!"

Skully covered the entire three-room shack in as many minutes. She wasn't here.

Lan's mother screeched at him in Vietnamese, the words spewing from between betel-nut-stained teeth. Older women chewed the mild narcotic to relieve the pain of gum disease. That would be Lan in a few years, old before her time if he didn't get her out of here.

Tears streamed down the woman's weathered face. "Go home, Joe!" she said in mangled English. "We not want your kind round here no more. No more! You make big trouble."

"Shh," her husband admonished.

Skully turned on him once again. "Just tell me where she is. I can take care of her. Take her to the States. I'm taking Bay, I can take you."

"Lan is gone."

"Gone? Gone where?"

"Gone."

"I don't believe you."

"It's true." Lan's oldest brother, Than, the one serving the south, entered the hut. "Xang took her. He'll kill her before he lets you have her. Now, get the hell out of here and leave my family in peace."

CHAPTER SEVEN

0700 Friday
THE BEACH; NAVAL AIR FACILITY
Sand Island, Midway Islands

BOWIE WOKE UP IN A GOOD mood. First morning on the island and she hadn't shot him in the back. Or even in his sleep. That had to be a good sign.

He decided to be bold and put on the sarong.

For Seabees a welcome party started at dawn—at least the preparations. They hauled empty oil drums out to the beach and packed them with ice and beer they'd had flown in from Hawaii for the occasion. They cut other drums down the center and welded them into makeshift barbecues.

He and McCain were on each end of a porcelain tub they were carrying down to the beach for mixing mojo, when Captain Harris arrived.

"Lieutenant Prince," Harris said. "You're late for morning muster. Have your men assemble down at the marina immediately. Don't bother changing."

"Yes, sir," Bowie said, but Harris had already left. "Where did he come from?"

McCain shrugged. "Must have flown in with the beer."

"He's got my curiosity piqued," Bowie admitted.

He rounded up the men with a series of calls via two-way radios. By the time they reached the marina, Bowie realized something was up. Two Coast Guard vessels were docked. The entire company had arrived ahead of him and were standing in formation, though with their nonregulation beachcomber wear, they looked like something out of *McHale's Navy*.

"Lieutenant Prince," Harris addressed him. "Since you couldn't make it to the World Free-diving Championships again this year, we decided to bring them to you. Make us proud."

The company parted and there sat Bowie's gear on the dock in front of the bigger of the two boats.

When Bowie didn't move, McCain slapped him on the back and said, "Let's get it in gear."

"Thank you." Bowie shook his C.O.'s hand. Maybe he'd been wrong about Harris. Gathering his wet suit and flippers, Bowie started to climb the dive boat's outboard ladder. "Hey," he said over his shoulder to McCain, "would you—"

"I already sent Katie to get her."

Trust had to be built. But today Bowie just wanted to show off.

"KATIE, I REALLY HAVE too much to do today to spend it down on the docks. And so do you," she reminded the girl. "Besides, after what happened yesterday I think we should keep clear of the Seabees and just let them do their job."

"Talk some sense into her, Will," Katie said, lifting her hand up in exasperation.

They'd cornered Tam in her house before she'd even had the chance to get dressed. She stood in her pjs with her morning tea, wishing they'd leave her alone.

"You've heard of the Super Bowl, the World Series, boxing's Heavyweight Champion of the World?" Will asked.

"Of course."

"Well, in the world of free-diving this is the title fight," Will explained.

"Really?"

Katie and Will both nodded.

"He wants you there," Katie said. "Besides, we've declared today a holiday. Everyone's taking the day off for the party. You wouldn't want to be the only one not there, would you? What if he fails? It would be all your fault!"

Katie-logic, of course, but Tam probably would blame herself if he failed. Katie and Will would certainly blame her. And if the lieutenant didn't fail, well, it wasn't like she could take credit for that, but it would be something to see.

"Okay, let me get dressed. It'll only take me a minute to put on my uniform."

"No!" Katie and Will both vetoed her intention.

"Let your hair down," Katie suggested. "It's a party."

So Tam put on a plain yellow one-piece swimsuit and a sarong. She added a yellow ball cap and picked up her carryall. In truth, she hardly ever wore her uniform, but she'd decided on a change of policy with the arrival of the Seabees.

The marina was crowded by the time they got there. Katie was right. There'd be no work done today.

"Warden." They were greeted by a Coast Guard petty officer in a dungaree uniform. "Lieutenant Prince asked me to make sure you had the best seat in the house."

Bowie stood on deck wearing the sarong she'd bought him in Hawaii. Or rather he was discarding his, leaving him in a Speedo. Next to pinkie rings and gold chains, it was one item she'd always felt shouldn't be worn by men. Seeing Bowie had her making an exception.

The petty officer directed Tam and her friends toward the smaller boat, but Bowie motioned her over as he scrambled down the ladder.

"Hold these for me?" He draped his dog tags around her neck, reminding her of the lei she'd given him in Hawaii. "Kiss for luck?" he asked, as if reading her thoughts.

"Don't you have to keep your pumper under control, sailor?"

He chuckled. And she realized it was good to see that smile back on his face. She blew him a kiss and backed away. He still had the bandage above his brow but had unwrapped his bruised knuckles.

She, Katie and Will, along with the Coast Guard crew, were joined by Captain Harris and Master Chief Cohen. Safety and medical divers, a camera crew and the judges were all on the other boat with Bowie. Everyone else had found places in dozens of crafts of all sizes docked at the marina.

By the time the boats were positioned in a semi-circle around the dive site it was midmorning. It was only when Bowie was in the water that Tam remembered her camera and dug it out of her bag.

"Warm-up's going to take about an hour," the petty officer told her.

"I've never seen fins that long."

"They're a lot longer and more flexible than scuba fins. For strong kicks," he explained. "The total weight of his gear is only about four pounds."

"And the floating lawn chair?"

"For breathing exercises. And those last deep breaths before he goes down."

"They've got the underwater cameras set up," Katie said excitedly.

Tam glanced at the monitors, but for the most part kept her eyes on the diver in the water.

"He can slow his heart rate to ten beats per minute with breath holds," Captain Harris informed her.

"Mammalian diving reflex," she said absently. But ten beats? The man had control. "How deep will he be going?" she asked.

"The men's constant ballast world record is 267 feet. Prince has already reached 270 feet in an unofficial dive," Captain Harris said. "Today he's going for a flag at 274 feet."

"What about the current world record holder? I bet he's pretty disappointed about this attempt."

"I imagine the retired Captain Prince is feeling pretty proud of his son right about now. He and his wife are watching online. There'll be a few seconds delay, but they'll see history in the making."

"His father?" Tam moved closer to the starboard side as Bowie went through his deep-breathing exercises. She aimed the video camera at him, surprised at the envy she felt. He and his father had a shared hobby, a shared life.

She didn't know what traits or interests she shared with her father. But she'd forged tentative bonds with the man who could help her find him.

She lowered the camera and reached up to encircle his dog tags in her hand. And found herself breathing right along with him. Her heart rate slowed, sixty, fifty, forty beats...

"Ready," the petty officer said, directing everyone's attention toward the screen.

Tam filled her lungs with a deep breath before he jackknifed into the dive. Powerful, thrusting kicks propelled his descent along the ballast line. Thirty, sixty, ninety seconds later, 270 feet.

"Ladies," the petty officer announced. "No man has ever gone deeper."

She felt the dog tags bite her palm as she silently urged him on. He grabbed the tag at 274 feet, turned and started his ascent. Three minutes into the dive she finally let out the breath she'd been holding as he broke through the surface and his body received the oxygen it craved.

He gave the thumbs-up sign and the crowd started to cheer. Tam would have, but she noticed Bowie was having trouble getting to the boat. When the medical and safety divers beside him began to drag him from the water her hands went cold, but the petty officer explained that was normal as during the dive the body had directed oxygen-rich blood away from his limbs and to his vital organs.

So there he was a few hundred yards away on another boat. And all she could do was wave to him in the distance.

1900 Friday
THE BEACH; NAVAL AIR FACILITY
Sand Island, Midway Islands

AFTER THE INITIAL EUPHORIA wore off, Bowie had taken a well-deserved three-hour nap to go with his record-breaking three-minute dive. He woke rejuvenated and ready to join the party.

He'd changed into a pair of loose-fitting khaki shorts and a wild print shirt that he could only assume would go with anything in his closet.

The eighty Seabees in his detachment, Coast Guard members from the dive boats and USNS *Bob Hope* merchant marines were out in full force when Bowie's sandals kicked up sand on the beach. It was the one place on the island where gooney birds didn't build a nest every few feet.

"Why is it always the guys with the biggest bellies and the hairiest chests who put on the grass skirts and coconut bras?" McCain asked, handing Bowie an ice-cold beer.

"Because the rest of us have better sense."

"I noticed you didn't wear your man skirt to the party. Good call."

"It's a sarong. They're gender neutral."

"Some commissioned salesgirl sell you that idea?"

"Something like that." Bowie scanned the crowd.

"*She's* manning the barbecue with Rusty." McCain pointed in the general direction with his bottle.

"Master Chief Cohen, the man who perfected the two-handed burger flip, let someone else near the grills?"

McCain shrugged. "Guess he's feeling *paternal* tonight."

"This I've got to see." Bowie chugged his beer, then tossed the bottle before heading over to the cooking duo.

Rosy-cheeked and perspiring from the heat, Tam manned a grill under the watchful eye of the master chief. He'd put her in charge of the hot dogs.

She laughed at something Rusty said. "Oh, I haven't laughed so much since—" She caught sight of Bowie and switched to Vietnamese.

Rusty chuckled. "I think you've earned your dinner now. Why don't you fix a couple of those hot dogs for you and the lieutenant?"

They both laughed louder at that. But she put her cooking utensils aside and met Bowie with a full plate.

She wore a simple pair of khaki shorts and a pink tank top.

"What was that all about?" he asked.

"I just shared our little hot dog incident."

He cocked a brow. "It wasn't that funny."

"I guess you had to be there," she said, leading the way to the shaded tables laden with condiments. They divvied up the dogs and loaded their plates.

"I *was* there, remember?"

"I may have elaborated just a little."

"Are you sure you don't mean exaggerated?" he asked as they found an empty corner of a table. "What can I get you to drink? We've got beer from around the globe. But trust me, stay away from the Ba Muoi Lam."

"I'll try." She smiled up at him. "A diet soda is fine."

Heading toward the nearest ice-filled drum, Bowie glanced over his shoulder. She'd been hanging around him too long. That sounded like innuendo.

But trust me, stay away from the "playboy."

I'll try.

He returned just in time to head off the swarm of drones descending on the queen. "I can't leave you alone for a minute."

"The odds are in a gal's favor around here. I would have left earlier, but the master chief took me under his wing. And I really did want to congratulate you on your dive today. I'm sure you've heard it a hundred times already, but that was amazing."

"Thanks," he said, feeling his chest swell. "I never get tired of hearing it." Not from her.

"I was wondering if you'd let me, or Will, rather, since he's the techno wizard, post some of your dive footage to my cyber classroom. I've never featured a person before, but I had this idea of working it in with some information about aquatic sea mammals."

"I'm sure that could be arranged."

"I'd also like to interview you about the experience, if it's not too much of an intrusion?"

"We could make a deal. I have maps and blueprints for the entire island, but I'd really like a guided tour. Things are going to settle down around here by Tuesday, when the ship will be gone. Think we could get together then?''

"I'll clear my calendar."

They talked until their food became cold and the tiki torches and bonfire blazed. He'd tuned out the rest of the world and simply focused on her face.

Tam was enjoying Bowie's company, but the volume of the party had increased in direct proportion to the amount of alcohol consumed. And when the Seabees started to mix the jungle juice she decided it was time to leave.

"I think I'm going to call it a night." She pushed to her feet and disposed of their plates.

"I'll walk you home," he offered.

"That really won't be necessary. I know the way."

"I'm headed in that direction," he insisted. "If you say no, I'm just going to follow you, anyway. I want to make sure that you get home safe."

She realized she'd probably lock her doors and windows tonight, something she hadn't felt the need to do before, and that took some of the enjoyment from her evening.

"Okay."

"After you." He made a sweeping gesture.

"I thought you were headed in *that* direction?"

"I am. I just don't know the way." Was he using that silver tongue to tell her to take the lead? That he'd cover her back? Or would he run for cover when things heated up?

He grabbed two beers and handed her one. She

took it and started home along the beach, though it wasn't the most direct path. Soon the party noises faded enough for them to hear the sound of the rushing water and clapping beaks again.

"What projects do you think you'll start with?"

"The runways are a priority. The night we met I learned firsthand that they're in bad shape. The drainage ditches alongside are backed up. I stepped up to my knees in muck."

She processed this bit of information. "That's why your pants were wet and your boots were dry." So he wasn't the one who'd left the footprint on Eastern.

"I had a spare pair...." he trailed off. "Is that why you thought I'd been to Eastern Island?"

"Well, somebody left a footprint."

"Footprint? Someone from the island?"

"No, there's really nothing over there. A couple of runways, a fuel depot and a few historical sites. Of course, you probably know that. But that's where I get my best turtle and seal footage."

"I don't want you back over there until I've had the chance to check it out."

Tam stopped to face him. "Don't be silly, it's my job to catch poachers." Not that she was convinced it was a poacher's print. When she'd returned to Eastern the following day, nothing had been taken. Which was why she'd figured it had to be him.

"Do you want me to make it off limits?"

She put her hands on her hips. "I don't take orders from you."

"Let's compromise," he offered. "Take someone

with you. If I'm available I'll go. If not, I'll find someone who is.''

''Fair enough.''

''You're not just agreeing to shut me up?''

''No, your request is reasonable,'' she said, cutting inland. They reached the road that wound around the neglected Navy housing units. For the most part, those living and working on the island chose to stay in the military barracks. But she'd preferred the privacy of the houses.

''Look at this place,'' he said. ''It's a whole other world.'' Overgrown lawns and gardens were starting to obscure most of the units. Soon it would be difficult to find any evidence of them. ''If you're living in this neighborhood, I gotta tell you the resale value on your house is zilch.''

''It's not like I invested a lot of money in the place.''

''Of course not,'' he agreed. ''You're squatting.''

''I have to live somewhere.''

''I never said you couldn't, only that I think you should let me check it out. Uncle Sammy wouldn't like it if I let one of his houses fall down on you.''

''That one's mine.'' She didn't have to tell him. He would have been able to pick it out by the mowed lawn and neat gardens—vegetables in the back, hibiscus and bird of paradise in the front with bougainvillea climbing the porch. ''See, nothing to worry about.''

''Why don't you let me be the judge of that. It is my job, after all.''

Tam followed him around her house. The front and

back porch lights were on but provided little light. Occasionally he'd pause to look at something more carefully. He seemed to concentrate on the foundation and the roof. When they reached her front porch again, he asked, "Roof leaking at all?"

"Only when it rains."

"If I'm not mistaken, it does that every day around here." He didn't even crack a smile.

"There's one, maybe two leaks at the most." She sat down on her stoop to finish her beer.

He joined her. "All right, we'll leave it open to further discussion at a later date."

"Agreed," she said, and steered him toward another topic. "I forgot to ask, what did your dad think of your breaking his record?"

He looked at her in surprise. "We only exchanged a quick, very public phone call. Local media covered the dive on his end. I'll probably call home later tonight." He checked his watch. "Which is morning in Florida."

"I'll bet he would have liked to have been here, though."

"Probably. He helped Harris with the details, arranged for the judges. But he gave me space to breathe because he wanted me to succeed. You know I could've just as easily failed." He gave her a sideways glance, then studied the bottle in his hand when she didn't say anything right away. "I was glad you were there to share that moment with me."

"I was glad I could be there," she admitted, touching his shoulder. He turned to her, but she pulled away. "You know I still have something of yours."

"My bird?"

"That, too. You should come see him." She transferred his dog tags from her neck to his.

He sat back expectantly for moment, then took a swig from his beer. "You know that's the third time we've exchanged something without a kiss."

If they counted his knife, her gun, his bird, it was more than that.

"Have you found out anything about my father?"

"Not much. Not yet." He took a swig of beer.

She accepted his answer because she didn't have any other choice. She pushed to her feet "It's late, I'm going to call it a night."

"Night." He stood and watched her all the way to the door. "I still don't like the way this porch sags," he said when she reached for the handle. "You should stay somewhere else tonight—"

"Now, what kind of example would that be for your men? Good night, Lieutenant."

She waved and could hear his good-natured laughter as she stepped inside and slammed the door for good measure. She leaned against the door and sighed. The house sighed with her. Then groaned. Then heaved.

And then there was a horrific sound of collapse. She opened the door and had to wave away the dust. Her porch was now on the ground. The lieutenant stood out of harm's way, just beyond the bottom step.

"You did this!" she accused.

"Do you think I'm going to bring a house down with you inside?" He held his hand out to her and helped her over the pile of shingles and debris.

"You're not staying here tonight. And that's an order."

"You can't give me orders."

"Try me."

She opened her mouth to protest, but thought better of it. He was right. She couldn't stay with the house like this. "All right, just let me pack a suitcase and get my toothbrush."

"No." This time she was inclined to listen to him. "I'll send someone for your things in the morning."

"I had three, maybe four leaks at the most," she mumbled, her glazed eyes transfixed on her house as he dragged her up the road. It was only when she could no longer see it that she realized he still held her hand.

BOWIE HAD DROPPED Tam off at Flynn's door. Before he'd left she had asked for a toothbrush, any toothbrush. So he'd set out on a mission to find one. He could have gone back to her house, he supposed, but he'd rather traverse that by the light of day.

On the way back to his office he called his parents on his cell phone.

"Morning," his mother's cheerful voice answered.

"Not here it isn't."

"Let me put you on speaker phone. It's Bowie," she said to his dad. They talked for a few minutes about the dive, but that wasn't what he'd called about. He'd expected his mom to raise hell about not returning her call last week, but she didn't, though she did take him by surprise.

"So who's the lucky lady?"

"What?" He stumbled on the dark path and stopped to better concentrate on his call.

"Your sister said you sent Mariah the most adorable muumuu. We both know *you* didn't pick it out, maybe the T-shirt for Aaron, but not the muumuu. So who is she?"

"My personal shopper?"

"Good one, son," his dad said, taking up his side.

"Actually, she's the reason I called. That, and I kind of wanted to talk about some stuff going on with the company. But first I want to know how you two managed to stay together all those years dad was away from home."

"You must be serious," his mother teased. Then launched into a long speech about commitment and relationships. As she rambled on and his dad occasionally added his opinion, Bowie realized it was their shared sense of humor *and* purpose that had kept them married and in love.

Bowie propped himself up against a nearby tree and listened.

He'd spent years with guys who cheated on their wives or girlfriends and married and divorced at the drop of a hat. They were good, hardworking guys. Guys he'd trust with his life, but not his money or his wife. And he'd seen the other side, too. The wives weren't always waiting when the guys got home.

He simply did not want any part of that.

But then there were the others. Guys like the master chief, who'd spent his last dime for a few days in Hawaii with his wife. Or Milton, who'd asked Bowie to find a way around the no-leave policy because his wife was due to deliver their first baby.

And then Bowie started to long for something he didn't have.

"You did say *she* was the reason you called," his mother reminded him. "We want to hear all about the girlfriend."

"Friend," he corrected her, it felt safer. "I'm doing a friend a favor. Dad, she's Amerasian and never knew her father. She has his picture, though. And I sure as hell recognized him. It's Skully—Rob Stevens. Before I tell her I need to know *why* he left her and her mother behind in Vietnam. Then maybe I can help bring them together. I just can't figure it out, it seems so out of character with everything you've ever told me about the man."

Neither of his parents said a word.

"Dad?" Bowie urged.

"Bowie," his mother said. "Are you sure Rob Stevens is this girl's father?"

"Impossible," his father said. "Xang killed Skully's wife and *son*."

"*Wife and son?*" Bowie repeated. "Are you sure?"

"I was there. Skully almost drove himself insane with grief and guilt."

"I guess I'd better check this out before I go any further. I'll call you back later. Can we keep it between us for now?"

"Of course," his parents agreed.

The mystery was far from solved, but as Bowie hung up the phone, he found a bit of hope in the information his father had given him. If a man believed his wife and child were dead, he might stop looking.

He entered the brig a few minutes later.

"What are you doing?" McCain asked, stretched out on his rack. They'd take up residence in the Commanding Officers Quarters as soon as Captain Harris boarded a plane tomorrow.

"Looking for an extra toothbrush," Bowie said, digging around in his seabag. "Have one?"

"Not an extra one."

"Me, neither." He grabbed the master key ring off a hook on the wall above his desk. "I guess the most logical place would be the medical-dental building." It was close. And brick. At least he wouldn't have to worry about it falling down around his ears.

They set out for the clinic with a flashlight, coming upon rats the size of cats more than once.

"Mighty Mouse lives," McCain said, throwing gravel at a rat that wouldn't scurry out of their way fast enough. "How are we supposed to eradicate supercritters?"

"Traps, I guess. I'll leave the details to you."

"Thanks a lot."

They arrived at the clinic and Bowie opened the door and reached inside to flip on the switch. The building had power, just not a lot of light bulbs, but enough worked, so he turned off his flashlight.

Half of the building had served as sick call, the other as dental. It was easy to distinguish the two.

"You try that room. I'll take this one," Bowie instructed. A dust-cloth-covered dental chair sat in the middle of the room Bowie had chosen. He hit the jackpot with the first drawer he opened. He grabbed a handful of wrapped toothbrushes and looked for anything else that might be useful. He loaded his pockets with floss and sample-size toothpaste, wondering what the expiration date was.

"Find anything?" McCain entered the room with a cardboard box tucked under his arm.

"Yeah. What've you got there?"

"A gross of condoms. And there's more where this came from."

"In case you haven't noticed, McCain, you're not going to need them. There are only six women on this island. Four of them are enlisted, which means they're off limits to you and me. As for the two civilians, one is way too young for you."

"And the other?"

"I saw her first."

McCain shoved the box to Bowie's chest.

"Grab another one," Bowie ordered.

"You busy Bee."

"FYI, I was thinking of the enlisted men. We can set one out in the barracks and one in the office." But he pocketed a couple just in case.

Showing up at the women's door with a gross of condoms was probably not the most brilliant idea he'd ever had. But at least he'd left his box in the hallway of the BEQ.

Except for E-6 and above, the guys were doubled up while the girls each had their own room. The bathroom schedule had been a little tricky, but he hadn't wanted to open up more than one barrack. So the girls had the head on the second floor and the guys on the first. There was also a laundry room on each floor, but that operated on a first-come, first-served basis.

Flynn answered his knock in an oversize jersey, eating a banana. Tam was still dressed and sat on the extra rack in the corner. All the other girls had gathered in that one room, including Katie. Bowie remembered a pajama party fantasy he'd once had.

"Hi, L.T., J.G., we were just talking about you. Do you want to come in?" Flynn offered a little breathlessly. Bowie stepped just inside the door and McCain moved into the doorway. Their nicknames had caught on with the rest of the Alpha Dogs so he was used to even the girls calling him L.T. now.

"Ladies," he said. "I come bearing toothbrushes. Anyone else need an extra one besides the professor?" He made sure Tam got everything she needed, then put the rest up for grabs. "Talking about me, huh?" he said in an aside to Tam.

"Trust me, the subject wasn't all that interesting. But it appears you have some groupies," she whispered back.

"What's in the box, J.G.?" Flynn asked.

"Condoms. Want some?"

"Sure." The girls rushed him as if he were throwing beads at a Mardi Gras parade. "Professor?" McCain asked the only person holding back. "Condom?"

"All right, we're leaving," Bowie announced, trying to push McCain and his big mouth out the door. "Good night, ladies."

"How many did you take, Lieutenant?" Tam's question stopped him.

"Some would say too many, others not enough," he answered.

"And you'd say?"

Bowie couldn't believe it. Here they were discussing condoms, when just yesterday morning protection and precaution were two words she hadn't associated with him.

She kept looking at him as if she were waiting for an answer.

"Two," he admitted.

She held his gaze while she picked out one, then two.

His gut clenched at her unusual method of seduction. He was ready to fall down on his knees in gratitude anytime now. "I meant ten," he said.

And she laughingly shoved him out the door.

CHAPTER EIGHT

0730 Saturday
ABANDONED HOUSING UNITS;
NAVAL AIR FACILITY
Sand Island, Midway Islands

TAM GOT CAUGHT TRYING to sneak back into her house through the French windows. "I just need to get a few things."

"I've been waiting for you," he said, handing her a hard hat and following her inside. "I thought we'd go house hunting today. Unless of course you like rooming with Flynn."

"Oh, please." She stuffed clean clothes into a duffel bag. "I'd rather have you for a roommate."

"That could be arranged."

"*That* was sarcasm," she said, staring him down. "They're teenagers. They kept me up all night."

"And I wouldn't keep you up all night?" He gave her that sexy dimpled smile as he leaned against the doorjamb.

"Of course you would." She slammed her bag into his chest and let him carry it. "But at least you might enjoy it."

He threw back his head and laughed. "Are you

always like this when you haven't had a good night's sleep?"

"*Always* is such a relative term," she said, following him outside. "Where do we start?"

"Anywhere you want. I brought a golf cart," he said, stuffing her duffel bag in the back.

Anywhere you want turned out to be a relative term, as well. What he should have said was *anywhere I say*. He'd scouted out a number of houses in advance. Unfortunately they couldn't agree on any one of them. What he considered structurally sound she considered ugly.

Any house that looked like it might blow over with a huff and a puff from a big bad wolf had been spray-painted on the front door with a fluorescent *X*. It was pretty clear that the neighborhood of housing units wouldn't exist much longer.

It was afternoon and she was tired and hungry. With her temper growing shorter all the time, she was ready to call it quits.

"Are you really trying to get me to share that little cell with you? Because if you are, you'd better start padding it. You're driving me crazy."

"Don't you trust me?" he demanded. "There's nothing wrong with this house. Look," he said, directing her attention to the water. "It has a nice view of the ocean. A leeward wind. A roof that doesn't leak and isn't going to fall down on you. What more could you ask for?"

"My house had an open porch, this one is enclosed. How would I even be able to enjoy the view or the breeze? There're tiles missing in the bathroom and kitchen. And the place is filthy. It would take me a month to even clean it.''

"Forget about all that for a minute, it's cosmetic. This house has a solid foundation. There's even bougainvillea. You didn't want the last house because it didn't have any. Well, there you go, bougainvillea.''

"I don't know—''

"I can open up the porch,'' he said, taking a screw driver from his utility belt and beginning to remove a screen.

Just a few short weeks ago he'd worn weapons on his utility belt. Now he wore tools. She had to admit, she could learn to love a man who knew how to use tools. An open porch with a view of the ocean and a leeward breeze would be heaven.

"Sold!''

THEIR NEXT STOP TURNED out to be her lab, where she fixed them both a cup of instant soup. She was pretty sure one package wouldn't hold him so she dumped two into an oversize mug for him and one into a regular-size mug for her. She put the kettle on the hot plate and waited for the water to boil.

In the meantime they had peanut butter on Ritz crackers to tide them over. "I told you I couldn't cook,'' she said, stuffing a cracker into her mouth.

He took the butter knife from her and spread peanut butter onto a cracker. "You managed last night. Besides, I've had worse.''

"Like what? What's the worst thing you've ever eaten?''

"I'm not sure what you'd call it, but it moved. Of

course C-Rats, C-Rations for the uninitiated, run a close second. And Meals Ready to Eat.''

''Yeah, that sounds pretty bad,'' she agreed. ''I'd have to say French fries top my list. Because they're so good and so bad for you. I can't stop at one. I have to supersize and then eat every last fry. It's a good thing there isn't a McDonald's on the island or I'd be fat as a house.''

''I doubt that.'' He eyed her appreciatively.

''It's true. I'm a pig. I stuff my face every chance I get. Of course, going to bed hungry for so many years—'' she paused, as if realizing what she'd said ''—makes one appreciate food.'' The kettle whistled and she went to check on it. As she poured the water she heard Crackers squawking up a storm in the back room. ''Your bird misses you.'' She handed him his mug.

''Do you mind?'' he asked, setting it aside and heading that way.

''Not at all. You should visit. Parrots develop close bonds with their humans, substituting them for mates. And they get rather destructive when denied contact.''

He removed Crackers from the cage and set the bird on his shoulder. The bird immediately calmed down.

''Parrots mate for life,'' she continued. ''Unfortunately, the average parrot has seven owners in its lifetime. Quite an adjustment for the bird. And of course she'll probably outlive you.''

''She?''

''Yes, your he is a she. The Thai government must

really like you. This bird is worth about ten thousand dollars on the open market.''

He fed Crackers some crackers.

''How come you know so much about birds?''

''You mean other than it being my job? I find them fascinating. Many species mate for life. And they work in partnership with each other. I think people could learn a lot from birds.'' She stroked the parrot's feathers. ''I do think it's a shame, however, that people feel the need to own something that was meant to fly free. Her wings have been clipped.''

''Now you're making me feel bad.''

''Just be a committed pet owner. I have my own reasons for making myself feel bad when it comes to parrots.''

''What? As a kid you went around shooting birds with a slingshot?''

''Something like that,'' she admitted, sipping from her mug. He looked as if he didn't believe her. And she wished it weren't true. She wanted very much to unburden herself. But not to just anyone. She wanted to tell those deep dark secrets to him.

''In Vietnam there were children who grew up on the streets, orphaned, abandoned. They were called *bui doi,* dust of life, because of their round eyes. Women were often pressured by families or future husbands to give up children fathered by American GIs, or go through life alone.

''These children survived, just barely. And one of the ways they did was to catch parrots and monkeys, even stray dogs, for the street vendors who would pay them what amounted to pennies. Vendors made a modest amount. But importers and exporters got rich. When I see a bird in captivity, it makes me think of those kids."

"If that was the only way to survive…"

"No one should profit at the expense of another. I caught a parrot once, sold it to a vendor. For a few minutes I felt rich. But I stayed around too long and saw it locked up in a cage. I felt sorry for it. Sorry that I'd done such a terrible thing when I wanted nothing more than to be like that bird and be free. Because it really depends on what you're selling."

"Tam?" he questioned softly. "Did you grow up on the street? Tell me more about your life. Tell me about your mother."

"I was lucky. I had a mother who loved me more than life itself. She made sure I had a roof over my head. And saw to it that I was fed, even if it meant skipping a meal herself. But if you're asking if I resent the fact that my American father abandoned my mother, the answer is yes."

"Is it possible your parents were married? Separated by some outside force?"

"It's possible *he* was married." She hung her head. "I feel so disloyal when I talk like that. She loved him so. She claims they were married. Along with the picture, he'd given her money and a piece of paper, making her his wife. It also had on it his name, rank and serial number. She couldn't read English, but I guess it's possible he assumed she'd recognize his name, at least. I don't know." Tam shook her head. "Anything's possible, right?" She searched his eyes for the answers. His eyes never lied.

"He probably swore out an affidavit, stating that they were married or that he intended to marry her."

"Are you sure?"

"It's likely. You know, you've never told me your mother's name."

"Lan. It means *flower*."

0930 Sunday—Mother's Day
TAM'S NEW HOUSE; NAVAL AIR FACILITY
Sand Island, Midway Islands

"THE SIX-BY IS FULL," McCain said, putting down his end of the faux-leather couch with faux-bamboo frame.

Bowie set down his end as well. A six-by was a canvas-covered truck with two bench seats that ran lengthwise and could carry six troops on either side. They used the truck to haul themselves to job sites. But it wasn't nearly big enough for this job.

"Come in, Master Chief. Over." Bowie spoke into a two-way radio. "Better send me a deuce 'n' a half."

"Copy," Rusty said. "One two-and-a-half ton ready to roll."

"Think that's going to do it?" McCain joked.

"I don't know, she's got a lot of junk." Just about everything he owned could be packed on his back. Except for the Harley he had to keep in storage six months out of every year. This time it would be a year before he got to ride it again. "Ever think you'll find that one place where you want to settle down?" Bowie asked McCain the question that had been burning in his own mind.

"Well, it sure as hell isn't here. Morale's already low. The men don't want to be here as it is. And once they realize the captain's abandoned ship again, we're going to have some real attitude on our hands."

"I've been thinking the same thing. We could rotate the squads into Hawaii for a little R and R. Each squad once a month. Out on a Thursday flight. In on a Tuesday flight."

"Maybe I'll get a chance to use those condoms, after all."

"Why don't you take care of the scheduling."

"That's one detail I don't mind your dumping on me."

"And we can take care of things on this end. We're here to restore the island, make it a habitat for birds and humans. Human habitats include golf courses, baseball diamonds—"

"Clubs," McCain said.

"Marinas, theaters…"

"I like the way you think." They bumped fists just as the deuce 'n' a half rolled to a stop on the potholed blacktop. At some point they'd have ten miles of road to pave.

They'd just finished loading the couch when Tam pedaled up on a bicycle. "What's going on?"

"It's moving day," Bowie said. "We're taking your things to their new home."

"Did you ever stop to think that maybe I don't want you going through my things?"

"We didn't open any drawers," he said, once again playing defense. "We just loaded dressers and desks as is."

"Trust me on this," McCain added, pressing a hand to his lower back for effect. "There were a few pots and pans in the kitchen cupboards we boxed. And a few items in the bathroom."

"I'm still going to need time to clean the new place—"

"Don't worry about," Bowie said, heading toward the golf cart parked along the residential road. "We got it covered. Come see for yourself."

She followed them over on her bike. They pulled up at her new house. The outside looked pretty much the same, except he'd removed the screens from the porch first thing, and there were a few men stripping the deck.

Was it too much to hope that she'd actually be pleased by something he did?

He watched for her reaction, which was still wary.

"Hope you like sea-foam green," he said, going inside. "We didn't have much to choose from. It will probably clash with your couch, but—"

She stood in the doorway in stunned surprise.

"You hate it."

"No, you're amazing…I mean, it's amazing. How did you—"

"We're Seabees, ma'am. Roos *Kan Do*." McCain tipped his boonie cap as he strode past.

"Of course, we're not finished yet," Bowie apologized. "And you'll want to keep all the windows open tonight, maybe even sleep somewhere else. But we'll be finished before then."

He showed her around the house. The painters were still in the second bedroom, one on each wall applying sea foam and just as many working on the white trim. Missing tiles in the bathroom and kitchen had been replaced and the floors were in the process of being stripped and buffed to a high gloss.

"My floors have never been so clean," she commented.

"I'm afraid we had to do the kitchen cabinets in haze gray," he told her. The floor tile was industrial, gray flecked, and it made a nice contrast to the sea foam and white. That's what the guys had told him, anyway. And they were all being good sports about the house.

The men started moving in furniture, and the small house got a little crowded, so Bowie and Tam stepped into the backyard, where he had another Seabee mowing the lawn.

"What can I say, except, thank you."

"Are you starting to think I'm not such a bad guy after all?"

"No, I'm starting to think you're a kiss-up," she teased.

All he could do was laugh. She had him pegged. But there was only one set of lips he wanted to kiss.

"Has this kiss-up earned himself a date for movie night?"

"Are you asking?"

"I'm asking."

"What's playing?"

"Ever hear of *The Fighting Seabees?*"

"No, I can't say that I have."

"Then you're in for a real treat. It's got John Wayne in it."

"I thought he played cowboys."

"Honey, Seabees *are* cowboys. I'll pick you up at seven."

2100 Sunday
THE THEATER; NAVAL AIR FACILITY
Sand Island, Midway Islands

"So WHAT'D YOU THINK?" Bowie asked as they exited the base theater.

Tam removed her glasses and tucked them away. "I think I just sat through the longest recruiting film in history, next to *Top Gun*, of course."

"Oh, come on, it wasn't that bad."

"I didn't say it was bad." She'd spent most of the movie watching Bowie watch the movie, but she did get the gist of the picture. It'd been a private screening. He'd opened the theater and run the projection booth—which is where they'd sat—just to show her the movie. "I just don't understand why he drove the whatchamajigger—"

"Bulldozer," he supplied for her.

"Yeah, that, into the fuel dump and killed himself."

"He didn't kill himself, he sacrificed himself and the fuel reserve so that the Japanese taking over the island wouldn't be able to use it."

"I understand that. But I wanted him to jump off at the last minute. He had every reason to live. That journalist was in love with him."

"She was engaged to another officer. He did the honorable thing."

"You're such a guy." Maybe she hadn't meant it as a compliment. But in his case it was.

"So what else is there to do on this island at twenty-one hundred hours?" he asked.

Tam suppressed a yawn. "Bed," she said. "And that wasn't an invitation," she added before he could utter a quick comeback.

"I get the hint," he said.

They were moving in the direction of her new house, but taking their time. He carried a flashlight but hadn't turned it on. Instead they walked in the moonlight. Clapping gooney beaks and crashing surf was their music.

They'd reached the front door of her new house. She'd had very little to do to settle in. "Did you want to come in?"

He arched a brow, clearly unsure of what her invitation involved. Well, she didn't know, either.

Bowie let the screen close behind him, but stood near the door as if gauging his welcome.

She felt rather awkward herself. "There's beer in the fridge. Make yourself at home. After all, you did make this a home." Lame, really lame. She had a master's for heaven's sake. Couldn't she come up with something better than that? Time to regroup. "I'll just be a minute," she said, walking into her bedroom.

The new-paint smell had all but disappeared, though she might pull her mattress onto the porch for the night. Maybe she could ask him to help. No, not a good idea getting him anywhere near the bed.

But before she went to bed, she had to make a phone call. Here it was Mother's Day and she had yet to speak to her mother. First she'd been busy. Then the phone lines had been busy.

She picked up the desk phone. Not even a dial tone, just a busy signal. The phone system on the island was basically one big party line. Not in the conventional sense, but outgoing lines could get tied up rather easily. And with all the Seabees and their support personnel, she imagined there were a lot of mothers on the receiving end of phone calls tonight. And a lot yet to be made.

Of course she hadn't recharged her cell phone. "Damn!"

"Something the matter?" He stood in the doorway and offered her a beer.

She took it. Twisting the top, she couldn't help but whine, "You don't happen to have your cell phone on you, do you?"

"Afraid not, I loaned it out. The guys all want to call home for Mother's Day. But they're having trouble getting out on these old phone lines."

"It's too late, anyway. It's after midnight in San Francisco. I'm a terrible daughter."

"It's never too late. And you just happen to be looking at a ham radio operator. There's a ham radio shack down by the watchtower, isn't there? What do you say we go check it out?"

"You're a lifesaver," she said. Like everything on the island, the ham radio shack was just a brisk walk away.

"It's locked," she said, noting the padlock in dismay once they got there.

He tried the door and it opened a crack; only the

padlock held it in place. "This is nothing," he said, shining the flashlight on the lock. "The door's rotten. The lock won't give, but I bet the door will." He put his shoulder into it and rammed the door.

It flew open. And he gave her the most adorable I-told-you-so look.

The unused shack was dusty, but the equipment worked. They brushed off a couple of chairs and sat down. He had them connected to another ham operator in no time, and eventually through the network they reached one in California not too far from home.

The lieutenant gave his operator number and introduced himself. "This is Lieutenant Bowie Prince calling from Midway Islands. Can you patch me through to a number in San Fran? We'll cover any long-distance charges. It's for a Mother's Day phone call home. Over."

"Be happy to, sailor. Was in the Navy myself, so this call's on me. Over."

"Thank you." He relayed the number Tam gave him, then advised her on ham protocol while the phone rang. "Sorry, it's not exactly private. You've got two operators, me and the other guy listening in. Keep it short. *Over,* is the signal for me to switch from *talk* to *listen,* so remember to say it. Ready?"

She nodded.

They heard her mother pick up. "Hello?"

The other operator explained what was going on.

"Hello, Tam?" her mother said. "Over."

"Mom, it's so good to hear your voice. I hope I didn't wake you. I just wanted to say happy Mother's Day. Over."

"You didn't wake me. It's good to hear your voice, too. Over."

They talked for a few more minutes before saying goodbye. Not really a conversation, but a connection.

After Lan hung up, Bowie thanked the stranger on the other end, exchanged a bit of information, then signed off.

Tam was so content she didn't even feel like moving. "Again, thank you."

"Here's the guy's address." He handed her a piece of scrap paper. "You may want to thank him, too."

"I think that deserves a kiss." She brushed her lips, soft like butterfly wings, across his. When she pulled back to look into his eyes, she could almost feel her heart taking flight. But what surprised her most was that he didn't swoop down on her. He gave her room to fly.

0100 Monday
LAN NGUYEN'S HOME
San Francisco, California

"YOUR DAUGHTER?" SHANE asked, hitting the eject button on the VCR.

"Calling to wish me a happy Mother's Day," Lan answered, hanging up the phone in the kitchen. She came into the living room just as the movie popped out. "I'm so sorry, I completely ignored you. And I missed the end of the movie."

"There'll be other movies. You only have one daughter." Shane boxed the two videos he'd brought over for the evening and pushed to his feet. "It's late, I should get going."

What she should do was beg him to stay the night, what was left of it, anyway. He treated her with such kindness and expected nothing in return. Maybe he hoped she'd return his affection, though he knew she wouldn't.

"Thank you for keeping me company."

"Not at all," he said, putting his arm through the sleeve of his leather jacket. She stepped behind him to help with the other sleeve as he switched the videos from one hand to the other.

"I almost forgot I have a check for you."

"How many times have I told you I don't want your money, Lan?"

"But you need it to keep your business going. If you won't take it for helping me, take it so that you can continue to help others," she insisted, retrieving the check from the breakfast counter.

She handed it to him. He glanced at the generous amount and furrowed his brows. A handsome man of forty-seven with only a bit of gray in his brown hair, he could look awfully stern at times. Hard living, she supposed.

He'd fought in Vietnam at seventeen. And at forty-seven he fought to reunite veterans and their families, his way of making peace with his past. Or so he'd told her.

"I'm going to find your husband, Lan."

"I know you will." He didn't have to add *dead or alive*. They'd already discussed it. She just wanted to find *her* peace with the past. And then maybe she could move on.

But what about Tam, would *she* ever find peace?

After Shane left, Lan wandered the rooms of her empty town house, turning out the lights. She'd chosen this city, Skully's city, thinking fate would bring them back together. But she'd never bumped into him on the street the way she did in her dreams.

In her bedroom, she changed into silky pajamas of her own design and picked up her sketch pad from the nightstand, but then couldn't settle into work.

The hours just before dawn were the hardest. She picked up an enlarged reproduction of Skully's photograph. From the picture, Shane had said Skully was probably Special Operations and would be difficult but not impossible to find. He said they were called "men with green faces."

She could hardly remember what that face looked like under all that paint. No doubt the lines had become a little more pronounced, a little harder. Or softer, maybe. His hair would be threaded with silver. Or even missing.

But his eyes would still be as blue as the China Sea.

She set his picture back on the nightstand, next to Tam's, and crawled under the covers. She was so happy her daughter had called, but Mother's Day shouldn't feel this lonely.

Fall 1972
Hanoi, Vietnam

BIAN XANG HAD TAKEN LAN to his home in Hanoi, where he was warden of the prisoner-of-war camp.

By the time they reached his residence, she was in full labor from the trauma and travel. Her feet were still swollen from the ant bites and all over her body she had little red marks.

Still, she fought the labor. "Please, Bian-san, swear you will not hurt my child."

He remained stern-faced as his mother and the other women of his household led her to a small bedroom. They were fussing over her, but not out of kindness.

"You were mine, betrothed to me. You betrayed me!" He pounded his chest and roared like a wounded cat. She knew he loved her and she would use that against him if she had to.

"Please, Bian-san. Please." She broke away from the women and fell to his feet. "I beg your forgiveness. Do anything you want with me. But please do not hurt my child. The child is innocent. It is the mother who is guilty."

She looked up and searched his face for any sign of forgiveness. A handsome man, he stood proud.

There were tears in his eyes, but he remained firm. "Fate will decide. I will not allow *his* bastard to live. But a daughter belongs to her mother."

"No, no!" she screamed, clutching her belly as the women once again hauled her to her feet.

The pains grew worse and she labored for many more hours, thinking Xang might kill her baby. Finally they took the child from her and wrapped it without letting her see if she'd borne a son or a daughter.

Then exhaustion claimed her and she slept. When she awoke Xang stood at the foot of the bed with the swaddled infant. "You have a daughter," he announced.

She wept for sheer joy, but when she held out her arms he didn't move.

"Bian-san, your promise," she reminded him, sitting up in the bed, preparing for the worst.

CHAPTER NINE

0600 Monday
TAM'S HOUSE; NAVAL AIR FACILITY
Sand Island, Midway Islands

TAM AWOKE TO THE SMELL of bacon and eggs and coffee. She crawled up onto her knees and peeked out her open bedroom door.

"Morning." Bowie stood in her kitchen in his utility uniform, moving with surprising efficiency between the stove and a tray sitting on her small kitchen table. "If you stay there, I'll bring this to you."

But she got up and went to him. The tray was laden with juice, coffee, tea. She picked up the juice and took a sip. "If you tell me you hand-squeezed this I may have to kill you."

"Crabby again, are we? I thought that was only when you were kept up all night." He added a plate with what appeared to be his famous western omelet and two crisp bacon strips laid out on each side of the eggs.

"So this is what a real breakfast looks like."

"Now, where are we going to eat it?" he asked as he buttered toast. "You ruined my surprise."

"You ruined your surprise when the smell of food

started coming from my kitchen. The deck?'' she suggested, picking up the tray.

He plucked the hibiscus flower from the tray and tucked it behind her ear. Her breath caught and she didn't exhale until they were outside in the open air.

She set the tray down on the patio table. He followed her to the door with a cup of coffee in his hand, then leaned against the frame. He seemed content to stand there and look out over the ocean.

''You are going to join me, aren't you?'' she asked, unloading the tray. Even though there was only one plate there was enough food to feed two. Or at least, feed her and whet his appetite.

''I have to be at the job site in an hour,'' he said, checking his watch. ''But breakfast with you was the plan.''

She sat first, then he sat across from her. When he didn't take the chair right next to hers she propped up her feet and prepared to enjoy her breakfast thoroughly.

She took a bite of the omelet, then offered one to him since they only had one fork between them. While they ate, she realized that, out of habit, she'd left her door unlocked, which explained his presence but not the food.

''You didn't find bacon in my fridge.''

''I stocked up for you. If you need anything, all you have to do is ask. We came with plenty of stores, but we also have the twice-a-week supply runs.''

''Thank you.''

''Support personnel should be arriving any day to open up the chow hall and Navy Exchange. In fact, we'll have chaplains, dentists, doctors and lawyers in and out periodically.''

He told her about his plans for the day. And did delicious things to her feet, which had somehow wound up in his lap. She reached over with a bite of egg, then a strip of bacon, anything to ensure he kept massaging.

But as much as she enjoyed it, in the back of her mind there was a little voice chanting, *hooch girl, hooch girl.*

0700 Sunday
TAM'S HOUSE; NAVAL AIR FACILITY
Sand Island, Midway Islands

BOWIE HAD SHOWED UP every day for a week to cook and eat breakfast with Tam, followed by a visit to his parrot before heading to the job site. On Tuesday she'd given him the guided tour of the island, and by Sunday he was feeling like one half of a married couple.

The thought scared him to death. Yet he couldn't bring himself to stop their morning ritual.

He'd arrived an hour later than usual, thinking she'd sleep in on Sunday.

"Tam," he called as he entered her house. He made a point of never crossing that line into her bedroom. Not that he didn't want to. Just that he could tell she wasn't ready.

Maybe Tam would want to go with him to the nondenominational services he'd arranged for that morning. They pretty much shared their plans every day, even made a point of bumping into each other or keeping in touch by two-way radio.

She didn't answer, and he walked right up to her bedroom door, expecting to find her snuggled under the covers. Empty. Her bed was made, her house neat. Where was she?

It took him more than an hour to find her, and by that time he'd started to worry. She still wore her pajamas and was stretched into some kind of tai chi pose.

She didn't look up when he stopped and stood beside her, but he could tell she knew he was there.

"Am I your hooch girl?" she asked.

"My what?" He'd never even heard of the term.

"Some guys call them their laundress, their house-keeper...temporary wife. Someone to play house with." She dropped her arms and looked right at him. "Are you thinking of moving in?"

He removed his hat, so she could really see his eyes. "The thought had crossed my mind, I mean there's nothing to stop us, but we're not there yet."

"But that's where all this is leading, right? You're making yourself comfortable while you're here. But you're not going to be here that long."

"Tam, I've treated you with nothing but respect."

"Of course you have. You're courting me. But for what purpose? To get me in the sack, or are we building a nest like those gooneys over there."

He spared a glance at the male and female albatrosses preening their downy baby. "That's a hell of a way to pressure a guy."

"Pressure? We can only go one of two ways, forward or nowhere. And I don't think you're ready to go anywhere. It's not fair for you to come around every morning and make me breakfast, promises—''

''What kind of promises?''

''Exactly!''

''Is this some female thing that will blow over in a week?''

''That's a man's answer to everything.'' She took a deep breath. ''I like what we have, but I don't want zero return on my investment when you ship out in a few months. Before we take this any further I need to know, would you give up the uniform for me?''

He shifted and looked down at his feet. ''Now, *that's* unfair. I'd never ask you to give up something to be with me.''

''I know. I shouldn't even ask. I'm just warning you now, that might be what it takes to hold me. And for me to hold you, I might have to give up some of my beliefs and ideals. We're opposites, and even though opposites attract, they aren't always right for each other.'' She crossed her arms. ''I don't want you to come around and make me breakfast anymore.''

He chose his next words very carefully as he put his cap back on. ''You're right, I don't see us going forward from here when you're unwilling to take one step in my direction. You won't have to worry about me coming around anymore.''

1900 Monday
Eastern Island, Midway Islands

A WEEK AND A DAY LATER, Tam had asked Bowie to meet her on Eastern Island. She'd been miserable every minute without him. As promised, he was there waiting for her. "Thank you for meeting me."

"I told you I would." He put aside the book he'd been reading and jumped to his feet, brushing the sand off his shorts. "Did you lug all that from the boat?" he asked, gesturing to the picnic basket, blanket and gunny sack she held.

"They're supplies. It's going to be a long night." In truth, they could have started out later in the evening, but sunset had seemed more romantic.

"Why are you wearing your sunglasses this time of evening?"

"Just sitting here watching the sunset and reading Tennyson, guess I forgot about them." He took them off.

"It's a beautiful sunset, isn't it?"

"So I've been told," he said, staring at her as if she had all the answers.

She busied herself unloading the picnic basket. "You can't see the colors, can you."

"Not without these," he said, holding up his sunglasses. "When I was a kid with a whole world of possibilities, a teacher broke the news I'd never be an astronaut, a pilot, a fireman, a policeman—none of the really cool jobs that a boy grows up dreaming about."

She sat on the blanket beside him. "So you picked from the very top of that list and chose demolition?"

"Something like that. I always want what I can't have."

"We have a lot in common because I always gravitate toward what's bad for me." Which is why she'd kept herself locked away from the rest of the world for so long. "Is this a step in the right direction?" she asked.

"Honey, this is two miles in the right direction," he said, acknowledging the actual distance between Sand and Eastern with a smile. "I want to kiss you, Tam."

"I know."

He brushed a strand of hair away from her forehead and followed the length to the end. It was as if he'd awakened every nerve ending in her body and they were all begging for his touch. "You're very beautiful. I'm not going to—"

She pressed her fingertips to his lips. "Don't swear you're not going to hurt me. Because you are."

Her fingers moved to his hair. She pressed her mouth to his. He stole her breath and replaced it with his. Over and over again.

Eventually she must have made a sound because he raised his head to look into her eyes.

She wanted him to say something. Anything.

"Now, that didn't hurt, did it?" he asked, stroking her face.

She reached up and touched his smiling lips. She couldn't help but smile back. "No, that didn't hurt."

She ran her hand across one broad shoulder and trapped him closer. Just as he opened his mouth to kiss her, he pulled back. "What the hell?"

Tam twisted for a better angle. A turtle hatchling dropped to the sand above the blanket and crawled away. "Don't move," she said when he would have rolled off her. "You might roll onto one."

There were hatchlings all around them, breaking through their sandy nests and heading toward the water by the hundreds.

Once she determined none of the little creatures would be crushed, they were able to sit up. "Grab the camera," she said, pushing to her feet and following the turtles to the water.

"How do you turn it on?" he called to her.

"It's already on!"

"Why, you little devil," he teased. He trode carefully, and starting at the nest he captured the progress of hundreds of tiny sea turtles on their way toward the ocean.

Tam stood ankle-deep in the surf, and he directed the camera on her.

"Not me, silly. The turtles," she said.

"I kind of like what's in my sights right now."

A wave crashed in to her and she fell to her knees, laughing as she tried to regain her feet. He rushed her then and she splashed him, mindless of the camera. He picked her up and spun her around, kissing her hard on the mouth until she was dizzy and breathless.

"You know," he said, "they filmed the love scene in *From Here to Eternity* on Midway because at the time it was too shocking to be filmed in Hawaii."

"You do love your movie trivia."

"I do," he agreed.

"Well, it *was* shocking when Burt Lancaster slapped Deborah Kerr."

"I'm actually more interested in acting out the rolling around in the sand bit."

Her breath caught. "Look, I'm sure, no, I *know* that you're a nice guy and all—"

"But you're used to my kind just passing through. What does that mean exactly, Tam? We've all been hurt before. What's life about except taking chances? I'm here *now,* I'm not hurting you *now.* So I'm here for six months and we don't know beyond that. You've been here what?—three years? And you have a contract for the next three, but do you know where you'll be sent next? The truth is, none of us knows what tomorrow will bring. We only have tonight."

"Pretty words, Lieutenant. But I can't be with a guy who only thinks about tonight."

"Okay," he said, pulling back slightly, shoving the video camera into her hands. "And I can't be with a woman who doesn't trust me. But we would have made a hell of a movie."

No doubt they would have.

He dunked himself completely and emerged soaked to the skin, his mismatched clothes clinging to his every muscle and sinew. Oh, the hell with it. Who knew better than she that there was no tomorrow?

She tossed the camera to the sand and rushed him. Despite the cooling off period, their kisses were heated, demanding, invasive. She started to unbuckle his belt.

He stilled her shaking hands. "You're not ready for this." He kissed her fingertips. "But I appreciate the effort."

What did he mean? Her body was beyond ready.

And his was once again hard with need. Was he rejecting her?

"What's the matter?" she asked, sensing she no longer had his complete attention.

"Nothing," he said. But he stared off into the distance, listening to something. "It's late. We need to head back."

He helped her pack, then hurried her to the boat.

"Don't tell me nothing if it's something. I have a rifle in the footlocker on board."

"No offense, but I'd rather have McCain as backup. And you safe on Sand Island."

0500 Tuesday
Eastern Island, Midway Islands

"WHAT ARE WE LOOKING FOR again?" McCain asked, shouldering his weapon.

"I don't know," Bowie answered, equally equipped for trouble. "But I heard an engine of some kind." He thought it might have been a boat, but he wasn't sure of the size or how far away it was.

They were standing in the middle of the fuel depot dwarfed by two million-gallon tanks. "We've combed every inch of this island." McCain bent to pick up something in the sand. "Are you sure it wasn't the blood rushing from your brain to other parts of your body?" He held out a wrapped condom.

Bowie grabbed it and put it back in his pocket. "Let's cut back across the airstrip, it was still dark when we checked it out before."

McCain heaved a sigh but followed Bowie.

Inland, there was a large sandy cove that harbored Hawaiian monk seals. They heard the barking even before they spied the basking seals.

"What is that?" McCain asked as they stood on the lava rock above the sand. Among the seals there was a large mass, a bloody mass. "Is it human?"

"I don't think so," Bowie called back, already scrambling down the rock.

McCain slid down right behind him and they ran headlong through the seals, only to be charged by a bull who sent them climbing back up the rock.

"Now what? He's not going to let us near it."

"We call for backup," Bowie said, unhooking his two-way radio from his belt and preparing to eat crow. "Warden, come in, over."

He explained the situation to Tam. He'd wanted her to tell him what to do over the radio, but she insisted she'd be right over. In a matter of minutes she was there, taking control of the situation.

"Keep downwind of the bull. And try not to make any sudden moves."

They reached the corpse of the dead seal, and she stooped beside it. Flies buzzed around the open wound.

"This seal wasn't killed for her pelt. A poacher doesn't come for just one. And this one hasn't even been skinned."

"Maybe we scared him off last night before he could do any more damage."

"Yeah, we were real scary," she muttered as she snapped some Polaroids. "No, this killing was more ritualistic. The seals are birthing, this one was pregnant. It looks like she delivered under stress. If there's a pup, it won't be far.''

She had them wrap the seal corpse in a sheet she'd brought with her and started looking around. The pup had died nearby. Covered in afterbirth and a layer of sand, it had already been attacked by scavengers.

''Poor little thing didn't stand a chance.''

Fall 1972
Hanoi, Vietnam

SKULLY HEADED NORTH with one purpose and one purpose only—to reach Lan. His seventy-two hours had come and gone. Only a fool would travel up country now. But he did what he was trained to do and moved among the shadows.

Just before he reached Hanoi his luck ran out. He was captured by a squad of NVA regulars who wanted to shoot him on the spot before realizing just who he was.

''*Mau len,* faster!'' The NVA urged Skully forward with a bayonet to his back.

His mind calculated his escape options. He had a chance against the five NVA. But if he went along with them, he'd make it to Hanoi alive. Even better, they would march him straight up to the gates of hell, the Hanoi Hilton.

Exactly where he wanted to be.

Xang would be there, maybe he was holding Lan captive. Skully didn't know for sure. And the only person who could tell him where she was, happened to be the devil himself. Lieutenant Bian Xang, warden of the Hanoi Hilton.

There was only one flaw.

He'd survived the war by following one rule: never walk into a situation without backup and an escape route. He didn't have either.

Upon reaching the prisoner-of-war camp they brought him straight to an interrogation room. The NVA had roughed him up pretty good by the time Xang entered the room. Beads of sweat ran down his forehead and stung the cuts on his face and chest.

"So we meet again," the general said. "However, I believe the advantage is mine this time." Xang fancied himself a MacArthur, carrying a riding crop that he beat rhythmically against his palm.

Skully sat like a stone and said nothing, biding his time.

"Look where they sent me after Parrot's Beak? Because of you some other general will lead the way to Saigon. I'm going to enjoy this."

It took four men to hold him down while another whipped the soles of his feet. Skully cursed and spit and taunted Xang, but he would not cry out.

"Dung lai!" Xang grew impatient and called a halt to the beating.

The regulars sat him upright in a chair facing the general.

"I almost forgot to tell you I have something of yours. Or should I say I've taken back what is mine."

"Where is she?" Skully spat out blood.

"Perhaps I should have framed that in the past tense. Forgive my imperfect English." A table stood between them, and Xang rested his palms against the flat surface. "Are you aware Lan gave birth to your bastard?"

"You're lying."

"You're doing the math in your head, yes? You've known her for what, nine months? Yes, I believe that is what she said. But this child was born at seven months. So maybe, maybe not yours. I couldn't take the chance."

Skully pulled his battered body up straighter.

His child.

"What have you done with them?"

"You don't really want to know. But I will keep you alive until you are begging for a merciful death. The way that Lan begged—"

Skully rushed Xang, knocking back his chair and turning over the table to reach the bastard. But the guards caught Skully first, and he remembered little after that.

The next thing Skully knew, his squad was picking him up off the floor and he was begging Tad Prince to kill him.

He'd lost the woman he loved and their baby.

There was no reason to live.

CHAPTER TEN

SHE'D BEEN RIGHT ABOUT Bowie not being the kind of guy who looked beyond the present. But Tam had other problems on her hands. Gooney birds were dying. She hadn't gotten the toxicology reports back yet to know if this was an epidemic of some sort, but she suspected an outbreak of parrot fever.

Because of that she'd kept her distance from Crackers. And the bird was squawking up a storm.

"What's with the bird?" Bowie asked from the other side of the screen door, where he stood holding a branch.

"She's lonely," Tam said as he stepped into her office.

"I need to build her an aviary outdoors. Cracker's chew toy arrived," he said.

"I can see that."

"This came for you. It's a controlled substance. I had to sign for it."

''Just an antibiotic. I wanted your medic to have it on hand in case we have an outbreak of psittacosis, parrot fever. In humans, it causes an acute intestinal infection.''

She kept herself busy so he'd get the hint and go. Several minutes passed and she heard a squawk, then a curse.

''What's going on in there?'' she asked.

''Crackers bit me.''

''Let me look at your hand.''

''Just a scratch,'' he said.

''It's not just a scratch.'' She opened the package he'd brought with him. Moving to a locked cabinet, she took out a hypodermic needle and began filling it.

''What are you doing?''

''Your medic can give you the shot or you can drop your pants for me.''

''You don't have to ask twice. Will one cheek do?'' He revealed a modest expanse of well-muscled glute.

''A cheek will do,'' she said, swabbing the spot with alcohol, then jabbing him with the needle.

''Professor,'' he said in a tight voice. ''You have the bedside manner of a Navy nurse.''

''Know a lot of Navy nurses, do you?'' she asked while disposing of the syringe in a nearby hazardous waste container.

''What's eating you?'' He rubbed the injection site.

She ignored him and changed the subject. ''It's not even bleeding.''

"Could have fooled me." He looked over his shoulder at her.

And she peeked at his ass. A tattoo was just visible above the edge of the lowered waistband of his briefs. "You have a tattooed butt?"

"It's nothing." He tried to turn away from her.

She held his gaze but snagged his waistband with her index finger. Demon-red eyes glared at her from a black skull and crossbones. She felt herself slip into unconsciousness.

Bowie caught her before she hit the floor.

"Tam!" he called, manipulating her into a sitting position. "Tam."

"I'm not even going to ask," McCain said, entering the office with the screen door slamming behind him.

"It's not what it looks like. She took one look at my tattoo and fainted."

"But how did your pants get down around your ankles in the first place?"

"She was giving me a shot."

"If you two want to play doctor, who am I to judge?" McCain teased, as Tam's eyelashes fluttered.

"Help me get her up," Bowie said, letting McCain help Tam to her feet while he readjusted his pants.

"I'm okay, I'm okay," Tam insisted. "I just felt a little light-headed."

"I wish my ass had that effect on women," McCain said. "I have the same tattoo. Wanna see?"

2000 Tuesday
BACHELOR OFFICERS' QUARTERS;
NAVAL AIR FACILITY
Sand Island, Midway Islands

"PSST!" KATIE WHISPERED from the bushes.

"What are you doing here?" Tam whispered.

"I'm trying to get a peek at that tattoo you told me about. They shower around this time every night. Right after they get off work."

"Katie!"

"It's not my fault they never pull the shades." She offered Tam the binoculars. "His room's on the top floor, corner. Two windows on each side."

"I'm not looking," Tam said in a harsh whisper.

"Don't say I didn't offer." Katie raised the binoculars. "Oh, yeah, that's a real nice tattoo."

"Give me those." Tam practically ripped them off the girl's neck.

"You can't go around spying on them while they get dressed," she lectured, glancing toward the window. The lieutenant appeared, a softly muted blur behind the sheers.

"Better make up your mind to do it before he puts his pants on," Katie said.

"All right, all right," Tam caved. He'd turned his back to her and bent to step into his underwear. Boxers, she noted. There. The tattoo, just as she remembered. Then gone.

"What are you two doing?" Will asked. "You know peeping is a crime."

"We weren't peeping!" Tam's voice rose to a squeak.

"We were just checking out his tattoo," Katie said.

"Can I see?" he asked, reaching for the binoculars.

"No!" Tam slapped his hand away. "He would not want you spying on him like that."

"But it's all right for you two?" Will was having a good time teasing them.

"Go away, both of you. The show's over."

She glared at them until they turned to leave, then she glared at their backs until they were out of sight. She was going to do what she came here to do. And that was ask the lieutenant about his tattoo. She took a deep breath, turned around, and walked smack-dab into his chest.

"Nice night," he said, hands behind his back, looking up at the stars.

She felt her cheeks heat. Good thing it was dark. "Yes, it is," she agreed.

"Binoculars? You out here bird watching?" He said it a bit too casually.

She sensed a trap, but plunged full steam ahead, anyway. "Yes, yes, I am…out here bird watching."

"What can you see with those things after dark? I've always found these more appropriate," he said, bringing a pair up to his face.

She stifled a scream. Two piercing red eyes stared back at her.

"Infrared," he said, lowering them. "With night vision you can see anything. Even a woman checking you out from behind the bushes. Especially when she's not very quiet about it."

"It just so happens—" she raised her voice "—I

was bird watching whether you want to believe it or not.''

"So show me the birds." She didn't need night vision to see that sexy smile of his.

"Follow me." She took off with her head held high. She couldn't believe he'd caught her peeping. She'd be mocked for the rest of her life.

She took him across the island where there wasn't much of anything except gooney birds.

"Mating season is in the fall. Every spring night, the proud parents preen their babies and tuck them in," she explained. "But young males try all season long to engage a partner by dancing around the single females. There are certain movements the young couple has to follow in order to complete the mating dance."

"And what happens if they miss a beat?"

"They move on to someone else. But the first time they get it right, they mate for life."

"What's happening over here?" he asked.

Tam moved to stand beside him. "She's a hybrid between a black-footed albatross and a Laysan albatross. The males aren't interested in her. She looks like a Laysan, but bigger, so she scares off the Laysan male. And if the bigger black-footed male tries to approach her, he doesn't have a chance. The Laysan and black-footed albatross have different dance steps. She's imprinted with the Laysan dance. It's likely the bigger black-footed male mounted a smaller Laysan female."

"So where are her parents?"

"They don't stay together. She's an accident caused by an overeager male and nature. Young males try to mount females, with or without the dance.''

And she had brought the lieutenant to this world where everything was about the propagation of the species. What was she thinking? Nature had never embarrassed or aroused her before. But here she was standing in the middle of fornicating birds and all she could think about was *the act*.

Bowie approached a lone male black-footed albatross and sprinkled on the ground some crumbs he took from his pocket. Soon he'd coaxed the male to follow the trail to the hybrid female.

''What are you doing?''

''Giving them a chance. I had crackers in my pocket for Crackers.''

''You can't feed the birds. I'm ordering you to stop this instant!''

''They steal the crumbs from our lunches all the time.''

The couple had started to dance. And he kept rewarding them with crumbs. If either turned to leave he'd stop feeding them.

''He's not going to get the moves right just because you're feeding him.''

''Maybe it won't matter to her if he misses a few beats.''

He'd run out of crumbs, and she had the satisfaction of seeing the male turn away. But a few minutes later he came back on his own and started his mating dance. Apparently the way to that gooney's heart was through his stomach.

''What did I tell you,'' Bowie boasted.

"The young gooney couple has to get the dance down before they can pair off," she explained, faltering, suddenly unable to act like the prim and proper professor. "When they do, they'll set up practice housekeeping. Next year they'll come back to that same spot to mate. That's just not likely to happen."

"But it could. She happened, and that wasn't likely."

She supposed it was possible. Anything seemed possible with Bowie.

"As you see, I was bird watching. They're only this active at night."

"Interesting hobby you have, Professor. So how come *watching* makes you so uptight?"

"I'm not uptight." She rubbed a hand across the back of her neck.

"We could sit down on the beach and I could work the tension out of those shoulders for you."

"I'm not tense," she said through tight lips.

He leaned back against a tree trunk, crossing his legs at the ankles. He was neither uptight nor tense. He could relax because he knew he had her backed into a corner.

"I was spying on you, okay? Is that what you want me to admit?"

"All you had to do was ask."

"I wanted to know more about your tattoo."

"With or without my pants on?"

She heaved a sigh and stalked off, ending up at a lone picnic table, weathered by the years it had been sitting there.

"I know I'm just a gooney missing a few beats,

but it would help if I knew whether or not you were dancing with me.'' He joined her at the table, and she boosted herself on top. ''We all have our defenses, mine just happens to be that I'm a wiseass. When you're the youngest in a family of overachievers, you get your attention any way you can.'' He sat down and began to rub her shoulders. ''I've tried to back off, but you're sending me mixed signals.''

She relaxed beneath his touch but remained silent.

''Like now,'' he said, leaning forward.

''I think I'm drawn to things that are bad for me.''

''One minute I'm a nice guy, the next I'm bad for you.''

''One isn't mutually exclusive of the other. You *are* a nice guy. You do nice things for people. You're friendly, funny. I could go on. But then there's me. The last thing I need is for a guy in a uniform to walk into my life and turn it upside down. The military is the antithesis of everything I am. Or ever want to be. I have tried hard to put my past behind me. I actually thought I'd succeeded until you came along.''

''What if fate stepped in to prove you can't run away from your past?''

''You may be right. Even though I don't want you to be,'' she agreed. ''You're like the missing pieces of a puzzle I've been trying hard not to solve.''

''Why wouldn't you want to put the pieces together? Then you'd have the whole picture.''

''I might not like what I see.''

''But that's better than not knowing, isn't it?''

''Your tattoo. Does it have any significance?''

''I'll show you mine if you show me yours.'' He

backed away from the picnic table, unbuttoning his shirt. "Get naked with me. We'll go for a swim." He tossed his shirt aside.

"I'm not—"

"I won't be able to see anything. If you want answers, Tam, you're going to have to come get them. Because I want answers, too." He kicked off his sandals.

"You lied to me about a lot of things, didn't you. Like the fact that your help doesn't come with a price tag! Like the fact that you know my father!"

"I know your father, but you're the one I want to know better." He unzipped his shorts, stepped out of them, then peeled off his underwear and stood naked before her.

"This isn't about sex, Tam. I have no condoms." He held his arms out to his sides and kept backing up toward the ocean. "This is about you and me getting down to the naked truth."

When the water reached his waist, he turned and dove in.

She sat there shaking, her heart pounding. Her flight instinct told her to run, but she couldn't move. She'd started this crazy dance. And she wanted answers bad enough to finish it.

She peeled off her clothes, knowing she couldn't trust him. Then she got up from the bench. She couldn't see him. But he was out there.

She started walking toward the water in her underwear. He treaded water not too far from where she stood. She met his eyes and removed her bra and panties just before she stepped in.

The warm water surrounded her. She swam toward him but stopped a safe distance away to tread water.

"Come here," he urged. "You know I could be there in just two strokes."

"You do your stroking from over there," she warned, even though she didn't think she was much of a threat to him naked.

He threw back his head and laughed. "Now, wouldn't you be embarrassed if I did."

"Would you?"

"No, not at all," he said seriously, taking that first stroke toward her. He was close, but not close enough to touch her. "The red eyes of the skull represent night vision. The tattoo was adopted by a group of sixty special ops who managed to hold off forty thousand North Vietnamese Army regulars staging at Parrot's Beak, Laos, thwarting their mission, which was to capture Saigon. Of course, Saigon did fall to an Army attacking from Parrot's Beak, just not that time." He paused. "We call ourselves the Sons of the Sixty. That's why McCain and I have this tattoo. There are others. And there are the originals, my father, your father... You want to know more, you have to tell me something about your tattoo."

She turned her head toward her left shoulder, then back to him. "Tit for tat," she said.

"I was thinking more along the lines of give-and-take. I'll stay out here all night if I have to, just give me something. That's all I'm asking for."

He swam in a circle around her. She turned with him, always keeping him in sight.

He stopped, then disappeared underwater. She

knew a moment of panic, kept turning, trying to catch a glimpse of him or some movement, expecting to feel him brush against her body.

But she didn't feel anything. The panic subsided for a moment, until she realized it had been a while since he'd come up for air.

"Okay, that's enough," she called out to the dark. "Bowie!" But moments turned to minutes. How many? Three, four, five? She swam toward the shoreline, trying to catch a glimpse of him on the beach. She stood to her navel in water, not knowing which way to turn. To the water? To the shore?

Her heart stood still.

The hairs on the back of her neck tingled.

He sliced the water behind her and pulled her to him. "Did you find your answers?" he whispered in her ear. "Which frightened you more, my leaving or my return?"

Her heart had started to beat again. She sagged against him, felt his heat, his hardness, his strength.

"Stay or go, Tam? What do you want from me?"

"You don't play fair."

"I have a hidden agenda," he said, trailing kisses from her neck to the tattoo on her shoulder. "Tell me about the butterfly."

"You don't want to know. You won't—"

"You're wrong. Every night I see you in my dreams exactly this way, rising up from the ocean. Naked to the waist. Your hair wet and draping your shoulders and back. Your body glistening with droplets of water. But always, always your secrets are hidden. I would die to know those secrets." One of his hands had cupped a small breast. "Open up to me, Tam. Tell me everything."

He stole her breath. He stole her sanity. "I can't! I can't!"

He let go abruptly. "Can't or won't?"

"Where are you going?" she demanded as he headed toward shore.

But he didn't answer. He walked with his head bowed and his shoulders slumped. "Don't you dare walk away after that!"

"At least I'm just walking, Tam," he called over his shoulder. "You're the one running."

She stood stock still. "You were always going to leave me, anyway."

"Maybe, maybe not. Maybe you were going to leave me. But we'll never know. Because one of us is too much of a coward to risk it."

2200 Tuesday
FISHERMAN'S WHARF
San Francisco, California

LAN HAD AGREED TO MEET Shane O'Connor for dinner. She'd been avoiding him because she thought it best not to lead him on. And until she knew for sure what had happened to Skully she would never be free to love another.

Her apartment had become too intimate a meeting place. But Fisherman's Wharf seemed harmless enough. That is until they were seated at a table overlooking the docks with twinkling bulbs lighting up the terrace like fireflies.

"A penny for your thoughts," Shane said, leaning over his dessert.

"Hmm? I'm sorry. My mind is still on work," she lied.

"Tough day?"

"Not at all," she answered honestly, thinking over all the *tough days* she'd had in her life. "It's a good day. A very good day." She smiled.

"Well, I have information that is going to make a good day even better." He slid an envelope across the table to her.

She picked it up with trembling hands.

"I haven't found him yet," he warned. "But it's a solid lead."

She'd wait to read it until she was alone. As she knew he would, Shane went on to tell her what he'd discovered.

"It seems there's a story behind that tattoo that traces back to only sixty men. We've narrowed the field considerably, Lan. From here on out, it's only a matter of time."

Spring 1975
Saigon, Vietnam

XANG HAD KEPT HIS PROMISE. Lan had named the daughter of her heart Tam. She'd lived as the man's concubine for more than two years now, not seeing her parents or her brothers in all that time.

And she hadn't stopped thinking of Skully.

Xang had become frustrated with her because she hadn't conceived. He'd taken a first and then a second wife. Neither union had produced any offspring. He would soon be looking for a third wife.

The American War was only a memory, but the South Vietnamese had held on to Saigon. That was why she'd chosen to run away from Xang. If she could get to the U.S. Embassy she might still have a chance to be free of him forever.

She'd walked for days along Highway 1, carrying her daughter and looking over her shoulder. She hadn't dared to take more than the clothes on her back and what food she could carry. But he never came after them.

The baby started to cry, and Lan sang her a lullaby until she quieted. There was no turning back now. She had no choice but to keep going. So she put one foot in front of the other.

The foot traffic moved with her at a hurried pace as if sensing her urgency, or maybe it was their own. Many simply died beside the road for one reason or another, their bodies left to rot. The closer she got to Saigon the more desperate she became.

There were rumors passing from person to person that the embassy had closed. The last American civilians and military were being shuttled by helicopter to ships. Refugee South Vietnamese were being evacuated as well, but papers and connections helped. There was simply not enough room on the helicopters. And not enough time.

Lan reached the locked gates of the embassy.

People were begging to be allowed in. She pushed her way to the front. A tree had been cut down from the middle of the parking lot so that the helicopter could land, the lucky ones inside the gate were lining up, being prioritized and airlifted out.

Until only the Marines remained to face the desperate crowds pressing against the gate.

When they started to retreat, Lan knew it was too late to save herself, but she still hoped to give her daughter a new life. "G.I.-san!" she cried out. She caught the eye of a young Marine. "My baby. Take my baby, *lam on,* please," she begged, holding up a screaming Tam so he could see her daughter. "My baby has round eyes!"

He hesitated, ready to follow his fellow Marines up the fire escape to the roof. Then he turned back to her and came toward the fence.

"*Cam on,* thank you," she choked out, squeezing her daughter between the bars.

He reached out to take her and a shot rang out. Lan pulled Tam to her body and watched in horror as the corporal who'd been close enough for her to read his name tag fell backward. Marines fired back above the heads of the crowd to the building across the street. Two other Marines rushed over to drag Corporal O'Connor's limp body away. But at that point there was still hope for O'Connor.

There was no hope for her.

"My baby has round eyes!" Lan shouted over and over again. But it was no use. The last helicopter came at dawn to pick up the waiting Marines, then left.

"My baby has round eyes," she whispered. Sinking to the ground, she rocked her baby back and forth. She didn't know what the future held. She knew only one thing. There was no tomorrow in Vietnam.

CHAPTER ELEVEN

1600 Tuesday
Honolulu, Hawaii

BOWIE HAD RENTED A CAR at the base and was heading along the highway on the leeward side of the island toward Stevens's residence.

He'd been summoned to Hawaii by both his C.O., Captain Harris, and Stevens.

But he had a mission of his own.

He'd met Captain Harris on the driving range of the Navy-Marine Golf Course and the news couldn't have been worse. The C.O. had prostate cancer. He'd been in Hawaii not because the greens were better than on Midway, but for treatment. He'd opted for an early retirement and the X.O.—Commander Bask— had been promoted to C.O.

Lieutenant Bowie Prince had made the shortlist for Lieutenant Commander and had been promoted to X.O.

Bowie would be heading back to Gulfport, Mississippi, with the main body of the battalion in no less than a week, then from there to Australia. So much for wishing away his dog-pile duty. He'd just as soon wish away his life as be separated from Tam.

Bowie double-checked the address he'd written down and pulled up at the curb of Stevens's home. He hadn't known how to break the news, so he'd consulted his own father. Tad Prince had offered to do it for him, but when Bowie declined, his advice had been to tell it straight.

The other war being waged inside him came from not telling Tam first. She was the one he'd offered to help. Then there was Tam's mother to consider. But it was Skully's responsibility to make things right. Bowie believed the only way Tam would be free to love him would be if she realized how much she'd been wanted by her father. And the only way she'd realize that would be for Skully to tell her.

Bowie got out of the car and walked to the front door.

Too late to change his mind now.

He rang the bell. An Asian woman, only a few years older than himself, answered.

Bowie held back his surprise as he introduced himself. "Lieutenant Prince. Mr. Stevens is expecting me."

"Come in, please." She ushered him in the front door and then out to the lanai, where Stevens sat at a patio table, reading the paper. "Can I get you something to drink? A beer, perhaps?" the woman asked.

"Yes, thank you…" Bowie hesitated. "Mrs. Stevens."

The young woman laughed.

"Cai isn't my wife," Stevens said. "She's my housekeeper and the wife of a dear friend. Have a seat, Prince."

"My apologies," Bowie said to the woman and to Stevens, before sitting down.

"That isn't necessary," Cai said. "Bay and I have been telling him for years he needs a wife. But he won't listen so he has to put up with me. I'll be right back with the two beers."

Cai returned moments later with their beers. He half rose out of his chair and she waved him back down.

"Thank you," he said. Just what he needed. More Ba Muoi Lam. Didn't anyone drink plain old Bud anymore?

"I'll be heading home to the kids now," she said. "Since my husband is away on *your* business," she said, with a bit of undertone that could have been a taunt or a reprimand.

As they drank their beer Stevens made small talk. But Bowie was only half listening as he rehearsed what he'd come to say.

"Rob, you and my dad go back a long way. He told me if I had something to say to you I should just come right out with it. I'm finding that easier said than done."

He had the other man's complete attention now. "Just spit it out, Bowie."

"I'm in love with your daughter." Bowie shook his head and started over. "That came out all wrong. What I meant to say was you *have* a daughter. Her name's Tam. She was born in Vietnam twenty-nine years ago. She's the game warden on Midway Islands."

Stevens looked at him like he'd had too much Ba Muoi Lam. "You're not making any sense. Bian Xang killed my wife and *son*...twenty-nine years ago," he said, as if just grasping the possibility.

"Lan Nguyen had a daughter. And if this is you, then you're the father." Bowie handed Stevens a scanned copy of the old Polaroid.

Stevens studied the picture in stunned silence. "I have a daughter. *Tam* translates to *heart* in English," he said finally. "Daughter of my heart." The man swallowed, tears welling in his eyes.

Bowie nodded and cleared his throat. He wasn't finished. "Skully..." The man shifted his gaze from some faroff place to focus on Bowie. "Lan Nguyen is alive."

Bowie thought Stevens would lose it then. But just the opposite was true. The ex-SEAL drew on his reserves to assess the situation. The woman he loved was alive. No more time for tears. Time for action.

"She lives in San Francisco. Here's the number," Bowie said, drawing from his pocket the scrap of paper he'd written it down on all those weeks ago in the ham operator shack. He set it on the table in front of Stevens. "I'd better get going. I've given you a lot to think about." Bowie stood. "I don't know what you want to do next, but I hope you'll call them soon. Tam needs you in her life."

"What was that you said about my daughter?"

"She's the game warden on Midway. I'd appreciate it, though, if you'd contact her soon."

"I meant that *other* thing you said. About being in love with my daughter."

"Yes, sir. From the moment I saw her. Now I just have to tell her that."

1900 Tuesday
STEVENS'S RESIDENCE
Barber's Point, Hawaii

SKULLY REMAINED SEATED long after Bowie Prince had left. He held on to that scrap of paper, but he'd long since memorized the number.

For the past thirty years he'd felt as if he'd been driven by only one thing, revenge. And now he couldn't even think how to get his ass out of the chair and over to the phone.

What would he say to her?

Should he even call? Or should he just find out her address and show up at her door?

Prince had said his daughter didn't yet know about him.

Did Lan? Did she think he was alive or dead? How and when had she arrived in the U.S.? How many years had they been this close, yet this far apart? He should have asked Prince more questions.

And why the hell was he sitting here when the woman he loved was just a phone call away?

Beating back questions that would only get answered in time, Skully picked up the phone. He punched in Lan's number with an unsteady hand.

"Hello?" a man answered. "Hello," the man repeated when Skully remained silent.

Skully hung up.

There was a wrinkle he hadn't thought of. What if Lan had found a life with another man?

Early Spring 1972
Da Nang, Vietnam

"SKULLY, STAND OVER THERE with the rest of the squad. You, too, Commander Prince. The wife sent me this new camera." H.T. set the timer and took his position with the rest of the men who made up Team Seven's Alpha Squad.

They'd just returned from a little place called Parrot's Beak. And a big mess.

The flashbulb popped and the photo zipped out.

The men gathered around to stare at the black square.

"Try it again. It didn't take," Skully said.

"It takes a minute," H.T. said, defending his new toy. "I'll take another one, anyway," He made everyone get back in position.

The second picture came out. By this time the image on the first had become visible.

"Told you it takes a minute." H.T. slipped one photo in the pocket of his fatigue shirt and handed Skully the other as an "I told you so."

Skully ducked inside their tent and put the picture in his footlocker. Prince sat down on his rack, reading a letter from home.

Mail call was the best part of coming back from the jungle, but unlike the other men Skully didn't have a wife or sweetheart waiting for him at home. So there'd been no sweet-smelling letter waiting for him. Though he couldn't complain about his mother's chocolate chip cookies.

When he next looked up, Tad Prince sat with his head in his hands. Skully didn't want to think his commander had received bad news from home, but he had to ask.

"Trouble?"

"No." Prince shook his head, sniffing back tears Skully pretended not to see. "First picture of my new son. James Bowie Prince, born February 14."

They'd been in Parrot's Beak on that day where no health-and-welfare message from the Red Cross would have been able to reach them. So Prince was just now finding out he was a father for the third time. He held the picture out for Skully. It was one of those close-ups taken from the hospital nursery.

"He's a cute kid. All that blond hair. Must look like the milkman," Skully teased his dark-haired friend.

"Get the hell out of here," Prince said with a chuckle. "You know damn well my wife is a blonde."

That he did. The whole squad had been in love with Lily Chapel Prince at one time or another. The commander's wife was a strong woman and a faithful partner, the kind Skully hoped to find someday.

"She named him after that knife of yours since it saved my ass from being shark bait a time or two."

That made him feel good. Skully turned to leave the tent and noticed the commander do something out of character; he pocketed the picture of his new son. As a rule they never carried anything personal that could be used against them when out on patrol, and they were headed back out today.

A short time later, Prince mustered them together and they headed back out. They were losing ground in Quang Tri again and their job was to get it back since it was located south of the DMZ. And less than a hundred miles from their current position.

They headed out to meet up with a ruff-puff who would basically take them in the back door to Quang Tri. Once there they'd be smack-dab in the middle of NVA troops and trying to confuse the hell out of the enemy.

Regional Force/Provincial Force, or the ruff-puff, were really just the village militia. Sometimes they weren't even armed. They just helped out where they could. The problem was a ruff-puff could be anyone. And anyone could pretend to be one. So it was the same basic principle as cops and informants—you liked to use a ruff-puff you knew and had a relationship with. But the last ruff-puff they'd worked with had been killed, so they knew they'd be meeting up with someone new today.

Skully was on point when the girl came out of nowhere. He almost shot her out of reflex. "*Dung lai,* halt!" he shouted as he stared into the most beautiful almond eyes he'd ever seen.

"I take you, Quang Tri?" she said, then turned around and disappeared, leaving him no choice but to follow or get left behind. He motioned to the guys behind him to pick up the pace. A new ruff-puff, especially a girl, put him on edge. He didn't like an unarmed child taking point so he stayed close by her side.

Once they reached their objective she vanished as quickly as she'd appeared. For days, the eight men caused the enemy as much trouble as possible.

It was after they'd cut the line of NVA regulars down the middle and had half of them turning tail and running north that the Army engaged from the south. Their job was to close off any retreat.

SKULLY HEARD the trip wire of a booby trap and lunged at Tad Prince, dropping them both to the ground. All he could think about was the picture of that newborn son the man carried in his pocket.

Skully roared as a nail embedded in his shoulder, but Bouncing Betty had missed her mark. On big guys like them riding a Betty meant they'd be singing soprano.

Skully rolled off his C.O.

Prince sat up. "I owe you one."

"You sure as hell do," Skully complained, breathing heavily, as Prince examined his arm.

The C.O. waved the rest of the guys on to the rendezvous point with the Army division coming through; meanwhile they ducked into a dilapidated barn that looked like it would fall down around their ears if they so much as sneezed.

Prince doctored his arm while Skully tried to keep from passing out. "How does that feel?" he asked, wrapping off the bandage.

Skully rotated his shoulder. "I'll live."

"Ready to roll?"

Just as they stood, the barn door creaked open. They both drew their weapons as a girl slipped inside.

For a long moment they just looked at each other.

Skully took one look at her battered face, torn clothes, the fear in her eyes and knew she'd been raped.

"Good Lord."

That she didn't scream was probably the thing that surprised him the most. The other was that he recognized those eyes.

"It's ruff-puff," he said to his C.O. "What do we do with her?"

"Don't let her leave. I'll check this out. NVA?" Prince asked the girl.

She shook her head.

"American?" Skully asked through tight lips. But again she shook her head. "VC?" he asked then. And she nodded. Prince slipped out the door.

She went straight to the corner and huddled there, her slight body shaking. Her eyes never left him.

God, what she must be thinking. "We're not going to hurt you," he'd said as best he could in her language.

Blood ran down the inside of her legs.

He ripped the bandanna from his head and soaked it, using his canteen. He offered it to her but she wouldn't take it.

She flinched when he touched her face with the cloth, but sat quietly through his ministrations. When he finished with that he started at one ankle and ended at her knee. Then handed the cloth and urged her to use it.

"I have a kid sister about your age." He just started rattling nonsense, trying to offer what little reassurance he could. "What's your name? Guess you don't feel like talking much right now, do you." He checked his pack for something more he could offer her and came up with the only thing decent in his C-Rats. "*Chop-chop,* eat, canned peaches?" he offered them to her. "They call me Skully."

She devoured the fruit and he enjoyed watching her eat.

"*Cam on,* Skully-san."

When Prince came back with the all-secure sign, they left to rejoin their squad, but he couldn't stop thinking about her. They'd won their objective. And he'd started making regular trips to that barn.

At first he just left canned peaches, then one day she was there waiting for him. Even that started out innocent enough.

But he kept going back.

He should have known better, he was much older than she was. But that first time she touched him, the way a woman touched a man, he was lost.

1900 Tuesday
Lan Nguyen's House
San Francisco, California

"WHO WAS THAT ON THE phone?" Lan asked, hitting the kitchen tap with her forearm so she could wash the dough from her hands.

"Hang-up," Shane O'Connor answered, fidgeting with the manila envelope in his hand.

"Okay, I'm done now. Sorry for making you wait. But I wanted to get the bread made—"

"Ever hear of a breadmaker?"

"I like to bake. It's just that I have no one to cook for now that Tam doesn't live at home. I suppose it's time I sent her a batch of cookies."

Shane was a quiet man, but he seemed unusually quiet today. He'd let her rattle on and on about nothing, as if he'd just wanted to hear her voice.

"Sit down, Lan," he said. And then she knew.

She set aside the dish towel and wrung her hands together. "You found him?"

He nodded.

She covered her mouth, then did sit down, but as soon as she did, she stood back up again.

"Are you ready for this?" he asked.

When she nodded he made her sit at the dining room table. He pulled out another chair and sat beside her.

He removed the contents of the envelope and handed it to her. "His name was Robert Stevens. Skully was a nickname. He was captured and taken to Hanoi in the fall of '72. I'm afraid he's still listed as MIA. I'm sorry, Lan. He never made it home."

"You mean he's dead," she said without emotion. "In my heart—" the tears started to fall "—in my heart, I thought he must still be alive. Because I can still feel him right here." She pounded her chest. "That's it. It's over."

Shane pressed a hankie into her hand. "Lan, there are organizations that specialize in the recovery and identification of the remains of Vietnam vets. I'll make inquiries if you'd like.''

''I think he'd like that. And I'd still like to take our trip to Vietnam, so we can continue looking for the rest of my family.''

He nodded. ''Stevens has family in the area. I thought maybe you'd like that information for your daughter. And I'll check with them. They may have recovered the remains themselves. And I'm sure they'd want to know about Tam.''

''Thank you,'' she said, but she was already in another place.

Early Spring 1972
Da Nang, Vietnam

''SKULLY-SAN, YOU NOT LIKE Lan?'' She held his face in her hands so that he had to look at her.

''I like you very much, too much, *nhieu lam,*'' he emphasized, removing her hands from his face.

He stood abruptly.

She reached for his belt. Desperate to make him stay, she worked to release it. ''*Lam on,* Skully-san. Let Lan love you.''

She'd started on his zipper. Even though she could feel his desire beneath her palm, he stilled her hand. How could he want her and still reject her?

He brought her slowly to her feet and pulled her into his arms. He covered her mouth with his. When he kissed her like that it didn't matter that there was no tomorrow in Vietnam.

This moment was all she needed.

CHAPTER TWELVE

"WAITING IS FOR THE BIRDS," Will said.

Or in this case the green sea turtle.

Because of the penlight clamped between her teeth as she scribbled in her pocket-size notepad, Tam let her assistant's comment flit by on the breeze. She didn't share Will's impatience, despite the lava rock digging into her numb rear end.

Tam scribbled furiously, wanting to get the encounter down on paper while still fresh in her mind. The tiny *Chelonia mydas* dug their way out of the holes and raced down the beach toward the water.

"'urry." Tam took the penlight out of her mouth. "Hurry, follow them with the camera," she directed Will. Easing her cramped muscles from sitting to standing, she followed the parade.

Remembering exactly why it was she had to reshoot this particular video made her warm all over. It also made her think about Bowie, who had gone to Hawaii on battalion business. She wasn't exactly sure when he'd be back.

He hadn't come right out and told her his *hidden*

agenda, of course. But he'd hinted that by connecting her with her past he'd uncover her long-buried heart. The question was, what were his intentions after that?

Once she and Will were finished filming, they loaded up their equipment. She headed back to the boat with the first load. A good twenty feet from the dock she spotted the shadowy figure of a man propped against her schooner. She came to a stop.

Instant relief washed over her.

The shadow had a long, lean, athletic build.

Relaxed.

She felt the tension ease from her own tight muscles. "Hello?"

"Hello," the shadow responded. The deep resonance of his voice registered even before his answer. If she expected him to say something more, he didn't.

And she couldn't. Her mouth had gone dry.

He pushed away from the boat. Heaven help her, she couldn't move her feet. Water lapped her ankles and rushed away again.

Having closed the distance by half, he stopped. They were simply two silhouettes in the pale moonlight, one male, one female. Neither moving. Neither breathing.

Except she had to be breathing.

The cloying perfume of gardenias filled her nostrils. Above that she could pick up his unique scent, all sand and sunshine, salt and sea. She wanted to close her eyes and breathe in deep.

He carried flippers and had obviously just been in the water. His wet suit glistened with reflected light. Unzipped to the navel, it gave her a glimpse of muscle only hinted at in the parts covered by skin-tight neoprene. In the daylight his slicked-back hair would be blond. Right now his features were simply shades of gray.

Reality check. So were his motives.

"Is that thing loaded?" he asked, the barest hint of amusement in his voice. He moved in closer until he stood just out of range of the inadequate spotlight on her video camera.

She looked at the camera in her hand and blushed.

"I thought I told you not to come out here alone," he said, changing the subject and sounding stern.

"I brought Will," she said in her own defense, even though the young man was apparently lagging behind.

"Hi, Lieutenant," Will said, walking past them both to load the equipment into the boat.

"Go ahead and take my schooner back, Will. The professor and I have unfinished business." He was talking to Will, but he looked at her when he said it.

Leaving Tam no doubt as to what he meant by "unfinished business."

"Aye, aye, sir." Will chuckled and gave a mock salute before hopping aboard the schooner and heading for Sand Island.

Bowie grabbed for the blanket, then headed toward her.

"Is that how you say hello? Grab a blanket and go?" she admonished as he slung an arm across her shoulders and led the way to *their* spot.

"I already said hello. Besides, I'm in a hurry."

"What's the rush?"

"There's no rush, no rush at all. We have the whole night ahead of us. Except I'm having a hard time waiting to give you this." He unsheathed his knife and presented it to her.

"Your knife?"

"It's an heirloom. And heirlooms should be passed on to heirs. I'm giving it to you so you never have any doubt of my intentions. Even if I take some time getting around to other things."

She stood holding his knife while he laid out the blanket. When he had it just the way he wanted it, he stripped her of the knife, her satchel and the camera. Then there was nothing between them except his wet suit and her clothes, and even that seemed like too much.

"Did you miss me?" he asked, pulling her to him.

"Yes."

"I missed you, too." He dipped his head and kissed her until she thought she would drown. He felt warm and wet and wonderful in her arms. He tasted of salt and sea and was the fulfillment of every craving she ever had.

"I finally figured something out," he said finally. *"Toi khong biet."*

Her breath caught and she pulled away. "Would you please tell the master chief to quit teaching you how to talk hookers into your bed?"

He just laughed at her.

"Do you have any idea what you just said to me?"

Her heart pounded against her breast as she looked into his eyes and waited for his answer.

"Yes, I do."

"Then say it to me in English," she said, still not sure she believed him.

"I love you, Tam. And I want to make love to you, not some hooker."

Her lower lip began to tremble. He brushed his mouth across it. "No tears," he said. "Don't you love me?"

"Yes," she whispered.

"I need to hear you say it," he coaxed.

"I love you, Bowie Prince."

"Say it again and again and again." With each *again,* he rewarded her with a kiss. "Are you going to let me make love to you tonight?" he asked. "Because I can be a patient man, but I don't think I can be patient about this."

In response, she tugged his zipper lower. "I'm not a very patient woman."

He stood back and divested himself of the wetsuit in record time, leaving him in his swimsuit and her overdressed.

She lifted her tank top over her head, and he reached out to slide his hand along her body. She came alive under his gentle touch.

She hadn't even unhooked her bra before he was slipping the straps from her shoulders.

"You are so beautiful," he said in a husky whisper.

She pressed into him, tugging his trunks down his thighs as far as she could reach before her hands trailed back up to his perfect backside.

"I hope to hell you left those condoms in your bag."

"About a half a dozen or so. I've been stocking

up.'' She teased him with her words and tortured him with her touch.

He undid her shorts and pushed them and her panties past her hips, letting both fall to the sand.

Kicking off his trunks, he sat back on the blanket. Holding her hands he urged her closer, but when she stooped to join him, he said, "Not yet."

He didn't touch her right away, and just when she thought she would die if he didn't touch her, he slid his hands to her hips and pulled her to him. She had nothing to do with her hands except hold on.

When she threw back her head and cried out, he tugged her down to his lap with a hot trail of kisses that ended at her mouth. She didn't know which one of them remembered the condom first, but they both fumbled for her satchel and they both came away with a prize.

She opened hers first, but she put it on so frantically it tore. He tossed it aside and managed to get the other one on. By that time she was more than ready for him, but he took things slow.

"Am I hurting you?" he asked.

"No."

"Then tell me what I am doing to you," he encouraged.

Heat flooded her face, and she buried her head into his neck.

"Not comfortable with pillow talk, huh?" he asked. "I like it, but mostly I just want you to set the pace. So we'll do whatever you're comfortable with."

Could she love him any more? "I just want to move or die."

TAM DIDN'T KNOW WHAT TIME it was when she awoke with a start. She thought she'd heard something, but then she realized her bladder had probably woken her up. Sand made a comfortable bed at night, but it was cold in the early morning. She managed to leave the warmth of Bowie's body behind, but just barely.

He was so adorable in sleep.

She was too embarrassed to just do her business nearby even if he was unaware, so she slipped on her tank top and panties and grabbed tissue from her satchel, then headed for a bush.

Silly really to get dressed on a deserted island just to take a pee, but even after the most amazing lovemaking of her life, she was not an exhibitionist. Not yet, anyway. Maybe with a little more tutelage from Bowie that could change.

She finished, now able to relax just a little bit. The moon hung overhead, but dawn had begun to lighten the sky.

The hand that closed around her mouth took her by surprise. At first she thought it was Bowie playing around. But these hands weren't gentle.

"It's been a long time, Tam. Have you missed me?"

She recognized the voice from her nightmares.

She struggled, making as much noise as she could, but it wasn't enough to wake Bowie. Then a terrible thought crossed her mind. What if he couldn't wake up? His body had been warm when she left, but…

Xang dragged her inland as she fought to be free. Her feet scraped over lava rock until they were raw and bleeding. Then there was no more rock beneath her feet, only runway.

Xang relaxed his hold as he dragged her toward the Cessna, and it was enough. She was able to get out one good scream.

Xang laughed at her. "Go ahead if you want him to die." He pulled out a handgun that looked very much like her own 9 mm Glock. "But don't worry. You and I are just going for a little ride."

He led her at gunpoint toward the plane, finding it no longer necessary to put his hand over her mouth. His threat had worked.

Tam didn't know whether to pray that Bowie had heard her scream or pray that he still slept. She just knew if she got on that plane with Xang, she'd die.

Then Bowie was between them and the plane. Thank God he didn't have the same problem with modesty that she had.

"Surely, Lieutenant, you could have put on some pants before you came to rescue the girl."

"Let her go, Xang. If you need a hostage, take me instead."

"That would be awkward, now wouldn't it? Since I don't need a hostage, I need bait. Care to tell her about the big fish I'm trying to lure, Lieutenant?"

Regret shone in Bowie's eyes. What were they talking about?

"No?" Xang continued. "Then I will. Ask your young man about your father."

Tam's heart dropped as she tried to comprehend what Xang had just said.

Bowie pleaded with his eyes. "Tam—"

"Then again, Tam knows all about secrets...." Xang caressed the side of her face with the gun barrel. "She once came to me begging for work...didn't you, my little *ba muoi lam?* Amazing what hunger will drive a girl to do."

Tam felt the sickening lurch in her stomach. She closed her eyes so she wouldn't have to see the look on Bowie's face when he realized what Xang had just revealed about her.

"Of course, virginity fetches a higher price than a used whore," Xang said harshly. "But Tam still belongs to me, and I don't give up what's mine easily."

Tam forced herself to look into Bowie's face, but the pity there was worse, much worse than condemnation. How could he love her now that he knew the truth?

Bowie had been inching his way closer as Xang spoke.

"That's far enough, Lieutenant." Xang pointed the gun at him and then at her. And Tam realized what Bowie was trying to do. He was trying to get Xang to point the gun at him. And Xang was taking the bait.

"Don't be John Wayne!" Tam shouted. "You can't get the girl if you're John Wayne!"

Bowie hesitated just long enough for Xang to push her inside the plane. But she wasn't sure he got her message because he still looked ready to spring into action.

And then Xang pulled the trigger, and Bowie fell to the ground.

Tam fought to reach Bowie, but Xang overpowered her and cuffed her to the seat with her own handcuffs.

"Don't worry, Tam. I don't want to kill the messenger, just slow him down a bit. Of course, if I did kill him, I suppose it would get my message across just the same."

Ho Chi Minh City, Vietnam

AFTER THE FALL OF SAIGON, Tam and her mother were taken to a North Vietnamese Reeducation camp. Until she was seven years old, Tam didn't know what it was like to live without being surrounded by barbed wire. The soldiers in their green fatigues were as familiar to her as the weapons they carried.

Her playground was a dirt exercise yard, but she never played for fear of drawing attention to herself.

Her home was a tent. Her bed, a mat she shared with her mother.

She had rice to eat, but never enough to fill her belly.

General Xang would come to visit them inside the camp. After they were released, he set them up in an apartment in Ho Chi Minh City, though her mother always referred to the city as Saigon in private.

They shared the small two-room apartment with another woman and her two children and the other woman's mother. Mama-san Tong would watch the children while the two women went off to work in the textile factory. It was hard work, but honest work, her mother would say. She was grateful to Xang for getting her the apartment and the job.

Tam learned she was different once she started school. She would go off every day in her traditional *ao dai* uniform, negotiating the bustling streets of Ho Chi Minh City to get to school.

And there she would be teased and taunted unmercifully. The other children spat on her and called her *bui doi,* dust of life. After her differences were pointed out, they were all Tam could focus on. She was taller and rounder than the other children, but what really gave her away was her round eyes. Maybe not round by Western standards. But round.

It was then that she started to notice other children with round eyes, street urchins mostly. She began to grasp the extent of what her mother had sacrificed in order to keep her.

When Xang came to visit, usually late at night, Tam was sent into the other room. She never questioned this. Having grown up around soldiers, she'd known what went on between men and women from a very young age.

Shortly after she turned fifteen her mother had arranged for her to get a job in the textile factory. A fortnight later, Xang came to visit, waking her and her mother as usual.

Her mother looked tired, but she nodded for Tam to leave the room. But before she could go, Xang grabbed hold of her wrist. He looked her over then sent her away. Tam hadn't liked the way he'd looked at her.

That night Xang and her mother fought.

The next morning they were turned away from the

factory. The same thing happened when they got back to the apartment.

Xang's orders.

They had nowhere to go and no food in their bellies. Nothing but the clothes on their backs. So they found themselves living on the streets.

Tam couldn't help but blame herself. If it wasn't for her, Xang and her mother would never have fought. She knew what they had fought about, knew what he wanted from her.

And also knew that her mother wanted her to have a better life than she'd had. She'd always told Tam stories about her father and about America. Even after all they had been through her mother had never given up hope that one day he would return for them.

Her mother looked for work every day, doing even the most menial of tasks. The one thing her mother had never considered was selling her body.

She would lecture Tam as they passed the *ba muoi lam* on the street. The girls were so pretty, and they wore the most beautiful silk *ao doi*. But sometimes they had blank stares from hanging around the opium dens.

What good was all their money if they spent it on drugs? And what good were their pretty clothes when their faces and bodies were worn out?

So Tam heeded her mother's warning.

She knew about the *ba muoi lam* and the opium dens, because Xang was in the business. It was her mother's threats to turn him in to the authorities if he touched her daughter that had caused him to turn them out. And by this time Xang was more powerful than any authority.

One day her mother found a good job as a live-in laundress. But the mistress of the house would only take one of them. So her mother wanted Tam to take it. Tam didn't want to take the job if it meant being separated from her mother.

With a great deal of persuading on Lan's part, Tam finally agreed. After a tearful goodbye, her mother left. It was later in the day that Tam met the master of the house. She didn't like the way he looked at her, but as she didn't care much for the way any man looked at her, she didn't pay much attention.

That night he tried to force himself on her and she ran back to the streets, back to her mother, like a child. But she was no longer a child; she never really had been.

Tam was tired of being homeless and hungry, and she was a realist. Their situation was hopeless. It was time she did something to elevate her status.

There was only one man she could go to for help. Xang.

So she went and begged him to take them back.

He agreed. He got them another apartment. Bigger and better than the other one. And though her mother seemed less than pleased with the whole situation, she accepted his help.

He showered them with gifts. And like any teenager, Tam took the new clothes and makeup without question. She didn't realize Xang was making her over for a reason.

Her mother did, however, and urged Tam to reconsider, especially once the rumors began about people looking for *bui doi* to take them and their mothers to America.

Tam was having too good a time to pay much attention. She had the life she'd always dreamed of. Then came the day Xang expected a return on his investment.

The evening had started out nicely. She'd gotten dressed up. He'd taken her out to dinner. But then they'd ended up at an opium den.

When she resisted, he forced her inside. No one seemed to notice or care that she was being dragged through the door. They were oblivious to everything.

There was a back room with men gambling over cards. And Xang intended to auction her off. She didn't know how she found the strength to break free from him, but she did. His laughter followed her to the door.

He thought she would be back because she had no options. He was wrong. She and her mother ran away for the second time that night, but now they had somewhere to go. America. And it was so far away he would never reach them.

She'd been wrong.

CHAPTER THIRTEEN

0700 Friday
Eastern Island, Midway Islands

BOWIE PICKED HIMSELF up off the ground. He staggered on unsteady legs, pressing his palm to his forehead in an attempt to relieve his bitch of a headache. His forehead was wet, and when he removed his hand he saw that it was slick with blood.

Thank God, he had a hard head. The bullet had only grazed him.

He heard the airplane engine in the distance.

"Tam!" He ran up the runway calling her name. The Cessna took off over the ocean and he felt panic like he'd never known.

Don't be John Wayne!

She'd been talking in code.

Live! And get the girl!

John Wayne.

Okay, so he didn't have to sacrifice himself to be the hero. But he did have to take action and hope that a plan came to him along the way. Because the girl he loved had sacrificed herself for him.

He had no idea where Xang was taking her. But he did have pieces to the puzzle.

Bowie took off at a sprint. He stopped only long enough to pick up his discarded knife. He ran over lava rock on his already-shredded bare feet. Other parts of his body had been scraped raw as well during his fall.

He reached the blanket and dumped the contents of Tam's bag onto it. No two-way radios. Xang had probably taken them. He only had his knife because it had been half buried beneath the blanket and the sand.

It sickened him to know that Xang had stood over them as they'd slept. But that was nothing compared to the churning in his gut when he thought of that man hurting Tam.

He hopped into his swim trunks, but left everything else and ran toward the boat, knowing what he'd find. The general had disabled that, as well. Bowie didn't waste time trying to fix a problem he couldn't solve.

He had one option and that was to swim the two miles back to Sand Island. Never mind that he was bleeding and that sharks fed at sunrise and sunset. He'd have to trust that the coral atoll would keep the big sharks out.

He strapped the Pirate to his thigh and dove in.

His body sliced through the ocean, one stroke, one kick at a time. He reached Sand Island exhausted, but picked himself up from the surf and hit the marina at a dead run.

"Will," he shouted. "Give me your walkie-talkie and get me the fastest boat this island has. Keep the motor running."

"Do you want me to call in the Coast Guard?" Will called back.

"Do it!" Bowie answered without breaking his stride. "McCain!" he called on the two-way.

"Where've you been? Over."

"Round up the squad, meet me at the armory, and I want it done yesterday!"

He'd reached the brig and slammed open the screen door, heading straight to the phone on his desk.

"What the hell happened to you, college boy?" The master chief sprang to his feet from behind his desk. "Looks like a bullet parted your hair."

"General Xang has Tam. McCain's rounding up the squad. I'm trying to reach Stevens," he said as he waited for the operator. "Will's standing by with a boat. Also contacting the Coasties."

"Slow down and have somebody look at that head of yours."

"I'm sorry, the line is busy," the operator said. Bowie slammed down the phone without a thank-you. The sound of his labored breathing filled his ears as he slowed down just enough to think for a second. He didn't have time to worry about his head.

In the stillness he heard an airplane. He rushed outside. Overhead an unmarked C-130 made its final approach. "Stevens!"

Cohen had followed him outside. "I'll get the men to the war room."

Bowie took off for the hangar. He reached the tarmac just as Stevens stepped down the ladder.

"What's happened?" Stevens asked. "I'm here to meet my daughter."

"Xang has her. You have to help me find her. I don't even know where to begin."

Stevens turned to the man behind him. "Have everyone assemble in the war room."

"It's a trap," Bowie warned.

"That's not going to keep me from walking into it."

"Me, neither."

Bowie was the first one up the stairs. He pulled a chart off the wall and spread it out on the conference table. "He's been right in our own backyard all along," Bowie said as the rest crowded around them, his own brother and sister-in-law included.

"What kind of trouble did you get yourself into this time, little brother?" Zach reached up to touch Bowie's matted hair.

Bowie jerked his head back and focused his attention on the chart. "He's using the depot on Eastern island to refuel." Tam had given him the idea with her John Wayne reference.

"We know he's been using small boats and planes," Stevens said, taking over the briefing. "What we don't know is which island he's using as a distribution center. That's probably where he's taken her." Stevens stood back and crossed his arms. "Now all we have to do is find it."

How did you find one small uncharted island in the middle of an ocean?

Think, think. Bowie supported his weight by leaning on the table. It was all that was holding him up.

"Let me look at your head, Bowie," Zach coaxed.

"You should have told me you worked for the CIA."

"What's to tell?" Zach studied Bowie's injury. "That doesn't look so bad. Bet it hurts like a bitch, though."

"I'll find a first aid kit," Michelle said, ducking out of the room.

His men arrived and took up what was left of the space. Stevens filled Bowie's men in on the situation. And they got back down to business.

Bowie had a flash of insight. "Midway got its name because it's midway between Hawaii and Japan, right? So he's refueling midway, right?"

"I think you're on to something. Keep going," Stevens encouraged.

Bowie pressed the heel of his hand to his head. "Well, we know he's not coming from Japan—"

"No, he's transporting the drugs out of Laos by cargo ship through the South China Sea...."

"And he'd want to make the switch over to smaller vessels sometime after the Philippine Sea...but stay clear of U.S. Coast Guard patrols around Palau, Guam, and the Mariana and Marshall Islands. Islands all south of the Tropic of Cancer."

"Midway is northeast of Hawaii.... We've been looking too far south," Stevens concluded. "Lay out the satellite photos of those islands to the east of Midway," Stevens instructed one of his men. "We're looking for a small airstrip, probably dirt."

Everyone began poring over the photos. When they were finished, everyone went so far as to check and recheck photos that had already been gone over.

"It isn't here," Bowie said in frustration, shuffling aside another picture.

"What you've got to look for," said Zach, "is an airstrip that's been camouflaged."

Bowie riffled through the photos again. How could he have been so stupid as to have missed it? "Like this one right here?"

"Got it!" Zach handed the photo to Stevens of a small island just outside of U.S. jurisdiction. If the island was being used as a distribution center, that was well camouflaged, too.

"Let's get to work," Stevens said. "We need a plan to get in. And one to get out again."

Michelle returned with a first aid kit and squeezed her way through the crowd to Bowie.

"Sit down and let me get a look at you," she said, pulling out a chair from the table. Bowie did as he was told.

"There," she said when she was done. "I put a butterfly bandage on it. Maybe you won't even scar."

"What do I care about a scar."

My little ba muoi lam.

Bowie remembered Xang's words, remembered the look on Tam's face. Bowie didn't know or care if what Xang said was true. All he cared about was that Tam was set free.

And soon.

He listened to the plans for storming the island. "Can I see that photo again?" Bowie asked. General Xang wanted Stevens on his terms. He'd chosen the place and time. How did they get back the advantage? "How would a Navy SEAL approach the island?"

"From the water," Zach said.

"Exactly."

"What's going on inside that brain of yours, Prince?"

"How close can we get to that island without being seen or heard?"

"Several miles. But not everyone here is trained for long-distance swimming."

"No, but I've got a whole squad of divers," Bowie said. "Some with underwater demolition training. What if we set explosive charges around the perimeter? We could create one hell of a diversion. We go in, get her out, blow the charges, confusion masks our escape. Then the boats can move in to pick us up."

"I like it," Stevens said.

"It gets better. That island is made up of lava rock. We can make them think a volcano is about to blow."

They set a timetable for the operation.

They'd wait for darkness, but the hours until then were agonizing.

Bowie had showered the blood out of his hair in the locker room down at the marina, but he hadn't bothered to shave. Or eat. He kept his body hydrated only because he knew he needed to.

Will had still had the engine running on the speedboat when Bowie had returned to the marina after the briefing. So Bowie didn't argue when the young man begged to captain them to the dive site; he'd earned his stripes.

The Coast Guard was standing by, too, again thanks to Will.

Bowie was putting on his frogman gear when Stevens entered the locker room and started suiting up.

"Think you're going to be able to keep up?" After all, the man was in his fifties.

"Just watch me," Stevens said.

When his brother joined them, Bowie started to get a little irritated. "What's going on here? You think I need baby-sitting?"

"Nope, just goin' for a swim," Zach said.

Bowie slipped on his hood and smeared his face with grease paint. "Maybe we'd better set our watches." And they did, down to the second.

"You know, if this goes off without a hitch, my daughter is going to owe you her life. And I'm going to owe you," Stevens said.

Live! And get the girl!

"Tam doesn't owe me anything. And neither do you. But you do owe her."

2400 Friday
UNCHARTED ISLAND
Northern Pacific Ocean

"TWO, ANY SIGN OF THE professor?" Bowie spoke through the headset of his transmitter.

"Negative," McCain told him.

He got the same from Zach and Stevens.

Each of them approached the island from a different direction. Bowie signaled to Brown and Jones. They were to secure the highest point on the island and serve as lookouts. Or snipers, whatever was necessary.

The rest of the squad were to set perimeter charges under Cohen's direction. They had enough C-4 to blow the island to kingdom come. As Bowie suspected, the center of the island was made up of porous lava rock. But there was also thick vegetation. And there didn't appear to be a soul around. What if she wasn't here? As his heart pounded against his chest he hoped and prayed he hadn't made a mistake.

Bowie followed an overgrown path inland.Within minutes, he pulled up short, spotting a trip wire an inch from his boot. Following the source of the wire, he identified the trap and stepped over it, then tripped it with the butt end of his weapon. The fulcrum action released the spiked Malayan gate. Had he been on the other side he would have been gored.

"At least I know we've come to the right place." Bowie released his breath.

He warned his men and disabled three more traps along the way before the sound of rushing water captured his attention. A waterfall. And a sentry. The man trudged across a fallen log over the top of the falls, then followed a path down the other side and disappeared.

"This is One," Bowie said over the transmitter. "I have visual contact. And what appears to be the entrance of a cave. Report."

"Two, negative," McCain reported from the south side.

"Three," Zach came through from the west. "Four Cessna Citations under camouflage netting. Two armed guards on the line. And another five playing poker in a Quonset hut."

Next Stevens reported from the north. "Four, I've got the mouth of a cave big enough to drive a boat through. I'm going to follow it and see where it leads."

"Copy," Bowie said. "Three, can you disable those planes?"

"The question is, can I get close to them."

"Try."

"Roger that."

"Two, head west to help. I'm going to check out this cave."

"Copy," McCain said.

Bowie followed the same path as the guard, keeping his back to the wall when they reached the other side. The entrance wasn't behind the waterfall as it first appeared, but next to it.

The cave was dark with no sign of movement. He crossed quickly to the other side and drew his weapon. The cave opened up to a cavern below, a natural north-to-south waterway slicing through the middle of the island. And cutting him off from the opposite bank.

Tiki torches staked to the ground and from sconces attached to the wall gave off an eerie and unnatural light. He heard voices and ducked behind an outcropping of rock. Two armed guards emerged from the opposite side of the cavern where a natural V shape opened into the overgrown core of the dormant volcano.

The guards passed by four high speedboats docked in the water and followed the waterway north along the western bank. If this was the same waterway Stevens was following, he'd meet up with those men somewhere inside the tunnel.

"Four, two men headed your way along the west bank," Bowie whispered.

Bowie followed the path down and waded across the waterway, using the boats as cover. He climbed up the west bank just as Stevens emerged from the tunnel.

"We're clear here," Bowie said in hushed tones as the two of them headed to the overgrown opening. "What happened to those guards?"

"I took care of them," Stevens answered.

Entering the core of the volcano was like something out of *Journey to the Center of the Earth.* Alive with natural sound and thick vegetation, the cave would have been fascinating to see in the daylight.

Behind them the bowl of the volcano rose straight up a couple of stories high. The mouth was so vast that from where they stood they couldn't make out how wide it was. They headed west along a freshwater stream to an encampment.

No wonder McCain hadn't been able to spot anything. The lip of the volcano had created a natural barrier between him and the base camp.

They veered off the path, using the thick foliage for cover.

"Stand by." Bowie spoke into the transmitter, readying the demolition crew. But since there was only one way in and out of this bowl, a diversion wouldn't do them much good until they cleared it.

There were several storage buildings, one large barracks, one medium size barracks and two small hooches. They could smell the weed burning from one. And two guards stood watch over the other.

Keeping to dense cover, they worked their way around. Bowie pointed to himself, leaving no doubt as to who would go in to see if she was there. He scrambled across the clearing in a crouch, then plastered himself to the wall and worked his way around the corner to peek inside the window of the hooch.

She was there! And alone. Gagged and bound to a chair in the middle of the room, which contained only a table and a propane lamp.

"Psst," he whispered. And when she turned her head he winked. Then he ducked back down and headed around the corner.

He signaled to Stevens to go around one side while he took the other. Bowie left the guards to Stevens and burst through the door.

Tam shook her head frantically.

Bowie stopped in his tracks. "Is the room booby-trapped?"

She nodded.

From the looks of things, so was she. One thing at a time, he told himself, willing his breathing under control. He looked over his shoulder at the Malayan gate ready to swoop down from the ceiling if he made one wrong move.

So much for rushing to the rescue.

He looked everywhere but couldn't see a trip wire, and he didn't dare move around the room. Or even untie Tam's gag to ask for help.

About the time he noticed that the floorboards under Tam's chair were different, a commotion started outside.

"We've gotta move now!" Stevens said at the door.

"Don't come in here," Bowie warned. He'd figured out the trap had been set when he'd entered the room. There were now two triggers. If they added or removed weight from either side, the trap would spring.

But he had to act.

The table was on his side. He crouched under it.

"Now would be a good time to trust me," he said to her.

Grabbing the table by two legs, he flipped it to his back and leapt across the divide, knocking Tam and the chair over and into a corner. He covered her with his body as the table took the brunt of the blow and splintered.

The propane lamp had overturned and a fire had started in the opposite corner.

Bowie untied Tam from the chair as quickly as possible and carried her from the burning room. Her feet were still bound, but she looped one arm around him and removed the gag with the other.

"Still think you're John Wayne," she accused.

"It's good to see you, too, honey."

Gunfire sounded behind them.

"Get her out of here," Stevens shouted as he returned fire.

Bowie ran toward the cavern opening with Tam in his arms, but realized he needed his hands free, since he didn't know what was waiting for them on the other side of that bowl.

He veered off the path and put her down. He also wanted a good look at the explosives strapped around her chest. While he was busy doing that, she untied her ankles. "I can run," she offered, reaching to take off the vest.

"Not yet. And not on those feet," he said. "Hop on."

He removed his pack and piggybacked her.

"They didn't follow," Stevens said. "That was too easy."

"Speak for yourself," Bowie said.

"I'll go through first. Don't follow unless I give the all clear," Stevens said. He stepped through and came back a few minutes later. "I don't like it, but I can't see anything."

They all stepped into the cavern. The boats appeared to be the fastest way out, so they hopped aboard one and started the engine. But just as they pulled away from the bank, a boat entered from the north and blocked their escape.

Xang laughed as his men started shooting.

Bowie threw himself over Tam while Stevens spun a hard left. Turning the boat one-eighty, he sped south.

"Now would be a good time for either of you to tell me if you had any reason to tell Xang I was color-blind." There should have been a whole mess of reference wires on this vest, but there were only two. A red. And a green. He knew that not because he could see the difference, but because he couldn't.

"What's wrong?" she asked.

The speedboat jumped across the rough surface, and it took all his concentration to cut the casing off each wire. "One of these is going to blow us up. And one isn't. I need you to point out which wire casing is red and which is green." His sunglasses wouldn't do him much good in a dark cave working by flashlight. He could feel his hands wanting to tremble and willed them to stay steady.

She pointed out the wires. His hand hovered over the green wire. Xang had wired her to an easy setup, giving him a fifty-fifty chance. If the man wanted to use Bowie's color-blindness against him, would he make it that easy?

"I trust you," she said, urging him to make the cut. "Get me out of this, please."

"Honey, did you ever hear the one about the jealous husband who gave his wife's lover a fifty-fifty chance? Behind the green door there's a tiger and behind the red there's a beautiful lady. The wife knows which is which. Which one would you choose for me?"

"The red door."

Without giving either of them time to think, he pulled her into his arms and cut the red wire.

"What if I'd have said green? I was thinking about it!"

"I still would have picked the red one," he said, holding her close. "I just wanted to hear how much you loved me."

She started crying, but Bowie turned his attention to helping Stevens.

"We're not being followed," Stevens said, slowing the boat to a crawl.

"He has it on remote!" Bowie tossed the jacket overboard. Not three heart beats later, it exploded. And then Stevens stopped the boat.

The south tunnel exit was barred. And beyond the bars the tunnel narrowed.

"Dead end," Tam said.

"Maybe not." Bowie grabbed a flashlight and jumped over the side. He could go under the bars and come up on the other side. "Let me check it out and see how long it takes to get through the tunnel." He checked his watch and dove under.

Tam waited in the boat, counting every agonizing second until Bowie surfaced. Not even he could hold his breath that long.

But then he was there.

"We can make it, but the cave gets tight. It's a stretch, almost four minutes one way," he said with labored breath.

"You're the only one here who can hold your breath that long," Tam said.

"I'll get you out of here," Bowie promised as he climbed back on board.

"Right now they're just waiting us out," Stevens said. "But eventually they'll figure out what we're doing in here and either come after us or go around."

"They weren't out there yet," Bowie told him.

"You swim out," Stevens said. "I've got a score to settle. I'm going to play chicken and see who swerves first."

"I'd just as soon take my chances on the boat," Tam said.

When Bowie hesitated, Stevens gave him a shove. "Get her out of here. When you're clear start the fireworks."

"Okay," Bowie agreed. "We'll meet you on the southern peninsula. Good luck."

Stevens nodded.

Tam and Bowie jumped over the side. Treading water, she watched for a while as the boat picked up speed and disappeared.

"Is he going to be all right?" she asked.

"Yeah."

"Are we?"

"I guarantee it." And then he kissed her.

Tam had never tasted anything so sweet in her life. But she was scared. "Maybe you should go and I could wait here."

"That's not an option. Relax. Take deep breaths." He placed her hand over his heart. "We're in sync, remember. If I can do this, you can."

She took one steadying breath, then the rest came easier.

"I'm not going to let go of you," he said. "And you don't let go of me, and we'll make it out."

Gunfire echoed in the cavern. She turned toward the sound, then back to him. She really didn't have any other choice.

One more deep breath and they were underwater. Even with the flashlight, it was dark. They cleared the bars easily.

The tunnel narrowed, and she gasped for breath.

Taking in water, she clutched at Bowie's wrist and panicked, starting to feel herself slip into unconsciousness.

And then they broke through the surface and precious air filled her lungs. She choked and gasped.

"Are you all right?"

She couldn't speak so she nodded. He practically had to drag her, but they made it to shore, then jogged the short distance along the sand to an airstrip.

Bowie put his headset on. "Is everyone accounted for?" He didn't speak for a moment, then said, "Stand by. Give me ten minutes, then let her rip."

"Where are you going?" she asked, clutching his hands so he wouldn't go.

"To keep a promise," he said, squeezing her hand.

"I want to go with you," she pleaded.

"Stay here. And when McCain comes with the boat get on it," he ordered. "Rob Stevens is your father. I'm going to go find him for you."

She stood there stunned. *Rob Stevens was her father.* She'd stared at his youthful picture for countless hours, yet hadn't recognized the flesh-and-blood man.

Bowie headed back in the direction from which they'd just come.

The sun broke over the horizon to the east. On a cliff above the cave she spotted two men. Stevens and another man. She hurried toward them.

Her father stood with his back toward the cliff. There was a ledge just below him, but beyond that a sheer drop. Xang pointed a gun at his head.

"No!" Tam screamed.

Xang turned, giving her father a chance to rush

him. Xang fired, and her father staggered. Xang took aim again, but before he could shoot, Bowie burst past her and lunged at Xang. She watched in terror as they both went over the cliff.

She ran to the edge.

Xang was falling to the rocky surf below. Bowie lay on the ledge, his head against a rock.

CHAPTER FOURTEEN

0900 Saturday
COAST GUARD HELICOPTER
Northern Pacific Ocean

TAM COULDN'T HOLD Bowie's hand, because the emergency medical technician refused to let her near him. So she held on to her father's hand instead.

She tried not to think how far they were from Hawaii and the nearest hospital. Or how battered and bruised Bowie's body had been when they had taken him from that ledge.

And when they landed at the helo pad at the Navy hospital, she tried not to cry out in sheer relief. The medical staff pulled his stretcher from the helicopter and headed to the emergency room.

His brother ran along beside the stretcher. His sister-in-law had given up her seat to Tam, otherwise she wouldn't have even been allowed on the flight, which could carry only four passengers and the crew.

Additional medical staff brought a wheelchair for her father because of the bullet that had grazed his arm. Tam stepped out of the helicopter behind him, ducking beneath the whirling blades.

He made a fuss about getting in the wheelchair but

did it just the same. Zach was just closing up his cell phone when they entered. Since she didn't have her father's hand to hold anymore, she held his.

"They've taken Bowie for tests," Zach told her. "I don't know what they're looking for, but I'm scared as hell at what they're going to find."

She didn't know who was comforting whom, so she squeezed his hand. "He's going to be all right. He has to be, because he's no John Wayne."

Zach looked shocked.

"It's a private joke," she told him.

"How long have you known Bowie?"

"All my life, it seems."

"I assumed you two were tight because of the will."

"Will?"

"I don't know if I should even be mentioning this now, but he wants to leave you a bird. Provided support as well."

"What? How?" She shook her head.

"I'm executor of Bowie's living will."

"I don't want to talk about wills."

"Frankly, neither do I."

They waited for hours. Her father had joined them in the waiting room, no longer a patient. The doctor finally came out.

"Your brother's been moved to the ICU. The good news is, there is good news. He hasn't broken anything—"

"And the bad news?" Zach asked.

"Head injuries are always a concern. But there is no skull fracture. He's bruised his brain, which is what caused the swelling. We've drained the excess fluid through a shunt and the swelling has subsided somewhat. He remains unconscious, but right now that's a good thing. We would have put him in a drug-induced coma to keep him as still and quiet if he wasn't.''

"When will he wake up?" Tam asked.

"We don't know," the doctor said. "His vitals are strong. He's breathing on his own. Those are all good things."

"When can we see him?" she asked.

"Next of kin only."

TWO MONTHS LATER, Bowie had yet to regain consciousness. But he'd been moved to a regular room, and Tam could hold his hand. The scary thing was that now the doctor was starting to talk about long-term care.

And if she didn't get back to the island soon she'd have to take a leave of absence or risk losing her job. Tam didn't know if sitting here holding Bowie's hand meant anything to him or not, but it meant something to her and she was afraid to let go.

She studied his long fingers. His nails needed cutting, maybe she'd mention it to a nurse or just trim them herself, next time. He had always kept them so neat before.

She kissed his knuckles and put his hand down on the bed. Then she stood and pressed a kiss to the scar on his forehead where the bullet had grazed him. His family patiently waited in the hall. His mother, father and sister had joined his brother the day after Bowie's accident.

When she left his room, Rob Stevens stood by the door. "How about some lunch?" he asked. He spent time every day sitting with her at the hospital, but recently he'd started coming around at lunchtime to make sure she ate.

She'd lost her appetite and had dropped a few pounds. "Lunch sounds good," she lied, and only picked at her food once they were seated in the cafeteria.

"Was your life hard growing up?" Rob asked.

She didn't know whether to think of him as Rob or Skully or Dad. They were still feeling their way around each other, but she appreciated his effort to get to know her.

"No," she answered in all honesty. "Life wasn't hard at all." Because now she had something to compare it to. Waiting was hard.

"And your mother?" he asked.

Curiously, it was the first time he'd asked about her. Tam didn't know if he was asking if her mother's life had been hard then. Or how she was doing now. She speared some lettuce with her fork.

"She's done well for herself."

"Remarried?" he asked. His sling still limited his movement, and he seemed to choose his movements as carefully as he'd chosen that word.

"No, she never remarried." She supposed she could have told him he was the love of her mother's life or try to explain that Lan was still searching for him, but she put the forkful of food in her mouth instead. Maybe she wasn't thinking clearly right now, but she had to know him better before she took the risk of telling her mother about him.

He nodded. When they said goodbye, she hugged him for the very first time, even held on to him for a bit. She supposed it was only natural that she feel so melancholy under the circumstance. But when he left she went into the nearest bathroom for a good cry.

After cleaning up, she decided to stock up on magazines in the gift shop. Maybe something she could read to Bowie. She also remembered the nail clippers. Killing time, she wandered around the little shop, which carried assorted sundries and over-the-counter medicines.

Tam didn't know why the home-pregnancy test made her heart stop until she counted backward to the last time she'd menstruated. She picked up one and read the back of the box, not yet convinced she was going to buy it. Or that she even needed it.

She purchased the test and went back to that out-of-the-way bathroom where she'd had her cry. Then she had another one after seeing the results of her test.

Positive.

She was pregnant with Bowie's baby. Now she would never have to let go. But when she didn't have anyone to share her joy with, that made her miss him all the more.

When she got back up to Bowie's floor, she ran into his family leaving the conference room with the doctor. Zach walked with his head hanging and his arm wrapped around his wife. His mother wiped at tears with a handkerchief. And even his tough-as-nails father looked pale.

"What's wrong? What's happened?" Tam demanded.

"Nothing's changed," he said, forcing a smile to reassure her. Though, it didn't work. "Bowie's being transferred to the VA. He'll be discharged from the hospital and medically retired from the Navy."

She wanted to scream at the unfairness of it all. The father of her baby was a healthy, vital man. Too young to be retired—never mind, spend the rest of his life in a care facility.

"If you'll excuse me." It must have been the baby giving her the strength to say those words. It certainly wasn't her.

Tam left them all standing in the hall and didn't shed one tear until she closed Bowie's hospital door behind her. And then she crawled right up in bed beside him.

She didn't know how she managed to choke out the words, but she did. "Hi," she whispered softly. "I know that it's a wonderful place where you are. So deep and so blue, that you just want to hold your breath forever. But first I need to tell you why you can't leave me. We're going to have a ba-baby," she stammered. "I can't do this alone. My mother was a strong woman, but I'm not. I can't think of the next thirty years without you." She pressed her head to his chest to muffle her tears.

She knew she had to lift her head, knew she had to get out of this bed, out of the room, but she just couldn't make herself move.

Finally she did lift her head, maybe hoping that by some miracle his eyes would be open, but they remained closed.

"I can't believe you left me with that stupid bird," she said, angry at him for disappointing her.

She got off the bed, dried her eyes and blew her nose. But before she could leave the room she had to kiss him one last time. She pressed her lips to his, trying to keep the tears from flowing again. "Good night, sweet Prince. *Toi khong biet,* I love you. And I will *never* forget you, you sure made sure of that."

She walked past his family without stopping or even slowing down. She didn't know when she would tell them about Bowie's baby. She only knew that she would. Just not today. Today was a day for tears.

"Tam?" Bowie's mother called out to her. "Are you going to be all right?"

She stopped and turned to face the woman. She managed a smile. "I'm going to be just fine."

She didn't feel like going to her rented room near the hospital. So she headed toward the Arizona Memorial. She wandered around the monument for a while, then found a bench where she could sit down and talk to her baby.

A pregnant woman strolled by on the arm of her lover, husband, friend, probably all of those things. Tam placed a hand over her flat stomach and tried to imagine the life growing inside her. She hoped her baby had green eyes, like his father.

"Someday I'm going to tell you all about your father. He was a sailor, a Seabee," she corrected herself. "He was so proud to wear that uniform. He loved John Wayne. And I loved him so much."

Before she spent the entire day in tears, she decided she had to do something constructive. There wasn't much of anything she could do about her own circumstances right now, but she could help two people very much in love find happiness.

She ran to the nearest pay phone and called her mother.

"Hello," Lan Nguyen said.

Tam had called her mother several times since Bowie's accident. But this time she told her mother everything that was in her heart. And about the baby. "Mama-san, I need you."

"I'll be on the next flight out."

Summer 2002
Honolulu, Hawaii

THE NEXT AVAILABLE FLIGHT from San Francisco to Hawaii was the next day. Tam hadn't told her mother about her father because she wanted it to be a surprise.

But maybe she should have. At her age, the woman could have a heart attack from shock.

"How do I look?" her dad asked for the hundredth time. "I should have worn a suit."

"You look fine," Tam reassured him for the hundredth time. She tried to see him as her mother might. A little older. A little grayer. But still hot.

And what would he think of her? A little wiser. A little heavier. But still very beautiful.

They waited near the baggage claim. Tam spotted her mother, but she didn't say anything. She just wanted to watch—to see the looks on their faces when they first saw each other.

That she had no doubt they would recognize each other was a testament to her own true love. Bowie could walk into her life right now or thirty years from now, and she would still know him.

Her father saw her mother first. Tam could tell by the way he stood up straighter. His eyes got bluer just focusing on her mother. And when Lan saw those blue eyes, she choked back a sob that would have made people stop and stare if they hadn't been in an airport.

They didn't run into each other's arms; there was a little more uncertainty than that. But they did meet halfway. And when her father took her mother into his arms and kissed her, Tam couldn't help but smile.

She turned to leave then. The two lovebirds would find their own way home. She was going back to her own nest. One that a certain Seabee had made sure was comfortable.

Summer 2002
Pearl Harbor, Hawaii

BOWIE OPENED HIS EYES. His stomach growled with hunger, and he didn't know where he was. It looked like a hospital. What was he doing in a hospital?

Did he have amnesia? There was such a thing as posttraumatic stress amnesia. Would he know that if he had amnesia? Would he know his own name?

The room got very busy very quickly. And he became easily confused with everyone trying to talk to him at once. If he was in a hospital, where were his family? His friends? Hell, where were the flowers and cards?

Someone put the bed into the upright position.

"Where is…" he tried to form the words but the question didn't come out right. The doctors and nurses were answering him. He just couldn't understand anything they were saying.

Then Zach burst into the room. His big brother crying?

"Tam?" Bowie managed to get the rest of the question out.

Zach hugged him, but Bowie couldn't seem to make his own arms respond the way he wanted them to. He grabbed onto Zach's sleeve. "Don't leave," he said.

"I won't."

When the doctors and nurses finally left him alone with his brother, Bowie asked Zach to explain everything to him all over again.

"What's wrong with me?"

"You had a closed brain injury. A blow to the head."

"Damage?"

"Some of your gross- and fine-motor skills. You're going to have to relearn some things, starting with the ABCs. Just give it time." His brother patted his hand.

Was Zach patronizing him?

Bowie was an engineer. He knew calculus, for heaven's sake.

He had a headache. And he was tired.

"I'm going to call Mom and Dad. Do you want me to call Tam?"

Bowie nodded. He wanted to see Tam.

Zach moved from the bed toward the door, and Bowie tossed back the covers. Swinging his legs over the side, he put his weight down and collapsed to the floor. A bedpan and some things from the nightstand crashed down beside him.

His brother rushed to his side. "Let me help you up," Zach said, grabbing hold of his arms.

"I had to go pee."

"You have a catheter," Zach reminded him.

He knew that.

He lay there for a minute in a crumpled heap, not cooperating with his brother, who was trying to help him up. He could walk. He wasn't paralyzed. He just had to relearn.

"Don't call Tam," he said. "I'm not ready to see her yet."

And he wasn't ready a month later after they'd moved him to a rehab hospital, and he took his first steps in physical therapy.

"You're pushin' hard today," his physical therapist said.

"I have a reason to push," Bowie said, inching his way between the parallel bars.

"I like a man who knows how to push," the older woman teased.

Bowie chuckled. It felt good to laugh again. And he'd been doing a lot more of that lately. He was even able to laugh at himself.

A month after that he'd graduated to a walker. The next month a cane. And then came the day when he didn't need any assistance at all. But he still wasn't ready to see Tam.

McCain stopped by his room at the rehab center. He'd been made X.O. of NMCB133 in Bowie's place. "Hey, how's it hanging?"

"It's hanging."

McCain filled him in on all the battalion news. Bowie liked to stay connected, and as soon as he was able he'd be right there in the thick of things. He hadn't been medically discharged from the Navy, but if he didn't get his act together soon he could be facing a medical review board.

"Calculus?" McCain picked up the book from his nightstand. "I thought you didn't like this the first time around?"

"I don't like it any better now." Which wasn't exactly true. He loved numbers and had a natural knack for mathematics, and it had all come back to him.

"How is she?" he dared to ask. As X.O., McCain didn't get to Midway Islands much anymore, and the Alpha Dogs had rotated to homeport. Another NMCB133 detachment had taken their place.

Bowie didn't want another Seabee to take his place with Tam.

Even if he still wasn't ready to see her.

"How do you want her to be?" McCain asked. "Because I could tell you anything, but until you go see for yourself, you'll never know."

"A man should have a future before he asks a woman to be a part of it."

"You have a future. Go get it. I put your name in for a new job...overlay manager of Midway Island. For the next three years. It's yours if you want it. Of course, the command was looking for a single guy to fill the slot because the tour of duty is unaccompanied. But if the guy's wife already lived on the island, what could they do about it?"

"I'll think about it," Bowie said seriously.

"What's there to think about?" McCain said, putting on his cover and taking his leave.

There was a lot to think about. But maybe he was doing his thinking in the wrong place.

Fall 2002
Sand Island, Midway Islands

"WHAT IS IT THIS TIME?" Tam asked, joining Will on the tarmac in front of the airplane terminal.

"What do you think is in that cargo hold?" Will asked.

"What is this, twenty questions?" Tam asked, easing the muscles in her back. "It's the regular log flight. Let's just hope there's toilet paper, since I have to pee every few minutes," she said, turning and heading for the terminal.

Once inside the nearest depot, she stepped between two waist-high stacks of empty pallets and dropped her bag. She dug through it for change for the Coke machine. Her hand came in contact with the invitation, and she took it out of the envelope to read.

"Trouble in paradise?"

Tam spun around.

Trouble? Oh, yeah. And she was looking right at him.

"Boyfriend trouble?" he asked, rephrasing the question.

"No," she said, looking him square in the eye. "My boyfriend's in a coma. If he wasn't I'm sure he'd pick up a phone and let me know."

She wasn't going to go easy on him. She'd spent the past five months walking around the island with all the Seabees shutting their big traps whenever she was within earshot. At first she thought it was the circumstances of her pregnancy. Single mother, father in a coma...nobody knew what to say to her, congratulations or condolences.

Then she realized nobody was saying anything at all.

Or she'd hear his name slip out and catch the guarded looks. Finally she came right out and asked her father, and he told her the truth.

She'd also told him that if news traveled both ways, she'd disown him. She didn't need some sailor thinking he had to put a ring on her finger because he'd knocked her up.

"I don't know what to say." He removed his cover. "Because I don't think I can make you understand why I didn't come...until now." He sounded humble, he looked anything but.

"Please just leave."

"I can't do that. I've been assigned to Midway for the next few years."

The color drained from her face.

"I'm sorry if that upsets you." He wrung his garrison cap in his hands. "I'm sorry if I waited too long. I loved you from the first moment I saw you standing right there in that exact spot."

Okay, now he looked humble. Tears stung the back of her eyes. She was making a man who'd risked his life for her beg. She knew why he hadn't called. It wasn't because he'd abandoned them.

"I know why you didn't call. But I'm still pretty damn mad at you." She was sniffling now, but she hadn't offered him any encouragement, so he made no move toward her.

Sometimes heroes needed a push in the right direction.

"Just say you love me."

"*Toi khong biet,* I love you, honey."

"*Toi khong biet, nhieu lam.* I love you, too much. And now I'm ashamed to say I let pride stand in the way of telling you something I should have told you a long time ago."

"You can tell me anything."

"Remember *that* night?" The one and only time they'd ever made love.

"How could I ever forget?"

"Trust me, you're *never* going to forget."

She gauged his response. He didn't get it.

Why did men have to have such thick skulls? Then again, maybe it was a good thing Bowie did.

She stepped out from behind the pallets, cradling her protruding stomach.

He stared at her middle.

"Say something," she said.

"I don't know what to say." He shifted his sea-green eyes to her face. "I'm in shock."

"Then just hold me."

He reached for her, and she met him halfway.

"We're going to have a baby," he said. "I'm going to be a father. You're going to be a mother." His tone softened. "We're going to be a family. I think we're missing something here."

"What could possibly be missing?"

He reached into his breast pocket and pulled out a diamond solitaire. "The ring."

EPILOGUE

February 14, 2003
Barber's Point, Hawaii

A CLIFFTOP WEDDING overlooking a Hawaiian sunset, what could be a more perfect setting for a wedding? Bowie escorted his mother up the white-carpeted aisle on his arm. "Bride or groom?" he asked.

"Where do you want to sit?"

"Groom. I get a better view of the matron of honor from here." He ushered his mother into the second row.

"It's *maid* of honor. Only married women are matrons of honor. So when are you going to marry the girl?" Lily Chapel Prince's whisper sounded like a hiss.

"You'll have to ask Tam. She didn't want to take away from her parents' big day."

"So what was wrong with last month, or the month before that?"

"We'll get there." He hoped. He'd been pressing Tam for that very same answer. He wanted to be married *before* the baby was born. And since Tam was already overdue their time was running out.

For months she'd been putting him off with one

excuse after another. Too close to her parents' wedding, too close to their baby's due date. He was kind of scared she was getting cold feet.

Seated in front of them were Rob's parents, his sister, Susan, and her family, which included her husband and four rowdy boys. On the bride's side were the rest of Tam's newfound family—Lan's brother, Bay, his wife and their three kids. Coworkers and friends filled the remaining seats on both sides.

A man sat alone in the back. Bowie guessed he was Shane O'Connor, the man Tam had told him about. Bowie couldn't even imagine what it would be like to watch Tam marry another man—he hoped to hell he never had to find out, but things weren't going exactly as he'd planned.

The chaplain, the groom and the best man, Bowie's father, chatted quietly under an arch of white flowers.

Zach and Michelle slipped into the seats on the other side of his mother. "Happy birthday, little Bo," Zach said.

"Have I ever told you how much I hate that name?"

"Speaking of names," Michelle said. "Have you picked out baby names yet?"

"Bay, boy or girl," he said. "It's Vietnamese for *seventh month* or *seventh son*. It's a family name."

"That's pretty," Michelle said.

"Very pretty," his mother agreed.

"She won't let me add Frisco to the birth certificate."

"Smart. Very smart," the women said in agreement.

A string quartet began the introduction. The small gathering of friends and family turned. Bowie reached under his chair for the video camera and focused it down the aisle.

Tam carried a small white nosegay, resting it on top of her expanding girth. She wore a flowing, ankle-length dress in a floral pattern that appealed to him.

She looked right into the camera as she strolled past, smiling just for him. He lowered the camcorder so he could see her beauty firsthand.

The first bars of the bridal march began. Everyone stood. And Bowie remembered to shift the camera as Lan Nguyen started down the aisle in a pale yellow dress.

By the time the bride reached the altar his thoughts had once again returned to Tam. He wanted a wedding just like this one. Except he and all his buddies would be dressed in their choker whites. And Tam would be wearing a long white bridal gown.

But they weren't reciting their vows today.

He wasn't going to kiss the bride. Well, he probably would give his soon-to-be mother-in-law a kiss. But he wasn't going to be kissing *his* bride today.

Tears glistened in Tam's eyes when her parents kissed. Then the happy couple ran back up the aisle. Lan turned midway and tossed the bouquet directly at her daughter, making sure she got the message. At least their families were on his side.

As the crowd dispersed for the reception, Bowie headed to the altar where Tam still stood. ''What's the matter?'' he asked.

"My back is killing me," she said, reaching around behind her.

"Let me do that for you." He pulled her to the circle of his arms and rubbed her back. "When's it going to be our turn?" he asked, hoping she'd ease his.

"You know I love you, Bowie." That was code for *back off, don't pressure me.* He was learning to interpret her language very well. He just wasn't fluent.

"Bowie," she said.

"Yes, honey?"

"I have a birthday present for you."

"You already gave me my present this morning. Remember?"

She blushed at the reminder. "This is an even better one, and it can't wait. You better pull the car around."

"Seriously?"

She nodded. "But don't make a fuss. I don't want to spoil the day."

"How could you possibly think the birth of our baby is going to spoil anyone's—"

"The car. Now. Please."

"Sit down, then. I'll be right back."

"Don't forget the suitcase."

He and Tam were both on leave, staying in Hawaii at the Stevens's home until after the wedding and the baby. It looked like both were happening today.

He was so excited he didn't know which way to turn. Or which dad to borrow the car from. They were both standing together so he walked up to them and said as casually as possible, "Dad, can I borrow the car keys?"

Both his dad and Stevens reached in their pockets for a set of keys.

"I've got it," Stevens said. "This one's a present for Bowie. It's a Porsche I owe him. Happy Birthday."

Well, that oughtta get them to the hospital fast.

Wait, this wasn't a race. Maybe he needed something more subdued for the ride.

"Thanks, Dad. And thanks, Dad," he said, taking both sets of keys.

He headed back toward Tam. She had the wooden folding chair in a death grip.

"Do you need me to carry you?" he asked.

She gave him a death-ray glare.

"No, okay, then Dad's car is just out front."

He walked and she waddled to the front yard as inconspicuously as possible to the front of the house, which had become a parking lot.

"Help!" Bowie screamed at the top of his lungs as panic set in. "I need keys! I need keys!"

The guests ran toward the front of the house. By this time Tam had doubled over, and he was trying to keep her on her feet.

"I forgot the suitcase," he shouted to his brother, who got right on it.

Stevens took charge and found the owner of the car closest to the exit, then grabbed the keys and got behind the wheel. Between moans and groans, Bowie managed to get Tam into the back seat and to crawl in beside her. Before he could shut the door his brother tossed in the suitcase.

Then Lan climbed in the front seat next to her husband of a few minutes. "Breathe, Tam, remember to breathe," she instructed.

Hey, that was his job.

But it sounded like good advice to Bowie. He released his tie and remembered to take a few breaths, before coaching Tam.

But they weren't rolling yet. Both the right side doors were still open and his mother was getting into the back seat.

"I've got the video camera," she announced, holding the camera and dropping Tam's satchel to the floorboards.

"Can we get going?" he asked impatiently.

"We're waiting on one more person," Lan said, just as the chaplain took the last seat up and closed the door.

The car started to move. Stevens was in charge of the driving. His mom and Lan were breathing with Tam. The chaplain was reciting wedding vows that nobody was listening to. And he felt left out.

"Mom, hand me the camcorder," Bowie asked.

"No wait!" Tam screeched.

He gave her a wounded look, and had to wait through a contraction for an explanation.

"Don't tape over the wedding video," she panted.

He scrambled for another tape. "Better?" he asked.

She nodded, then screamed louder than anything he'd ever heard before.

His instructions changed from "Breathe" to "Don't push, don't push."

"Tell him to shut up!" Tam pointed at the chaplain. "I'm not getting married in the back of a car while I am in labor!"

Bowie tried to explain that they didn't have a license, anyway, so it really didn't count, but secretly he was saying his "I do's."

"Don't you want to be a married woman before your baby is born?" Lan asked.

"No, I don't! I don't ever want to get married to a man who would do this to me!"

Both mothers said, "She doesn't mean it."

Somehow they got to the hospital where they'd taken their Lamaze classes. They hadn't gone to the Navy hospital, because Tam wasn't his wife.

Breathe, Bowie. Breathe!

They spilled from the car. He half carried, half dragged Tam to the nearest wheelchair attendant. And then they were off. Their preregistered paperwork wasn't in the computer so he had to stop by the office and fill out forms all over again.

Then it was up to the maternity ward where his mother handed him the camcorder. A nurse threw a gown at him and then pushed him into the birthing room.

Tam already had her feet in stirrups. A doctor stood at one end of the gurney, a nurse was at the other. Bowie arrived just in time to see the head crowning.

He remembered to focus the camcorder on the coming attraction and his son was born, screaming at the top of his healthy little lungs.

He had a newborn son.

Tam cried, then laughed as she held their baby. He felt like crying and laughing, too. He just couldn't decide which to do first.

"Do you want to hold your son?" she asked.

"And my wife," he said, looking deep into her eyes to see what might be missing.

She winked at him, and he breathed a sigh of relief. They'd be okay. They traded. He got the baby and she got the video camera.

Bowie stroked Bay's downy black head. He looked like his mother. Then he yawned and opened his eyes. "Hey, I think his eyes are blue, like your dad's."

"All baby's eyes are blue. I was kind of hoping they'd turn out to be green."

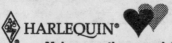

Harlequin invites you to experience the
charm and delight of

COOPER'S CORNER

A brand-new continuity
starting in August 2002

HIS BROTHER'S BRIDE
by *USA Today* bestselling author
Tara Taylor Quinn

Check-in: TV reporter Laurel London and noted travel
writer William Byrd are guests at the new Twin Oaks
Bed and Breakfast in Cooper's Corner.

Checkout: William Byrd suddenly vanishes and while
investigating, Laurel finds herself face-to-face with
policeman Scott Hunter. Scott and Laurel face a painful past.
Can cop and reporter mend their heartbreak and get to the
bottom of William's mysterious disappearance?

Princes...Princesses...
London Castles...New York Mansions...
To live the life of a royal!

**In 2002, Harlequin Books lets you escape to a
world of royalty with these royally themed titles:**

Temptation:
January 2002—*A Prince of a Guy* (#861)
February 2002—*A Noble Pursuit* (#865)

American Romance:
The Carradignes: American Royalty (Editorially linked series)
March 2002—*The Improperly Pregnant Princess* (#913)
April 2002—*The Unlawfully Wedded Princess* (#917)
May 2002—*The Simply Scandalous Princess* (#921)
November 2002—*The Inconveniently Engaged Prince* (#945)

Intrigue:
The Carradignes: A Royal Mystery (Editorially linked series)
June 2002—*The Duke's Covert Mission* (#666)

Chicago Confidential
September 2002—*Prince Under Cover* (#678)

The Crown Affair
October 2002—*Royal Target* (#682)
November 2002—*Royal Ransom* (#686)
December 2002—*Royal Pursuit* (#690)

Harlequin Romance:
June 2002—*His Majesty's Marriage* (#3703)
July 2002—*The Prince's Proposal* (#3709)

Harlequin Presents:
August 2002—*Society Weddings* (#2268)
September 2002—*The Prince's Pleasure* (#2274)

Duets:
September 2002—*Once Upon a Tiara/Henry Ever After* (#83)
October 2002—*Natalia's Story/Andrea's Story* (#85)

Celebrate a year of royalty with
Harlequin Books!

Available at your favorite retail outlet.

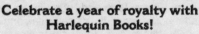

HARLEQUIN®
Makes any time special ®

HSROY02

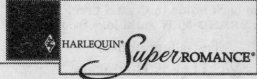